MEANWHILE

MR. WELLS HAS ALSO WRITTEN THE FOLLOWING NOVELS:

The Wheels of Chance.
Love and Mr. Lewisham.
Kipps.
Tono-Bungay.
Ann Veronica.
Mr. Polly.
The New Machiavelli.
Marriage.
The Passionate Friends.
The Wife of Sir Isaac Harman.

Bealby.
The Research Magnificent.
Mr. Britling Sees It Through.
The Soul of a Bishop.
Joan and Peter.
The Undying Fire.
The Secret Places of the Heart.
Christina Alberta's Father.
The World of William Clissold.

THE FOLLOWING FANTASTIC AND IMAGINATIVE ROMANCES:

The Time Machine.
The Wonderful Visit.
The Island of Dr. Moreau.
The Invisible Man.
The War of the Worlds.
The Sleeper Awakes.
The First Men in the Moon.

The Sea Lady.
The Food of the Gods.
In the Days of the Comet.
The War in the Air.
The World Set Free.
Men Like Gods.
The Dream.

NUMEROUS SHORT STORIES COLLECTED UNDER THE FOLLOWING TITLES:

The Stolen Bacillus.
The Plattner Story.

Tales of Space and Time.
Twelve Stories and a Dream.

THE SAME SHORT STORIES WILL ALSO BE FOUND IN THREE VOLUMES

Tales of the Unexpected.
Tales of Wonder.

Tales of Life and Adventure.

A SERIES OF BOOKS ON SOCIAL, RELIGIOUS AND POLITICAL QUESTIONS

Anticipations (1900).
A Modern Utopia.
The Future in America.
New Worlds for Old.
First and Last Things.
God the Invisible King.
The Outline of History.
Russia in the Shadows.

The Salvaging of Civilisation.
Washington and the Hope of Peace.
A Short History of the World.
The Story of a Great Schoolmaster.
A Year of Prophesying.
Democracy under Revision.

And two little books about children's play, called "Floor Games" and "Little Wars."

MEANWHILE

(*The Picture of a Lady*)

BY H. G. WELLS

NEW YORK

GEORGE H. DORAN COMPANY

ONE day about the time of the general strike in England I visited the celebrated garden of La Mortola near Ventimiglia. As I wandered about that lovely place, I passed by an unknown little lady sitting and reading in a shady corner. Her pose reminded me of another little lady who has always been very dear to me. She was making notes upon a slip of paper as she read. I noted how charmingly intent she was upon her book and wondered what it was that held her so firmly. I never discovered. I do not know who she was and I have never seen her again. In all probability she was a tourist like myself and quite unaware that she was destined, in my fancy, to become the mistress of all the beauty about her. She in part and in part the lady she had recalled. I went my way to the beach and sat there and as I mused on things that were happening in England and Italy and the world at large, that remembered and reinforced personality mingled with my thoughts, became a sort of frame for my thoughts, and this story very much as I have shaped it here presented itself suddenly to my imagination. It jumped into existence. Much of it had been in my mind for some time lacking a form and a personification. Then all at once it was alive. I went home and I began to write. The garden of this book is by no means a replica of the garden of La Mortola, which was merely the inspiring point of departure for this fantasia of ideas, this picture of a mind and of a world in a phase of expectation. Gorge and Caatinga you will seek at La Mortola in vain. But all sorts of things grow upon that wonderful corner of sunlit soil, and this novel, which I dedicate very gratefully to the real owners of the garden, gratefully and a little apologetically because of the freedoms I have taken with their home, is only the least and latest product of its catholic fertility.

H. G. WELLS.

CONTENTS

BOOK THE FIRST

THE UTOPOGRAPHER IN THE GARDEN

THE UTOPOGRAPHER IN THE GARDEN

THE SECTIONS

The Utopographer in the Garden

§ 1

THE room was long and lofty, a room of scar-
let hangings and pale brown stone, unillumi-
nated as yet by any of its red-shaded electric
lights. There were two great Italianate fire-places
with projecting canopies of carved stone; in one, the
olive logs were unlit, in the other the fire, newly
begun, burnt and crackled cheerfully; its leaping
tongues of flame rejoiced and welcomed the evening.
Bare expanses of the beeswaxed floor, sharp edges of
the massive furniture, metallic studs and rods and
handles and a big inkstand of brass responded by a
gay waving of reflections to these glad Hallos. The
curtains were not drawn, and the outer world by contrast with this intimate ruddy tumult seemed very
cold and still and remote. The tall window at one
end gave upon the famous garden which rose steeply
behind the house, terrace above terrace, a garden half
phantasmal now in the twilight, with masses of pallid
blossom foaming over old walls, with winding steps,
mighty old jars, great dark trees happily placed, and
a profusion of flowers, halted and paraded, by the
battalion, by the phalanx, their colours still glowing,
but seen beneath deeps of submerging blue, unsubstantial and mysteriously profound as they dissolved
away into the gloaming. The other window stared

out at the unruffled Mediterranean, dark ultramarine under the fading afterglow of a serene sunset.

A small, fragile, dark-haired woman in a green dress crouched musing in one corner of the long sofa before the fire; her hands clutched the back and her cheek rested on her hands; the reflections danced upon her necklace and bracelet and earrings and the buckles of her shoes, caressed her pretty arms and lit her eyes. Her expression was one of tranquil contentment. In that big room she was like some minute bright insect in the corolla of a gigantic red and orange flower.

At the sound of footsteps in the passage without she sighed, and moving lazily, turned an expectant face to the open door behind her.

There appeared a very exquisite little gentleman of some sixty-odd years. Grey hair streaked with brown flowed back gracefully from a finely modelled face that ended in a neatly pointed beard. The complexion was warm and delicate. At the first glance you would have said he is Spanish and he is wax; and he was neither. But indeed it was as though a Velasquez portrait had left its proper costume upstairs and dressed for dinner. For a moment this pleasant apparition stood clasping its white hands with a sort of confident diffidence, and then came forward with an easy gesture. "Ah-ah! My hostess!" he said.

She held out her hand to him with an indolent smile and did not seem in the least surprised that he took it and kissed it.

"Come and sit down by the fire here," she said. "I am so glad you have come to us again, Mr. Plantagenet-Buchan. Did they look after you carefully? We got back from Monte Carlo scarcely half an hour ago."

Mr. Plantagenet-Buchan strolled round the sofa, held out his carefully cherished hands to the blaze, and decided after due consideration to stand rather droopingly by the fireside. "You are sure I am not inconvenient?"

"You just complete us. There was one room free."

"That pretty room in the tower. Every way, east, west, north and south, one has a view."

She did not explain that dear accommodating Miss Fenimore had been bustled up to the dependence when his telegram came. She had other things in her mind. "You arrived in the afternoon?"

"I lunched on the train. I hired an irresistible automobile at the station. It was painted aluminium colour and adorned with a banner bearing the mystical word 'Shell.' And such a courteously exorbitant driver! Although it was sight-seeing day for your gardens and the road at your gates was choked with cars and char-à-bancs, all your servants, even the porter lady, received me as though I was the one thing they needed to round off their happiness. Your major-domo almost fondled me. Yes, Bombaccio with the Caruso profile. Yours is the perfect household."

"You have seen none of your fellow guests?"

He reflected. "I have a slight suspicion— Formally, no. Your major-domo gave me tea in my own room and afterwards I strolled about your gardens and heard them praised in most European languages as well as my mother tongue. One or two Germans. I may be old-fashioned but I don't feel a European show-place is complete without an occasional 'prachtvoll' or 'wie schön!' I've a sneaking pleasure in

15

their return. I feel I may be bullied for it but I can't help having it."

His hostess made no attempt to bully him.

He became enthusiastic over some flower in blue spikes, that was new to him.

The lady on the sofa disregarded the blue spikes. "There were one or two people about," she reflected aloud. "There was Lady Grieswold. She won't go to Monte Carlo because she loses her head. And always afterwards she is sorry she didn't go to Monte Carlo because it might have been one of her good days. Did you see her? But probably she went for a walk up in the hills with Miss Fenimore, to avoid Mr. Sempack. And then there was Mr. Sempack."

"Sempack," said Mr. Plantagenet-Buchan. "Sempack?" and consulted his toes.

"Yes," said the lady with a sudden hopefulness in her manner, "Mr. Sempack?" Her eyes were less dreamy. She wanted to know.

"In some connection—"

"Yes. But in what connection?"

Mr. Plantagenet-Buchan went off at a tangent. "As I have walked about the gardens— A presence . . . Most of your sight-seeing visitors are transitory; they make a round and they go. Or they make two rounds and go. But there has been *one* individual—"

The lady thrust out her pretty profile in expectation.

"Rather like a dissenting minister," he tried, feeling his way. "With that sort of hat. And yet not a real dissenting minister, not one of God's dissenting ministers."

Her eager face assured him he was on the right track.

"A dissenting minister, let us say, neither born nor created, not a natural product, but—how shall I put it?—painted by Augustus John! Very fine but slightly incredible. Legs—endless legs and arms. I mean as to length. Tree-like."

He considered judicially. "More ungainly—yes, even more ungainly—than Robert Cecil."

"Yes," she said in a loud whisper and glanced guiltily over her shoulder at the open door behind her. *"Him!"*

Mr. Plantagenet-Buchan folded his arms and bit a knuckle. "So *that* is Mr. Sempack! I saw him. Several times. We kept on meeting. The more we tried not to meet, we met. We sat about in remote corners and even then fate seemed to draw us together. Sempack!"

"You know about him?"

"I've heard of the great Mr. Sempack, yes."

"He writes books," she supplied helpfully.

"Real books, dear lady. Not books you read. Not novels. Not memoirs. Books that are just books. Like Santayana. Or Lowes Dickinson. Or Bertrand Russell."

"You've read some?"

"No. I've always hoped to meet him and save myself that duty. It *is* a duty. They say— They say he talks better than he writes. How did he come here?"

"Philip met him. He brought him along from the Roquebrune people."

"Why?"

"Philip wanted to know if there was going to be a coal strike. He's *fussed* about the coal strike."

"Did Mr. Sempack tell him?"

"Philip hasn't asked. Yet."

"I don't think that's Sempack's sort of subject, but one never knows. He might throw some side-lights on the matter."

"So far," said the lady, with reflective eyes on the fire, "he hasn't been very *much* of a talker. In fact— He hardly talks at all."

"Not his reputation."

"Intelligently out of it."

"Something not quite conducive in the atmosphere."

"He seemed almost to be beginning once or twice. But—perhaps they interrupt. He sits about in the garden in that large dispersed way of his, saying he's perfectly happy and refusing to go anywhere. Sometimes he writes in a little notebook. I don't think he's unhappy but he seems rather a waste."

"You'd like him to talk?"

"We never do get any talk here. I'd love to hear —discussion."

"Now I wonder," said Mr. Plantagenet-Buchan and consulted his ring again. "What did I see, the other day?" He stuck up a finger and held it out towards her. "Utopias!" he said. "Quite lately. It must have been in some review. Quite recently. In the *Nation* I think. Or the *Literary Supplement*. Yes. I have it. He has been reading and writing about all the Utopias in the world. He's a Utopographer!"

The lady seemed to weigh the possible meanings

of the word. "But what has that to do with the coal strike?"

"Nothing whatever that I can see."

There was a momentary pause. "Philip jumps at things," she remarked.

Mr. Plantagenet-Buchan knitted his brows. "Utopographer? Or was it a Utopologist? Or Uto-politan? Not a bad word, Utopolitan. No—it was Utopographer. I read it in one of the weeklies downstairs, the *Spectator* or the *Nation* or the *Saturday*. We might lead the talk rather carelessly towards Utopias and see what happened."

"We have some awful interrupters here. They don't listen and suddenly they shout out something about something else. Something—just silly. It may put him off his subject."

"Then we must pull the talk back to the subject."

"*You* may. But he's difficult. He's difficult. They disregard him and he seems to disregard them and effaces everything from his mind. When they interrupt he just loses them in thought and the meal. But he's not unhappy. He likes being here. He says so. He likes Philip. He likes Catherine. It is quite evident he likes Catherine. I think he has been talking to Catherine a little—in the garden."

"Is Lady Catherine here?"

"Lovelier than ever. Her divorce has made her ten years younger. She's twenty-five. She's eighteen. And—it's funny—but she evidently finds something attractive about Mr. Sempack. And naturally he finds something attractive about her. He isn't at all the sort of man I should have expected her to find attractive. But of course if she goes and carries him off and makes him talk about his Utopias

or whatever they do talk about when she gets him
alone, there will be no getting him to talk at large.
He'll be drained."

Her consultant quite saw that.

"We must think of a plan of campaign," he
brooded. "Broaching the talker. As a dinner table
sport. Now what have we given? An interest in
Utopias. I don't think we must use the actual word,
'Utopia' . . . No . . . I wonder if I should find
that review downstairs."

From far away came the sound of high heels
clicking on a marble staircase. His hostess became
very rapid. "That's Catherine!" she said in paren-
thesis. "The other people." She ticked the names
off on her fingers ineffectively. "There's a Colonel
Bullace. A great admirer of Joynson-Hicks. He
wants to organise British Fascists. Keep the working man down and save him from agitators and all
that. Adores Mussolini. His wife's a darling.
Rather a prosy darling if you let her talk, but endlessly kind. Then there's a couple of tennis-play-
ers. They just play tennis. And improve Philip's
game. It tries him dreadfully having his game
improved, but he *will* do it. What a *passionate* game
tennis is nowadays, isn't it? Mathison's the name.
And Geoffrey Rylands is here—Philip's brother. A
foursome. Too good for any of the others. And
there's dear Miss Fenimore. Lady Grieswold I told
you. And young Lord and Lady Tamar. He's at
Geneva, doing things for the League of Nations.
Such a fine *earnest* young couple. Oh! and there's
Puppy Clarges and some one else—let me see . . .
I said the Bullaces, didn't I? . . ."

The clicking heels halted in the doorway.

"Lady Catherine!" said Mr. Plantagenet-Buchan.

A tall young woman, with a lovely body sheathed in pale gold, dusky-haired, dark-blue eyed, smiled at them both. She had a very engaging smile, impudent, friendly, disarming. Her wide gaze swept the great room.

"Isn't Mr. Sempack down?" she asked her hostess.

And then remembering her manners she advanced to greet Mr. Plantagenet-Buchan.

"Come and conspire with us, Catherine," said Mrs. Rylands after a little pause for reflection. "Mr. Plantagenet-Buchan says Mr. Sempack is a great talker. So far—except perhaps to you—he's buried his talent. Come and tell us how we are to get him talking to-night."

§ 2

THEY did it between them and there was wonderful talking that night, a talk that delighted Mrs. Rylands altogether. It was like the talks her mother used to tell of in the great days of Clouds and Stanway, in the happy eighties when Lady Elcho and all the "Souls" were young and Lord Balfour was "Mr. Arthur" and people used to read Robert Louis Stevenson's *Talk and Talkers* in the hope of improving their style. Mr. Plantagenet-Buchan was bright and skilful and Lady Catherine was characteristically generous in giving away a vintage that might have been reserved for her alone, and Philip most unexpectedly helped with one intelligent question and Lord Tamar with two. Mr. Sempack once started, proved to be as great a talker as his reputation demanded, he could interest and inform and let in contributors while keeping them in order, and the evening was tremendously entertaining and quite different from any other evening over which Mrs. Rylands had presided at Casa Terragena.

There were moments of difficulty. The Mathisons were visibly disconcerted and alarmed by the strong, persistent drive towards such high-brow and devastating topics as what was going to happen to the world, what could be made to happen to the world, and how things could be made to happen. Their eyes met in only too evident protest against such "rot." The evening before they had had quite a good time, comparing notes with Geoffrey Rylands and Puppy Clarges about the different tennis courts upon the Riviera and shouting, "Oh! *that's* a scorcher if you like!" or "Talk about a cinder track!" and expressing opinions about the ankles of Miss Wills and the terrible and scandalous dispute about the balls and whether Suzanne was ever likely to marry, nice sensible stuff, as it seemed to them. Now they were pushed aside. They couldn't get in. Nor could Geoffrey nor Puppy help them. These four were scattered among the high-brows. Colonel Bullace was interested—positively interested, in a hostile way indeed, but interested. Once he interrupted. And Mrs. Bullace got loose for a time with a story about how down in Ventimiglia that day she had attempted to rescue a donkey from ill-treatment by a man it didn't belong to, and who wasn't, as a matter of fact, ill-treating it, and indeed who possibly had never been aware of the existence of the donkey until she called his attention to it, and how nice everybody had been about it, and had taken her part when the man became insulting. She began it unexpectedly and apropos of nothing. "Ow," she said suddenly, "*such* a funny thing!" But that had been a lacuna, and the great talk was joined up again before she had nearly done.

The great talk had reassembled itself after every interruption and triumphed over all that might have slain it in its immaturity and grown into a great edifice of interest. After dinner and a little interlude the men came up, and while the low-brow contingent was excreted to the bridge tables, the interested people gathered as a matter of course round the fire and went on talking. They went on talking and it was a great success, and little Mrs. Rylands felt that even Lady Elcho or Lady Sassoon, bright stars in her mother's memories, could never have presided over a better one. And at midnight, they were still talking, Mr. Sempack talking, Mr. Plantagenet-Buchan talking, Catherine talking, the Tamars both interested (unless *she* was pretending awfully well), Philip hanging on every word—unexpected Philip could be at times!—Miss Fenimore drinking it in. But she would drink anything in; it was her rôle. Even Colonel Bullace, whenever he was dummy, came and listened, and he was mostly dummy with such a chronic over-caller as Lady Grieswold for a partner.

It was wonderful how varied and yet how consistent the great talk was, how its topics went about and around and interwove and remained parts of one topic. Mrs. Rylands was reminded of a phrase Mr. Plantagenet-Buchan had used once for some music, "a cathedral of sound." This was a cathedral of ideas. A Gothic cathedral. Everything said had a sort of freedom and yet everything belonged.

§ 3

THAT evening had been tremendously entertaining, a glory, a thing to remember, but though the spirit may be extremely spirited the flesh is often weak.

At midnight Mrs. Rylands suddenly gave way. Right up to the moment of her crisis her attention had been held quite pleasantly, then suddenly it vanished. Abruptly she went like sour milk in thundery weather. Fatigue smote her and an overwhelming desire to close and put away the great talk and go to bed.

There was no phase of transition. It was like a clock striking suddenly on her brain. It said, "Enough. You have listened enough. You have looked intelligent enough. They have all had enough. Pack them off to bed and go to bed yourself."

She sat up on one of the pedestals that stood on either side of the fire and nothing in her pensive and appreciative pose betrayed the swift change within her. A moment before she had been a happy hostess blessing her gathering. Now she waited like an assassin for the moment to strike, and all her soul was hostile. And they went on, Mr. Sempack talking, Mr. Plantagenet-Buchan talking, Catherine talking, the Tamars interested (unless *she* was pretending awfully well), Philip hanging on every word and Miss Fenimore drinking it in. They might go on for *hours* yet—hours!

24

Mrs. Rylands invented something. She invented it in an instant. It flashed into her mind completed and exact. She would have it made directly she got to London, and bring it back with her next winter. A solid looking brass clock to go with the big ink-stand on the table. It should strike—just once in a day. Every twenty-four hours it should strike, slowly, impressively, imperatively—midnight. Never anything else. Midnight. Or perhaps to bring it home to them, fourteen or fifteen. Or four and twenty sound and full. The evening curfew. Why had no one thought of such clocks before? And sometimes one would put it on and sometimes one would put it back, and if it had a little stud somewhere that one could touch—or make Philip touch—without any one else noticing it, one might prevent it striking. . . . Or just blow everybody to bits by making it strike. . . .

In the natural course of things the bridge players started the go-to-bed break-up before half-past eleven, but to-night the bridge was bewitched it seemed. It made a background of muffled sounds to the great talk. Every one was overcalling over there; that was quite plain; tempers were going to pieces; and the games were holding out obstinately beneath vast avalanches of penalties that impended above the line. Sounds of subdued quarrelling came from Mrs. Bullace and Lady Grieswold. Each had arrived at the stage of hatred for her partner. At the other table Geoffrey was losing facetiously to the Mathisons, a close-playing couple, and Puppy was getting more and more acridly witty. Who was it sitting just hidden by the bowl of roses? Mr. Haul-bowline, Mrs. Bullace's partner. It was Mr. Haulbowline that Mrs. Rylands had forgotten when she had given the list of her guests to Mr. Plantagenet-Buchan. Why did one always forget Mr. Haulbowline?

The current of Mrs. Rylands' thoughts was interrupted. Something she realised had taken her by the cheeks and throat, something she knew she must control at any cost, a tension of the muscles. Just in time she bit her finger and suppressed the yawn, and then with a stern effort brought her mind back to the great talk. Now it was Mr. Sempack who was talking, and it seemed to her he was talking as though the only person in the room was Lady Catherine. Was that imagination? It was remarkable how those two entirely incongruous people attracted each other. They certainly did attract each other. When Mr. Sempack looked at Lady Catherine his eyes positively glowed.

It was astonishing that any woman could be attracted by Mr. Sempack. He was so entirely different from Philip. It was wonderful how cleverly Mr. Plantagenet-Buchan had hit him off. Of course now that he was in evening dress he was not so much like a dissenting minister, but he was still incredibly gawky. It was clever of Mr. Plantagenet-Buchan to have thought of Lord Cecil. Mr. Sempack really was more gawky than Lord Cecil; *much* more. How Mr. Plantagenet-Buchan observed things! And how acute and intimate it was of him—since he was American—to call him Robert Cecil still. Gawky! Mr. Sempack was the gawkiest man she had ever looked at. He became monstrous as she scrutinised him. He became a black blot on the scene, that had the remotest resemblance to a human form. His joints made her think of a cow, just as Philip's always made her think of a cat. It was awful to think how he could be joined together at the joints. Her pensive pose permitted her to examine his foot; his far-flung foot as he sat deep in the sofa. He had crossed his legs and his foot seemed to be held out for inspection. It waved about as if it challenged comment. His shoe reminded her of a cattle boat adapted to passenger service. His socks fell in folds over his ankle. Probably this man whom every one was listening to as if he was an oracle, had never found out there were such things as sock suspenders in the world. An oracle who had never heard of sock suspenders! It was quite possible. Men were incredibly stupid—especially intellectual men—about everything of practical importance in the world. Even what they knew they couldn't apply, whereas a woman could apply even what she didn't know. . . . They didn't know when to leave off. . . . Or, she suddenly amended, they left off too soon. Above the sock an inch of healthily hairy skin displayed itself and then a thin edge of Jaeger underclothing. Undyed, all-wool, slightly frayed underclothing. And Catherine found him attractive!

Very probably if Philip wasn't looked after he'd— No, it was impossible. He was like a different sort of animal. He would pull up his socks by instinct.

Mrs. Rylands, with an expression of intelligent attention, considered her guest's face. No one could have guessed from her quiet eyes that her reason had fled and only an imp was left in possession.

His bones, this imp remarked, positively ran wild under his skin as he talked. What could one call

such features? Rambling? Roughhewn? It was
like a handsome face seen through a distorting mirror. It was like one of those cliffs where people find
a resemblance to a face. There was a sort of
strength, a massiveness. The chin. It was a hygienic
chin; the sort of chin people wear so as to give fair
play to every toe. . . .

Mrs. Rylands had a momentary feeling that she
was falling asleep. What had she been thinking
about? About his chin—chins and toes— She
meant his chin was like the toe of a sensible boot,
not pointed. It was really a double chin. Not a
downwards double, not fat, but a sideways double
chin. "Cleft" did they call it? And the nose one
might call shapely—different on each side, but
shapely on each side. A nose with a lot of character
—but difficult to follow. And big! Like the nose
Mr. Gladstone grew in his late days. For people's
noses grow—longer and longer—all their lives.
This nose—how would it end? Something thoughtful about those deep overhung eyes there was, and
the wrinkles made them seem kindly and humorous.
But why didn't some one tell a man like that to get
his eyebrows cut? There was no need to have such
eyebrows, no need whatever. Unkempt. Sprouting.
Bits of hair on his cheeks too. A face that ought to
be weeded. She would not look at his ears—for fear.
Some woman ought to take him in hand. But not
Catherine! That would be Beauty and the Beast.
How venturesome Catherine was!—had always
been!

His voice was not unpleasant. Perhaps it was his
voice that attracted Catherine.

He was saying: "Work. We have to work for the

sake of the work and take happiness for the wild
flower it is. Some day men will grow their happinesses in gardens, a great variety of beautiful happinesses, happinesses under glass, happinesses all the
year round. Such things are not for us. They will
come. Meanwhile—"

"Meanwhile," Lord Tamar echoed in a tone of
edification. Just the word. He was really looking
up at Mr. Sempack. He, too, was attracted. Lady
Tamar's emotional response also was very convincing.

But what were they talking about? Her garden?
Happiness in little pots, happiness bedded out?
Mrs. Rylands blinked to make sure she was awake.

Then came a pause and Mr. Plantagenet-Buchan
delivered himself. "I perceive I have been meanwhiling all my life. Meanwhiling. . . . Have I
been living? You make me question it. Have I
just been meanwhiling away my life?"

He paused and seemed faintly dissatisfied with
what he had said. "Eheu! fugaces," he sighed.

It sounded awfully clever. And rather sad in a
brilliant sort of way. But what it meant now, was
another matter. She had lost the thread long ago.
Bother! Mrs. Rylands roused herself to smile
brightly at Mr. Plantagenet-Buchan. Anyhow, it
was as if they were coming to some sort of conclusion and she felt she must offer him every en-
couragement. Then, with a sudden determination,
she stood up. She could endure this talk no longer.
After all, it was her house. The bridge parties far
away down the room came to her aid, belatedly like
Blücher, but now they came.

"Game!" shouted Puppy. "And the two hundred

and fifty ought to save us from the worst of it.
We're well out of it, partner!"

A great stirring of chairs. Both bridge tables on
the move. Mr. Plantagenet-Buchan also standing
up. Lady Tamar standing up. Every one on the
move, thank God! Philip guiding Colonel Bullace
quite needlessly to the drinks on the far table. Mr.
Haulbowline following Colonel Bullace, unobtru-
sively but resolutely, like a pointer following a Scotch
terrier. Suddenly the men remember that Puppy
will take a whisky, Mr. Haulbowline stands aside and
Colonel Bullace pours out her allowance with an air
of having approached the tray for that sole purpose.
The other tray? The other tray is all right.
Geoffrey is getting lemonade for Lady Catherine. . . .

Now was the moment for the hostess to say: "We
have had a wonderful talk to-night, Mr. Sempack.
You scatter ideas like a fir tree scatters pollen."

She had thought of that in the interlude after dinner, while all the women were saying things about
him. He did scatter ideas. She had said it over to
herself several times since, to make sure it was still
there. But what she said was: "You scatter pollen
like a freeze scats ideese. I hope you will sleep
well, Mr. Sempack, and not hear too much of the
sea."

She said her little sentence rather rapidly and me-
chanically, because she had repeated it over too often;
she touched his knuckly hand and smiled her sweetest
and left him bowing. In the passage she let her
yawn loose and the happy thing nearly dislocated her
pretty jaw.

It was only when she was undressing that she

realised with a start what it was she had said. Never!
But she was horribly certain about it. "Freeze scats
ideese?" or had it been "Fleeze"? What could he
have made of it? Perhaps now, with that vast serious expression of his on that vast serious face, he was
repeating it over to himself upstairs.

It was hopeless even to try to make Philip understand what she was laughing at. So she just
laughed and laughed, and then Philip lifted her up
in his arms and kissed her and soothed her, and she
cried a tear or so for no particular reason, Philip being
such a dear, and then she was put into bed somehow
and went to sleep.

And the last thing she heard was Philip reproach-
ing himself. "I ought to have sent you to bed before, my little wife. You've tired your dear self
out."

§ 4

TO many hearers the great talk that was set
going in Casa Terragena by Mr. Sempack,
would have seemed far less wonderful and
original than it did to Mrs. Rylands and the group
of young people with her that listened to him. For,
after all, it was little more than a gathering together
and a fitting together of the main creative suggestions
for the regulation of human affairs that have accumulated so richly in the last few score years. It did
not seem in the least wonderful to Mr. Plantagenet-
Buchan, though he allowed it to interest and amuse
him. Mr. Plantagenet-Buchan was quite sure he had
heard it all before, but then, like most highly cultivated and Europeanised Americans, he had trained

himself to feel in that way about everything, and to smile gently and to intimate it quietly, with a sort of conspicuous unobtrusiveness. He knew that the one thing forbidden to an American was to be naïve. An American to hold his own must not rest under that suspicion. He must never be naïve, never surprised, never earnest. Only by the most inflexible tortuosity, by the most persistent evasiveness, by an exquisite refinement sustained with iron resolution, and a cynicism that never fails to be essential, can he hope to establish his inaccessible remoteness from either Log Cabin or White House; and maintain his self-respect among the sophistication of Europe.

So Mr. Plantagenet-Buchan played the part of a not too urgently needed prompter to Mr. Sempack, helped him out discreetly, and ticked off his points as he made them with the air of one fully prepared for everything that came.

The ground effect of Mr. Sempack upon which all his other effects were built, was his large and unchallengeable intimation of the transitory and provisional nature of the institutions and customs and usages, the forms and appliances and resources amidst which he and his interlocutors were living. He not only had the quality of not really belonging to them himself and of reaching back before they existed and forward to when they would have gone, but he imposed the same quality of relative permanence upon the thoughts of his hearers. He had the quality less of being ephemeral than of sitting with his hearers and watching everything else go by.

The human mind discovered itself relatively immortal amidst evanescent things. This beautiful house became like a tent that would presently be folded up and taken away and the celebrated gardens like a great bouquet of flowers that had been brought from the ends of the earth, just to be looked at and to delight for a little while and then to die and be dispersed. The house was built about a Saracenic watchtower for its core; wherever its foundations had extended buried fragments of polished marble and busts and broken provincial statuary had recalled its Roman predecessor; but at the touch of Sempack these marble gods and emperors became no more than the litter of the last tenant, his torn photographs and out-of-date receipts. The Via Aurelia ran deeply through the grounds between high walls, and some one had set up, at a bridge where the gardens crossed this historical gully, a lettered-stone to recall that on this documented date or that, this emperor and that pope, Nicolo Machiavelli and Napoleon the First, had ridden past. These ghosts seemed scarcely remoter than the records of recent passages in the big leather-bound Visitors' Book in the Hall, Mr. Gladstone and King Edward the Seventh, the Austrian Empress and Mr. Keir Hardie.

Occasionally tombstones that had stood beside the high road were unearthed by changes in the garden. One inscribed quite simply "Amoena Lucina," just that and nothing more, was like a tender sigh that had scarcely passed away. Mrs. Rylands had set it up again in a little walled close of turf and purple flowers. People talked there of Lucina as though she might still hear.

Over everything hung a promise of further transformations, for the Italians had a grandiose scheme for reviving the half obliterated tracks of the Via Aurelia as a modern motoring road to continue the

Grande Corniche. Everything passed here and everything went by; fashions of life and house and people and ideas; it seemed that they passed very swiftly indeed, when one measured time by a scale that would take in those half disinterred skeletons of Cro-Magnon men and Grimaldi men who lay, under careful glass casings now, in the great cave of the Rochers Rouges just visible from the dining-room windows. That great cave was still black with the ashes of prehistoric fires, as plain almost as the traces of yesterday's picnic. Even the grisly sub-man with his rude flint-chipped stakes, was here a thing of overnight. His implements were scattered and left in the deeper layers of the silted cave, like the toys of a child that has recently been sent to bed. With a wave of his ample hand Mr. Sempack could allude to the whole span of the human story.

"Utopias, you say, deny the thing that is," said Mr. Sempack. "Why, yesterday and to-morrow deny the thing that is!"

He made Mrs. Rylands feel like some one who wakes up completely in the compartment of an express train, which between sleeping and waking she had imagined to be a house.

Colonel Bullace had to hear that his dear British Empire had hardly lasted a lifetime. "Its substantial expansion came with the steamships," said Mr. Sempack; "it is held together by the steamship. How much longer will the steamship endure?"

Before the steamship it was no more than the shrunken vestiges of the Empire of George III. Most of America was lost. Our rule in India was a trader's dominion not a third of its present extent. Canada, the Cape were coast settlements.

Now Colonel Bullace was of that variety of Englishman which believes as an article of faith that the Union Jack has "braved a thousand years the battle and the breeze" since 1800. If any one had told him that the stars and stripes was the older of the two flags he would have become homicidal. A steamship Empire! What of Nelson and our wooden walls? What of John Company? What of Raleigh? What of Agincourt? He had a momentary impulse to rise up and kill Mr. Sempack, but he was calling his hand, a rather difficult hand, just then and one must put first things first.

And while Mr. Sempack made respect for any established powerful thing seem the delusion of children still too immature to realise the reality of change, at the same time he brought the idea of the strangest and boldest innovations in the ways of human life within the range of immediately practicable things. In the past our kind had been hustled along by change: now it was being given the power to make its own changes. He did not preach the coming of the Great Age; he assumed it. He put it upon the sceptic to show why it should not arrive. He treated the advancement and extension of science as inevitable. As yet so few people do that. Science might be delayed in its progress or accelerated, but how could its process stop? And how could the fluctuating extravagances of human folly resist for ever the steady drive towards the realisations of that ever growing and ever strengthening body of elucidation? There was none of the prophetic visionary about the ungainly Mr. Sempack as he sat deep and low on the sofa. He made the others seem visionaries. Simply he asked them all to be reasonable.

For a time the talk had dealt with various main aspects of this Millennium which Mr. Sempack spoke of so serenely, as a probable and perhaps inevitable achievement for our distressed and confused species. He displayed a large and at times an almost exasperating patience. It was only yesterday, so to speak, that the idea of mankind controlling its own destiny had entered human thought. Were there Utopias before the days of Plato? Mr. Sempack did not know of any. And the idea of wilful and creative change was still a strange and inassimilable idea to most people. There were plenty of people who were no more capable of such an idea than a rabbit. His large grey eye had rested for a moment on Colonel Bullace and drifted pensively to the Mathisons.

"The problem is to deal with them," Mrs. Rylands had reflected, following the indication of the large grey eye.

"They will all die," said Lord Tamar.

"And plenty more get born," said Philip, following his own thoughts to the exclusion of these present applications.

"You don't consult the cat when you alter the house," said Mr. Sempack.

"But is such concealment exactly what one might call—democracy?" asked Mr. Plantagenet-Buchan in mock protest.

"You don't even turn the cat out of the room when you discuss your alterations," said Mr. Sempack, and dismissed democracy.

It was only nowadays that the plan before mankind was becoming sufficiently clear and complete for us to dream of any organised and deliberate effort to realise it. The early Utopias never pretended to be more than suggestions. Too often seasoned by the deprecatory laugh. But there had been immense liberations of the human imagination in the last two centuries. Our projects grew more and more courageous and comprehensive. Every intelligent man without some sort of kink was bound to believe a political world unity not only possible but desirable. Every one who knew anything about such matters was moving towards the realisation that the world needed one sort of money and not many currencies, and would be infinitely richer and better if it was controlled as one economic system. These were new ideas, just as once the idea of circumnavigating the world had been a new idea, but they spread, they would pervade.

"But to materialise them?" said the young man from Geneva.

"That will come. The laboratory you work in is only the first of many. The League of Nations is the mere first sketch of a preliminary experiment."

Lord Tamar betrayed a partisan solicitude for his League of Nations. He thought it was more than that.

Parliaments of Nations, said Mr. Sempack, offered no solution of the riddle of war. Every disagreement reopened the possibility of war. Every enduring peace in the world had been and would have to be a peace under one government. When people spoke of the Pax Romana and the Pax Britannica they meant one sovereignty. Every sovereignty implied an internal peace; every permanent peace a practical sovereignty. For the Pax Mundi there could be only one sovereignty. It was a little hard for people who had grown up under old traditions of nation and empire to realise that and to face its consequences; but there was always a new generation coming along, ready to take new ideas seriously. People were learning history in a new spirit and their political imaginations were being born again. The way might be long and difficult to that last Pax, but not so long and difficult as many people with their noses in their newspapers, supposed.

"If one could believe that," sighed Lady Tamar.

Mr. Sempack left his politics and economics; his sure hope of the One World State and the One World Business floating benevolently in their mental skies; and talked of the reflection upon the individual life of a scientific order of human affairs. It was remarkable, he thought, how little people heeded the things that the medical and physiological and psychological sciences were saying to them. But these things came to them only through a haze of distortion, caricatured until they lost all practical significance, disguised as the foolish fancies of a race of oddly gifted eccentrics. There was a great gulf fixed between the scientific man and the ordinary man, the press. So that the generality had no suspicion of the releases from pain and fatigue, the accessions of strength, the control over this and that embarrassing function or entangling weakness, that science could afford even now.

Still less could it imagine the mines of power and freedom that these first hand-specimens foretold. Contemporary psychology, all unsuspected by the multitude, was preparing the ground for an education that would disentangle men from a great burthen of traditional and innate self-deception; it was pointing the road to an ampler and finer social and political life. The moral atmosphere of the world, just as much as the population and hunger of the world, was a controllable thing—when men saw fit to control it. For a moment or so as Mr. Sempack talked, it seemed to Mrs. Rylands that the room was pervaded by presences, by tall, grave, friendly beings, by anticipatory ghosts of man to come, happy, wise and powerful. It was as if they were visiting the past at Casa Terragena as she had sometimes visited the sleeping bones in the caves at Rochers Rouges. Why had they come into the room? Was it because these friendly and interested visitants were the children of such thoughts as this great talk was bringing to life?

"There is no inexorable necessity for any sustained human unhappiness," said Mr. Sempack; "none at all. There is no absolute reason whatever why every child born should not be born happily into a life of activity and interest and happiness. If there is, I have never heard of it. Tell me what it is."

"Bombaccio," said Mr. Plantagenet-Buchan, glancing over his shoulder to make sure that the servants were out of the room, "is a Catholic. He believes there was a Fall."

"Do *we*?" asked Mr. Sempack.

Puppy Clarges made a furtive grimace over her cigarette at Geoffrey, but the doctrine of the Fall went by default.

"But then," asked Mrs. Bullace, "why isn't every one happy now?"

"Secondary reasons," Mr. Plantagenet-Buchan asserted. "There may be no invincible barrier to an earthly Paradise, but still we have to find the way."

"It takes a long time," said Philip.

"Everything that is longer than a lifetime is a long time," said Mr. Sempack. "But for all practical purposes, you must remember, so soon as we pass that limit, nothing is very much longer than anything else."

Mr. Plantagenet-Buchan, after an instant's thought, agreed with that as warmly as if he had met a long lost friend, but at the first impact it reminded Mrs. Rylands rather unpleasantly of attempts to explain Einstein.

"It does not matter if it uses up six generations or six hundred," Mr. Plantagenet-Buchan endorsed.

"Except to the generations," said Philip.

"But who *wants* this world of prigs?" came the voice of Geoffrey in revolt.

"I do for one," said Mr. Sempack.

"It would bore me to death."

"Lots of us are bored almost to violence by things as they are. More will be. Progress has always been a battle of the bored against the contented and the hopeless. If you like this world with its diseases and frustrations, its toil and blind cravings and unsatisfied wants, its endless quarrellings and its pointless tyrannies and cruelties, the pettiness of its present occupations in such grotesque contrast with the hard and frightful violence to which it is so plainly heading, if you like this world, I say, defend it. But I want to push it into the past as completely as I can and as fast as I can before it turns to horror. So I shall be against you. I am for progress. I believe in progress. Work for progress is the realest thing in life to me. If some messenger came to me and said with absolute conviction to me, 'This is all. It can never be any better,' I would not go on living in it for another four and twenty hours."

Geoffrey seemed to have no retort ready. His face had assumed the mulish expression of a schoolboy being preached at. This fellow, confound him! had language. And splashed it about at dinner time! Long sentences! Bookish words! Philip might as well have let in a field preacher. Field Preacher, that's what he was. That should be his name. Geoffrey nodded his head as who should say, "We've heard all *that*," and helped himself in a businesslike way to butter. A fellow must have butter whatever trash he has to hear. You wouldn't have him wait until all the jawing was finished before he took butter.

"Not much to quarrel with to my mind," said Mr. Plantagenet-Buchan, "in a world that can give us such a sunset as we had to-night. This spacious room. And all these lovely flowers."

"But there will still be sunsets and flowers, in any sort of human world," said Mr. Sempack.

Mr. Plantagenet-Buchan was a little belated with his reply, but it opened profound philosophical issues and he liked it and was content. "Against a background," he said, "perhaps not dark enough to do them justice."

§ 5

AFTER the move upstairs, when all those members of the party who lived and were satisfied with the present, the Bullaces and the Mathisons and Geoffrey and Lady Grieswold and Puppy and Mr. Haulbowline, had gone apart to their happiness in bridge, the talk about Mr. Sempack and his great world of peace, justice and splendid work to come, had turned chiefly on the quality of the obstacles and entanglements that still kept men back from that promised largeness of living. The persistence of his creative aim impressed Mrs. Rylands as heroic, but it was mingled with a patience that seemed to her almost inhuman.

"There is a time element in all these things," said Mr. Sempack. "In one newspaper downstairs there was a report of the conference of some political organisation, I think the Independent Labour Party, and they had adopted as their 'cry,' so to speak, and with great enthusiasm, 'Socialism in Our Time.' The newspaper made a displayed head-line of it. What did they mean by that? Humbug? Something to catch the very young? Or a real proposal to change this competitive world into a communistic system, change its spirit, its intricate, undefined and often untraceable methods in twenty or thirty years? Face round against the trend of biology in that short time. Take nature and tradition by the throat and win at the first onset. A small group of ill-informed people. Fantastic! To believe in the possibility of change at that pace is as absurd as not to believe in change at all."

A distant "Hear Hear!" came from the bridge table.

"*Table,* partner!" the voice of Lady Grieswold reproved.

Colonel Bullace made no further sign.

"Nevertheless all these changes are going to be made and they may be made much sooner—I am sure they will be made much sooner—than most of us suppose. Change in human affairs goes with an acceleration. . . ."

He went on with this reasonableness of his that balanced so perplexingly between cold cruelty and heroic determination. The world was not ready yet for the achievement of its broader and greater changes. Knowledge had grown greatly, but it had to grow enormously and be enormously diffused before things could be handled on such a scale as would give a real world peace, a world system of economics, a universal disciplined and educated life. The recent progress of psychology had been very great, but it was still only beginning. Until it had gone further we could do no more than speculate and sketch the developments of the political life of mankind and of education and religious teaching that would usher in the new phase. There was a minimum of time needed for every advance in thought and knowledge. We might help and hurry on the process up to a certain limit, but there was that limit. Until that knowledge had been sought and beaten out, we were workers without tools, soldiers without weapons. Meanwhile—

"Easy for us to sit here and be patient, but what of the miner, cramped and wet, in the dark and the foul air, faced with a lock-out in May," said Philip.

"I can't help him," said Mr. Sempack serenely.

"Immediately," said Philip.

"Heaven knows if I can ever help him. Why should I pretend? If he strikes I may send a little money, but that is hardly help. Why pretend? I am no use to him. Just as I couldn't help if presently there came a wireless call—have you a wireless here?"

43

"In the kitchen," said Mrs. Rylands. "They like the music."

"To say that some shiploads of people were burning and sinking in the South Atlantic. No help is possible at this distance. Just as there is nothing that any of us can do for the hundreds of thousands of people who are at this present moment dying of cancer. It is no good thinking about such things."

The landscape of Mr. Sempack's face hardly altered. There may have been the ghost of a sigh in his voice. "It is no good getting excited by such things. It may even do harm.

"The disease of cancer will be banished from life by calm, unhurrying, persistent men and women, working, with every shiver of feeling controlled and suppressed, in hospitals and laboratories. And the motive that will conquer cancer will not be pity nor horror; it will be curiosity to know how and why."

"And the desire for service," said Lord Tamar.

"As the justification of that curiosity," said Mr. Sempack, "but not as the motive. Pity never made a good doctor, love never made a good poet. Desire for service never made a discovery."

"But that miner," said Philip and after his fashion left his sentence incomplete.

"The miner is cramped between the strata—in the world of ideas just as much as in the mine. We cannot go and lift the strata off him, suddenly, in the twinkling of an eye. He has his fight to fight with the mine-owner, who is as blind. In his fashion. Which is—physically at least, I admit—a more comfortable fashion."

Philip's troubled eyes rested for a moment on his pretty wife.

"The miners are finding life intolerable, the mine-owners are greedy not only for what they have but more; the younger Labour people want to confuse the issue by a general strike and a push for what they call the Social Revolution."

"What exactly do they mean by that?" asked Lord Tamar.

"Nothing exactly. The Communists have persuaded themselves that social discontent is a creative driving force in itself. It isn't. Indignation never made a good revolution, and I never heard of a dinner yet, well cooked by a starving cook. All that these troubles can do is to ease or increase the squeeze on the miners and diminish or increase the totally unnecessary tribute to the coal-owners—at the price of an uncertain amount of general disorganisation and waste. My own sympathies are with the miners and I tax my coal bill twenty-five per cent. and send it to them. But I cherish no delusions about that struggle. There is no solution in all that strife and passion. It is just a dog-fight. The minds of people have to be adjusted to new ideas before there is an end to this sweating of men in the darkness. People have to realise that winning coal is a public need and service, like the high road and the post office. A service that has to be paid for and taken care of. Everybody profits by cheap accessible coal. A coal-owner's royalties are as antiquated as a toll gate. Some day it will be clear to every one, as it is clear to any properly informed person now, that if the state paid all the costs of exploiting coal in the country and handed the stuff out at prices like—say ten shillings a ton, the stimulation of every sort of production would be so great, the increase, that is, on taxable wealth would be so great, as to yield a profit, a quite big profit, to the whole community. The miners would become a public force like the coast-guards or the firemen . . ."

"You think that is possible?" asked Philip.

"I know. It's plain. But it's not plain to every one. Facts and possibilities have to be realised. Imaginations have to be lit and kept lit. Certain obstructive wickednesses in all of us——"

Mr. Sempack stopped. He never finished a sentence needlessly.

"But coal winning isn't confined to its country of origin," said Philip. "There is the export trade."

"Which twists the question round completely," said Lord Tamar.

"When you subsidise coal getting in England you subsidise industrial competition abroad," said Philip.

"Exactly. While we still carry on the economic life of the world in these compartments and pigeon-holes we call sovereign states," said Mr. Sempack, "we cannot handle any of these other issues. Nothing for it but makeshift and piecemeal."

"Till the Millennium," said Philip.

"Till the light grows brighter," said Sempack, and added meditatively: "It does grow brighter. Perhaps not from day to day, but from year to year."

They went on to talk about the moral training that was needed if modern communities were to readjust their economic life to the greater and more unified methods that were everywhere offering themselves, and when they talked of that Mr. Sempack made the schools and colleges of to-day seem more provisional and evanescent even than our railways and factories. Beyond their translucent and fading forms, he evoked a vision of a wide, free and active life for all mankind. In the foreground, confusions, conflicts, wastes, follies, possible wars and destructions; on the slopes beyond the promise and a little gathering band of the illuminated, who questioned, who analysed, who would presently plan and set new methods and teaching going. Nothing in the whole world was so important as the mental operations, the realisations and disseminations of these illuminated people, these creative originatory people who could not be hurried, but who might so easily be delayed, without whom, except for accident, nothing could be achieved. Where was the plain and solvent discussion needed to liberate minds from a thousand current obsessions and limitations? Where were the schools of the new time? They had not come yet. Where were the mighty armies of investigators? Nothing as yet but guerrilla bands that wandered in the wilderness and happened upon this or that.

The self-discovery, the mutual discovery, of those who constituted this illuminated minority, became the main theme. They dawned. As yet they did but dawn upon themselves. They fought against nature within themselves and without. They fought against darkness without and within. Large phrases stuck out in Mrs. Rylands' memories of this talk, like big crystals in a rock.

"The immense inattentions of mankind . . ."

"Subconscious evasions and avoidances . . ."

"Our alacrity for distractions . . ."

"The disposition of the human mind to apprehend, to assent and then to disregard, to understand and yet flag and fail, before the bare thought of a translation into action . . ."

"The terror of isolation because of our insecure gregariousness. We try to catch every epidemic of error for fear of singularity . . ."

"Minds as wild as rabbits and as ready to go underground . . ."

"When you want then to hunt in a pack," Mr. Plantagenet-Buchan had assisted at this point. . . .

"The disposition of everything human to inflame and make a cancer about a minor issue, that will presently kill all the wider interests concerned . . ."

The great talk rambled on and all its later phases were haunted by the idea that embodies itself in that word "Meanwhile." In the measure in which one saw life plainly the world ceased to be a home and became the mere site of a home. On which we camped. Unable as yet to live fully and completely.

Since nothing was in order, nothing was completely right. We lived provisionally. There was no just measure of economic worth; we had to live unjustly. Even if we did not rob, "findings keepings" was our motto. Did we consider ourselves overpaid, to whom could we repay? Were we to relinquish all it would vanish like a drop in the thirsty ocean of the underpaid and unproductive. We were justified in taking life as we found it; in return if we had ease and freedom we ought to do all that we could to increase knowledge and bring the great days of a common world-order nearer, a universal justice, the real civilisation, the consummating life, the days that would justify the Martyrdom of Man. In many matters we still did not know right from wrong. We did not so much live as discuss and err. The whole region of sexual relations for example was still a dark forest, unmapped; we blundered through it by

48

instinct. We followed such tracks as we found and we could not tell if they had been made by men or brutes. We could not tell if they led to the open or roundabout to a lair. We followed them, or we distrusted them and struggled out of them through the thorns.

"But a glimpse now and then of a star!" said Mr. Plantagenet-Buchan—his best thing, he reflected, that evening.

"Or a firefly," said Lady Catherine.

The psychologist, the physiologist, would clear that jungle in time. In time.

All sorts of beautiful and splendid things might happen in this world. (The large gaze of Mr. Sempack rested for a moment on Lady Catherine.) But they happened accidentally; you could not make a complete life of them. You could not take a life or a group of lives and give it a perfect existence, secluded and apart, in a blundering world. Man was a social creature and you could not be gods in Italy while there remained a single suffering cripple in China or Peru; you could not be a gentleman entirely, while a single underpaid miner cursed the coal he won for you. The nearest one could get to perfection in life now was to work for the greatness to come. And not trouble too much about one's incidental blunders, one's incidental falls from grace.

"Work," he said and reflected. "We have to work for the work and take happiness for the wild flower it is. Some day men will cultivate their happinesses in gardens, a great variety of beautiful happinesses, happinesses grown under glass, happinesses all the year round. Such things are not for us. They will come. Meanwhile—"

"Meanwhile," echoed Lord Tamar.

Came that pause just before Mrs. Rylands asserted herself.

And then it was Mr. Plantagenet-Buchan had made his rather sad little summing-up; his sense of the gist of it all, given with his very formal and disciplined laugh, bright without being vulgar. "I perceive I have been meanwhiling all my life. Meanwhiling . . . Have I been living?" (Shrug of the shoulders and gesture of the hands.) "No, I have been meanwhiling away my time."

And for once his own bright observation pierced back and searched and pricked himself. But it wasn't real enough to end upon. Unsatisfactory.

"Eheu! fugaces!" he sighed, an indisputably elegant afterthought. Though something Greek would have been better. Or something a little less—familiar. But then people were so apt to miss the point if it was Greek or unhackneyed. And besides he had not on the spur of the moment been able to think of anything Greek and unhackneyed. Compromise always. Compromise. Meanwhile.

He became preoccupied and noted nothing of Mrs. Rylands' remarkable good-night speech to Mr. Sempack.

For quite a long time he sat on his bed in his charming room in the tower before he began to undress, brooding in a state of quite unusual dissatisfaction upon himself, regardless of the beautiful views south, north, east and west of him, the coast and the mountains and the silhouetted trees. He liked to think of his existence as a very perfect and polished and finished thing indeed and he had been wounded by his own witticism about "meanwhiling away his life." And this was entangled with this other unpleasant and novel idea, that if one's refinement was effective or even perceptible it couldn't really be refinement. Some of these Europeans achieved a sort of accidentalness in their refinement. They left you in doubt about it. Should one go so far as to leave people in doubt about it? Was there such a thing as being *aggressively* refined?

Presently Mr. Plantagenet-Buchan stood up and regarded himself in his mirror, varying the point of view until at last he was ogling himself gravely over his shoulder. He stretched out his hands, his very remarkable white hands. Then he pirouetted right round until he came into his thoughtful attitude with his arms folded, as if consulting his diamond ring.

He was comparing himself with Mr. Sempack. He was struggling with the perplexing possibilities that there might be a profounder subtlety than he had hitherto suspected in the barest statement of fact and opinion, and a sort of style in a physical appearance that looked as though it had been shot out on a dump from a cart.

His discontent deepened. "Little humbug!" he said to the elegance in the mirror. Its expression remained unfriendly.

He touched brutality. "Little *ass!*" he said.

He turned from the mirror, sharply, and began to undress, methodically, after his manner.

§ 6

NEXT morning Mrs. Rylands could better grasp the great talk and its implications. She lay in bed and contemplated it as she sipped her morning tea and it looked just as it had looked before she gave way to her fatigue, a very fine talk indeed and immensely interesting—to Philip and every one. She forgot her last phase and the awful things she had thought about Mr. Sempack and remembered only her happy plagiarism from Mr. Plantagenet-Buchan, a "cathedral of ideas." It was indeed like a great cathedral in her memory. It had sent her to bed exhausted it is true; but is anything worth having unless it exhausts you? It had stirred up Philip. That diabolical lapse had faded from her mind like a dream that comes between sleeping and waking.

It was impossible she found to recall how the talk had developed, but now that hardly mattered. The real value of a talk is not how it goes but what it leaves in your memory, which is one reason perhaps why dialogues in books are always so boring to read. Even Plato was boring. Jowett's Plato had been one of the acutest disappointments in her life. She remembered how she had got the "Symposium" volume out of her father's library and struggled with it in the apple tree. She had expected something like a bag of unimagined jewels. In any talk much of what was said was like the wire stage of a clay model and better forgotten as soon as it was covered over. But what was left from last night was a fabric plain and large in its incompleted outline, in which she felt her mind could wander about very agreeably and very profitably whenever she was so disposed. And in which Philip's mind might be wandering even now.

This morning however she had little energy for such exploration. She approved of the great talk and blessed it and felt that it had added very much to her life. But she surveyed it only from the outside.

The chief thing in her consciousness was that she was very comfortable and that she did not intend to get up. She would lie and think. But so far it seemed likely to be pure thought she would produce, without any contamination with particular things. She was very comfortable, propped up by pillows in her extensive bed.

She was, also, had she been able to see herself, very pretty. She was wearing a silk bed-jacket that just repeated a little more intensely the sapphire colour beneath her lace bedspread. It was trimmed with white fur. Her ruffled hair made her look like a very jolly, but rather fragile boy. A great canopy supported by bed-posts of carved wood did its utmost to enhance the importance of the mistress of Casa Terragena. The dressing table with its furnishings of silver and shining enamel and cut and coloured glass, enforced the idea that whatever size the lady chose to be, it was the duty of her bedroom to treat her as an outsize in gracious ladies. The curtains of the window to the south-east still shut out the sunlight, but the western window was wide open and showed a stone-pine in the nearer distance, a rocky promontory, and then far away the sunlit French coast and Mentone and Cap Martin.

The day was fine but not convincingly fine. Over the sea was a long line of woolly yet possibly wicked little clouds putting their heads together. But so often in this easy climate such conspiracies came to nothing.

She wasn't going down to breakfast; she did not intend indeed to go down until lunch. She was taking the fullest advantage of her state to be thoroughly lazy and self-indulgent and lie and play with her mind. Or doze as the mood might take her. Philip and Catherine and Geoffrey and dear Miss Fenimore and everybody, let alone Bombaccio the majordomo and his morning minion, would see that everybody was given coffee and tea and hot rolls and eggs and bacon and fruit and Dundee marmalade, according to their needs. They would all see to each other and Bombaccio would see to all of them. Just think. She would not force her thinking or think anything out, but she would let her thoughts run.

This onset of maternity about which feminists and serious spinsters made such a fuss, was proving to be not at all the dreadful experience she had prepared herself to face. Soft folds of indolent well-being seemed to be wrapping about her, fold upon fold.

After all bearing heirs to the Rylands millions was a very easy and pleasant sort of work to do in the world. Almost too easy and pleasant when one considered the pay. Smooth. Gentle. Living to the tune of a quiet murmur. She remembered something her Sussex aunt, Aunt Janet Nicholas, Aunt Janet the prolific, had once said. "It makes you feel less and less like being Brighton and more and more like being the Downs." The Downs, the drowsy old Downs in summer sunshine. The tiny harebells in the turf. The velvet sound of bees. A peacefulness of body and soul. And yet one could think as clearly and pleasantly as ever. Or at least one seemed to think.

She had an idea, a by no means imperative idea, that presently when she had done with realising how comfortable she was, her thoughts might after all take a stroll about the aisles and cloisters of the overnight discussion, but instead she found herself thinking alternatively of two more established prepossessions. One was Philip and his interest in the talk and the other, which somehow ought to be quite detached from him and yet which seemed this morning to be following the thought of him like a shadow, was—*Stupids*.

Philip's interest in this discussion had surprised her, and yet it was only the culminating fact to something that had been very present to her mind for some little time. She was convinced—and she had always been convinced—that Philip's mind was a very vigorous and able one, a mind of essential nobility and limitless possibilities, but so soon as she had got over the emotion and amazement of the wonderful marriage that had lifted her out of the parental Hampshire rectory to be the mistress of three lovely homes, and begun really to look at Philip and consider him not as a love god but as a human being, she had perceived a certain restrictedness in his intellectual equipment. Apparently he had read scarcely anything of the slightest importance in the world; he had gone through the educational furnaces of Eton and had a year at Oxford before the war, unscathed by sound learning of any sort. The smell of intellectual fire had not passed upon him. Not a hair of his head had been singed by it. He was amazingly inexpressive and inarticulate. If he knew the English language, for some reason he cut most of it dead. And he opened a book about as often as he took medicine, which was never.

Yet he seemed to know a lot of things and every now and then she found she had to admit him not only cleverer but more knowledgeable than she was.

If he had read little, he had picked up a lot. He had
been a good soldier under Allenby, they said, especially in the East. In spite of his youth men had
been glad to follow him. And in spite of his
silences all sorts of intelligent people respected him.
Mr. Plantagenet-Buchan and Mr. Sempack betrayed
no contempt nor pity for such rare remarks as he
made. They were infrequent but sound. He con-
ducted, or at any rate helped to conduct, business
operations that were still extremely vague to her,
operations that she had gathered had to do mainly
with steel. When he went into Parliament, and he
was nursing Sealholme to that end, he would, she
was sure, be quite a good member of Parliament.
And yet—she knew it and still her mind struggled
against the admission—there was something that was
lacking. A vigour, an expansion. His mind refused
to be militant, was at best reserved and a commentary.
Dear and adorable Philip! Was it treason to think
as much? Was it treason to want him perfect?

Her own family was an old Whig family with
traditions of intellectual aggressiveness. She had
cousins who were university professors, and her
home, so close and convenient for Oxford, had
been actively bookish and alive to poetry and paint-
ing. She had listened to good talk before she was
fifteen. She had not always understood but she
had listened soundly. She had grown up into the
idea that there was this something eminently desirable that you got from the literature of the world,
that was conveyed insidiously by great music, and
by all sorts of cared-for and venerated lovely things.
It went with a frequent fine use of the mind, a conscious use, and it took all science by the way. It was

an inward and spiritual grace, this something, that was needed to make the large, handsome and magnificently prosperous things of life worth while. She had not so much thought out these ideas to their definiteness, as apprehended their existence established in her mind. And when all the storm of meeting this glorious happy Philip and attracting him and being loved by him and marrying him and becoming the most fortunate of young women subsided, there were these values, still entrenched, reflecting upon all that she had achieved.

There in the middle of her world ruled this sungod, this dear friend and lover, active, quietly amused, bringing her with such an adorable pride and such adorable humility to the homes of his fathers, giving, exhibiting; and yet as one settled into this life, as day followed day, and one began to realise what the routines and usages, the interests and entertainments amounted to, there arose this whisper of discontent, this rebellious idea that still something was lacking.

The life was so large and free and splendid in comparison with anything that she might reasonably have hoped for, that it brought a whiff of ingratitude with it even to think that it was also rather superficial.

It wasn't, she told herself, that this new life that made her a great lady wasn't good enough for her. It was far too good. Her estimate of herself was balanced and unexacting. She had never been able to make up her mind whether she was rather more than usually clever or rather more than usually stupid; she was inclined to think both. It wasn't a question of how this new life became her, but how it became Philip. The point was that it was somehow not good enough for Philip. And, if it wasn't a paradox, as if Philip wasn't as yet quite good enough for himself.

And still more evasive and subtle was her recent apprehension of the fact that Philip himself knew that somehow he wasn't quite good enough for himself. This new perception had reached back, as it were, and supplied an explanation of why Philip had come out of a world of alert and brilliant women, to her of all people. Because about her there had been a sort of schoolgirl prestige of knowledge and cleverness, and perhaps for him that had seemed to promise just whatever it was that would supply that haunting yet impalpable insufficiency. Instead of which, she reflected, here in this almost regal apartment, she had given him a dewy passion of love, worship, physical, but physical as tears and moonlight, and now this promise of a child.

Had he forgotten, in his new phase of grateful protectiveness, what need it was had first brought them together?

Quite recently, and after being altogether blind to it, she had discovered these gropings out towards something more than the current interests of his happy and healthy days. He was questioning things. But he was questioning them as though he had forgotten she existed. He was, for example, quite markedly exercised by this question of a possible coal strike in England. With amazement she had become aware how keenly he was interested in it. For all she knew the Rylands' millions were deeply involved in coal, but it wasn't, she was assured, on any personal account that he was interested.

Beyond the question of the miners, there was

something more. He was concerned about England. She had thought at first that, like nearly all his class, he took the Empire and the social system, and so forth, for granted, and the secret undertow of her mind, her memories of talk at the parental table, had made it seem a little wanting in him to treat such questionable things as though they were fundamental and inalterable. But now she realised he was beginning to penetrate these assumptions. There had been an illuminating little encounter, about a week ago, with Colonel Bullace—on the night of Colonel Bullace's arrival.

Philip never discussed; he was too untrained to discuss. But he would suddenly ask quite far-reaching questions and then take your answer off to gnaw it over at leisure. Or he would drop remarks, like ultimatums, days or weeks after you had answered his questions. And a couple of these rare questions of his were fired that night at Colonel Bullace.

"What's all this about British Fascists?" asked Philip, out of the void.

"Eh!" said Colonel Bullace and accumulated force. "Very necessary organisation."

Philip had remained patiently interrogative.

"Pat's pretty deep in it," dear Mrs. Bullace had explained in her simple disarming way.

The picture of the scene came back to Mrs. Rylands. It was a foursome that evening; the Bullaces had been the first of this present party to arrive. She recalled Colonel Bullace's face. He was like a wiry-haired terrier. No, he was more like a Belgian griffon—with that big eyeglass, he was more like a one-eyed Belgian griffon. What a queer thing it must be to be a nice little, rather silly little woman

like Mrs. Bullace and be married to a man like that,
a sort of canine man. She supposed—for example—
one would have to kiss that muzzle. Embrace the
man! Mrs. Rylands stirred uneasily under her lace
bedspread at the thought. He had talked about the
dangers of Communism in England, of the increasing
insubordination of labour, of the gold of Moscow,
and the need there was to "check these Bolsheviks."
All in sentences that were like barks. She did not
remember very clearly what he said; it sounded like
nonsense out of the *Daily Mail*. It probably was.
What she remembered was Philip's grave face and
how, abruptly, it came to her again as though she had
never seen or felt it before, how handsome he was,
how fine he was and how almost intolerably she loved
him.

"You mean to say, you would like to provoke a
general strike now? And smash the Trade Unions?"

"Put 'em in their place."

"But if you resort to 'firmness' now—if Joynson-
Hicks and his fellow Fascists in the Cabinet, and your
Daily Mail and *Morning Post* party, do succeed in
bringing off a fight and humiliating and beating the
workers and splitting England into two camps—"

Philip found his sentence too involved and
dropped it "How many men will you leave beaten?"
he asked. "How many Trade Unionists are there?"

Colonel Bullace didn't seem to know.

"Some millions of them? Englishmen?"

"Dupes of Moscow!" said Colonel Bullace.
"Dupes of Moscow."

"A day will come," added Colonel Bullace de-
fiantly, "when they will be grateful to us for the
lesson—grateful."

Philip had considered that for a moment and then he had sighed deeply and said, "Oh! Let's go to bed," and it seemed to her that never before had she heard those four words used so definitely for calling a man a fool.

And afterwards he had come into her room, still darkly thoughtful. He had kissed her good-night almost absent-mindedly and then stood quite still for a minute perhaps at the open window looking out at the starlight. "I don't understand all this stuff," he said at last, to himself almost as much as to her. "I don't understand what is going on and has been going on for some time. This British Fascist stuff and so on. . . . I wonder if any one does? These work-people—and their hours and lives, and what they will stand and what they won't. It's all —beyond anything I know about."

He stood silent for a time.

"Wages went down. Now—unemployment is growing and growing."

"Nobody seems to know." It was like a sigh.

"Suppose they smash things up."

Then in his catlike way he was gone, without a sound except the soft click of the door.

Perplexed Philip!

Perplexing Philip!

She looked now at the window against which he had stood and wondered how she might help him. He was the most difficult and comprehensive problem she had ever faced. This social struggle that it seemed hung over England had risen disregarded while she had been giving herself wholly to love. She did not know any of the details of the coal subsidies and coal compromises, that had produced

61

this present situation about which everybody was growing anxious. It had all come on suddenly, so far as her knowledge went, in a year or so. And now here she was, useless to her man. It was no good pestering him with ill-informed questions. She would have to read, she would have to find out before she approached him.

It was queerly characteristic of Philip that he had pounced upon Mr. Sempack at the Fortescues' at Roquebrune and brought him over, without a word of explanation. She guessed Mr. Sempack had talked about coal and labour at Roquebrune. Philip had something instinctive and inexplicable in his actions; he seemed to do things without any formulated reason; he had felt the need of talk as a dog will sometimes feel the need of grass and fall upon it and devour it. But she reproached herself that he should have had to discover this need for himself.

Talk. That she reflected had been one of the great things that had been missing in the opening months of married life. This morning it was clearly apparent to her that so spacious and free a life as hers and Philip's here in Casa Terragena had no right to exist without a steady flow of lucid and thorough talking.

That was a final precision of something that had been evolving itself in her mind since first she had been taken up into the beauty and comfort of this Italian palace. From the outset there had been a faint murmuring in her conscience, a murmuring she spoke of at times as her "Socialism." She squared this murmuring with her continued intense enjoyment of her new life by explaining to herself that people were given these magnificent homes and

famous and entrancing gardens and scores of servants
and gardeners and airy lovely rooms with luminous
views of delicately sunlit coastlines, so that they
might lead beautiful exemplary lives that would
enrich the whole world. For the dresses and furnishings, the graces and harmonies of life at Casa Terragena were finally reflected in beauty and better living
all down the social scale. No Socialist State, she was
sure, with everything equal and "divided up" could
create and maintain such a garden as hers, such a
tradition of gardening. That was why she was not
a political socialist. Because she had to be a custo-
dian of beauty and the finer life. That had been her
apology for her happiness, and it was the underlying
motive in her discontent and in her sense of something wanting, that their life was not sustaining her
apology. They had been given the best of everything and they were not even producing the best of
themselves. They were living without quality.

That was it, they had been living without quality.

Tennis, she reflected, by day and bridge by night.

He was not living like an aristocrat, he was living
like a suburban clerk in the seventh heaven of
suburbanism.

He was doing so and yet he didn't want to do so.
He was in some way hypnotised against his secret
craving to do the finest and best with himself. And
he was trying to find a way of release to be the man,
the leader, the masterful figure in human affairs she
surely believed he might be.

How to help him as he deserved to be helped,
when one was clever and understanding perhaps but
not very capable, not very brilliant, and when one
was so easily fatigued. How to help him now par-

ticularly when one was invaded and half submerged
by the needs of another life?

That was a strand of thought familiar now to Mrs.
Rylands and it twisted its way slowly through her
clear unhurrying mind for the tenth time perhaps or
the twentieth time, with little variations due to the
overnight talk and with an extension now from
Philip to a score of great houses she had visited in
England and wonderful dances and assemblies where
she had seen so many other men and women after his
type, so expensive, so free and so materially happy.
With something inexpressive and futile shadowing
their large magnificence. And interweaving with
this and embracing it now with a suggestion almost
of explanation, was a still more intimate strand in her
philosophy, her long established conviction that there
was a great excess of Stupids in the world.

Stupids were the enemy. This grey film that
rested upon things, this formalism, this shallowness,
this refusal to take life in a grand and adventurous
way, were all the work of Stupids. Stupids were
her enemies as dogs are the enemies of cats.

Her conception of life as a war for self-preserva-
tion against Stupids dated from the days when she
had been a small, fragile, but intractable child, much
afflicted by governesses in her father's rambling Warwickshire rectory. Stupids were lumps. Stupids
were obstacles. Stupids were flatteners and diluters
and spoilers of exciting and delightful things. They
told you not to and said it was dinner time. They
wanted you to put on galoshes. They said you
mustn't be too eager to excel and that every one
would laugh at you. "Don't over-do it," they said.
In the place of your lovely things which they

64

marred, they had disgusting gustoes of their own.
They made ineffable Channel-crossing faces when
one said sensible things about religion and they
abased themselves in an inelegant collapse of loyalty
before quite obviously commonplace people, and
quite obviously absurd institutions. And they wanted
you to! And made fusses and scenes when you
didn't! Oh! *Stupids!* She met them in the coun-
try-side, she met them again at Somerville College
where she had imagined she would be released into
a company of free and vigorous virgins.

And now in this new life of great wealth and distinction, in which it ought to be so easy for men and
women to become at least as noble as their furniture
and at least as glorious as their gardens, there were
moments when it seemed to her that Stupid was
King.

She came back to her idea of Philip as awakening,
as endeavouring to awake, from something that hypnotised him, that had caught him and hypnotised him
quite early in life. He had been caught by Stupids
and made to respect their opinions and their stand-
ards; he had been trained to a great and biased
toleration of Stupids, so that they pervaded his life
and wasted his time and interrupted his development.
The Stupids at school had persuaded him that work
was nothing and games were everything. The
Stupids of his set had insisted that most of the English language was a mistake. The Stupids of this
world set their heavy faces against all thought. She
saw Philip as struggling in a sort of Stupid quick-
sand, needing help and not knowing where to find it,
and she herself by no means secure, frantic to help
and unable.

What if she were to try to do more than she did in making an atmosphere for Philip? The irruption and effect of Mr. Sempack had set her enquiring whether there were not perhaps quite a lot of other stimulating people to be found, and whether perhaps it wasn't a wife's place to collect them. Mr. Plantagenet-Buchan of course was clever, clever and dexterous, but he did not stimulate, and there were moments when Philip stared at some of Mr. Plantagenet-Buchan's good things as though he couldn't imagine why on earth they had been said. Tamars were intelligent but self-contained, they liked to wander off about the garden, just the two of them, she evidently listening to an otherwise rather silent young man, and Lady Catherine again was intelligent but quite uncultivated, a mental wild rose, a rambler, a sprawling sweet-briar. Philip seemed to avoid Tamar, which was natural perhaps since Tamar showed an equal shyness of Philip, but also he and Lady Catherine avoided each other, which was odd seeing how charming they both were. But all the others of the party—?

The little face on the pillow meditated the inevitable verdict reluctantly. The loyalty of the hostess battled against an invincible truthfulness. . .

Stupids! . . .

She had got together a houseful of Stupids . . .

Pervasive and contagious Stupids. The struggle overnight to get the great talk going had been a serious one, exemplary, illuminating. Nowadays people like the Bullaces, the Mathisons, and Puppy Clarges, seemed to assume they had the conversational right of way. They had no respect for consecutiveness. They hated to listen. They felt effaced unless they had something to vociferate, and it hardly mattered to them what they vociferated.

How stupid and needless Colonel Bullace's intervention had been? And how characteristic of all his tribe of Stupids!

He had pricked up his ears at the word Utopia and coughed and turned a rather deeper pink; and after the third repetition and *apropos* of nothing in particular, he had addressed Mr. Sempack in an abrupt, caustic and aggressive manner. He cut across an unfinished sentence to do so.

"I suppose, Sir," he had said, "*you* find your Utopia in Moscow?"

Mr. Sempack had regarded him as a landscape might regard a puppy. "What makes you suppose that?" he asked.

"Well! isn't it so, Sir? Isn't it so?"

Mr. Sempack had turned away his face again. "No," he said over his shoulder and resumed his interrupted sentence.

Then Bombaccio, wisest and most wonderful of servants, had nudged Colonel Bullace's elbow with the peas and the new potatoes and diverted his attention and effaced him. But surely it was wrong to have people in one's house at all if they required that amount of suppression. Yet how often in the last few months had she heard talk effaced by Stupids like Colonel Bullace. Full of ready-made opinions they were, full of suspicions, they would not even assuage by listening to what they wanted to condemn.

Dear Miss Fenimore again was a demi-Stupid, a Stupid in effect, an acquiescent Stupid, willing perhaps but diluent to everything that had point and quality, and Lady Grieswold had been knowingly and wilfully invited as a Stupid, a bridge Stupid to gratify and complete the Bullaces. Her bridge was awful it seemed, but then Mrs. Bullace's bridge was awful.

The Mathisons were a less clamorous sort of Stupid than Colonel Bullace, but more insidious and perhaps more deadly. They did not contradict and deny fine things; silently they denied. These Mathisons had been brought along by Philip and Geoffrey and they were to exercise him at tennis. They did, every day. For two of his best hours in the morning and sometimes after tea Philip strove to play a better game than the Mathisons, with either Geoffrey or Puppy as his partner. It tried him. It exasperated him. He detested and despised Mathison, she perceived, as much as she did, but he would not let him go and he would always play against him. He could not endure, and that was where the Stupids had him fast, that a man so inferior as Mathison, so cheapminded, so flat-mannered, should have the better of him at anything.

They all conspired to put it upon Phil that his form at tennis mattered. She would go down to the court helplessly distressed to see her god, hot and over-polite and in a state of furious self-control, while Puppy and the others—who was it?—Miss Fenimore and some one? Mr. Haulbowline! that shadow, sat in wicker chairs and either applauded or regretted—working him up.

She smiled and affected interest and all the time her soul was crying out: "Philip, my darling! It's the cream of your strength and the heart of your day you're giving to the conquest of Mr. Mathison. And it doesn't matter in the least. It doesn't matter

in the very least, whether you beat him or whether
you don't."

Geoffrey too it seems played a better game than
Philip. But that was an accepted superiority.

Geoffrey was a deeper, more complex kind of
Stupid altogether than these others. And yet so like
Philip; as like Philip as a mask is like a face. Geoffrey
was the bad brother of the family; he had been sent
down from Eton; he did nothing; he looked at his
sister-in-law askance. Philip was too kind to him. He
drifted in and out of Casa Terragena at his own invitation. A moral Stupid, she knew he was, with challenge and disbelief in his eyes, and yet with a queer
hold upon Philip. And an occult understanding with
Puppy. When Geoffrey was about, Philip would
rather die than say a serious thing.

And then as the accent upon all this Stupid side of
the house-party was Puppy Clarges, strident and
hard, a conflict of scent and cigarette smoke, with the
wit of a music hall and an affectedly flat loud voice.
She was tall as Catherine, but she had no grace, no
fluency of line. Her body ran straight and hard and
then suddenly turned its corners as fast as possible.

No, they made an atmosphere, an atmosphere in
which it was impossible for Philip to get free from
his limitations. It was his wife's task—if it was any
one's task—to dispel that atmosphere. Drive it out
by getting in something better—of which Mr. Sempack was to be regarded as a type.

It wasn't going to be easy to change this loose
Terragena atmosphere. It was not to be thought of
that a wife should set brother against brother . . .

Her mind was too indolent this morning to face
baffling problems. For a time it lost itself and then

she found herself thinking again with a certain unavoidable antagonism of Puppy Clarges. Why was
a girl of that sort tolerated? She was rude, she was
troublesome, she was occasionally indecent and she
professed to be unchaste. Yet when Mrs. Rylands
had mentioned the possibility of Puppy moving on
somewhere, if other visitors were to be invited, Philip
had said: "Oh, don't turn out old Puppy. She's all
right. She's amusing. She's very good fun. She's
so good for Lady Tamar."

The shadow of perplexed speculation rested upon
the pretty face against the pillows. It was not so
much that Mrs. Rylands disliked Puppy as that she
failed so completely and distressingly even to begin
to understand the reaction of her world to this an-
gular and aggressive young woman.

Puppy boasted by implication and almost by plain
statement of her lovers.

Who could love that body of pot-hooks and hang-
ers? Love was an affair of beauty; first and last
it had to be beautiful. How could any one set about
making love to Puppy? When men made love—
Mrs. Rylands generalised boldly from the one man
she knew—when men made love, they were adorably
diffident, they trembled, they were inconceivably,
wonderfully tender and worshipful. Love, when
one dared to think of love, came into one's mind as
a sacrament, a miracle, a mutual dissolution, as whispers in the shadows, as infinite loveliness and a glory.
Love was pity, was tears, was a great harmony of all
that was gentle, gracious, proud and aspiring in existence, towering up to an ecstasy of sense and spirit.
But Puppy? The very thought of Puppy and a
lover was obscene.

And she had lovers.

How different must be their quality from Philip's! The idea came from nowhere into Mrs. Rylands' mind that life had two faces and that one was hidden from her. Life and perhaps everything in life had two faces. This queer idea had come into her mind like an uninvited guest. She had always thought before of Stupids as defective and troublesome people against whom one had to maintain one's life, but against whom there was no question whatever of being able to maintain one's life. But suppose there was something behind the Stupid in life, nearly as great, if not quite as great as greatness, nearly as great, if not quite so great as nobility and beauty.

Suppose one lay in bed too long, and held emptiness of life, idleness, shallowness, noise and shamelessness, too cheaply? Suppose while one lay in bed, they stole a march upon one?

The mistress of Casa Terragena lay very still for some moments and then her hand began to feel for the bell-push that was swathed in the old-fashioned silk bell-pull behind her. She had decided to get up.

§ 7

THERE was a waterless part of the gardens at Terragena that was called the Caatinga. Nobody knew why it had that name; there was no such word in Italian and whatever justifications old Rylands had for its use were long since forgotten. Possibly it was Spanish-American or a fragment from some Red Indian tongue. The Caatinga was a region of high brown rocky walls and ribs and buttresses and recesses and hard extensive flats of sunburnt stone, through which narrow winding paths and steps had been hewn from one display to another; one came into its reverberating midday heat through two cavernous arches of rock with a slope of streaming mesembryanthemum, fleshy or shrivelled, between them, and a multitude of agaves in thorny groups, of gigantic prickly pears in intricate contortions, of cactuses and echinocactus, thick jungles of spiky and leathery exotics, gave a strongly African quality to its shelves and plateaux and ridges and theatre-like bays. Only the wide variety of the plants and an occasional label betrayed the artificiality of this crouching, malignantly defensive vegetation. "African," said some visitors, but others, less travelled or more imaginative, said, "This might be in some other planet, in Mars or in the moon." Or they said it looked like life among the rocks under the sea.

Some obscure sympathy with a scene that was at once as real as Charing Cross and as strange as a Utopia may have drawn Mr. Sempack to this region, away from the more familiar beauties and prettinesses of Casa Terragena. At any rate, he made it his resort; he spread out his loose person upon such rare stony seats as were to be found there and either basked meditatively or read or wrote in a little notebook, his soft black felt hat thrust back so that its brim was a halo.

And thither also, drawn by still obscurer forces, came Lady Catherine, slightly dressed in crêpe georgette and carrying an immense green-lined sun umbrella that had once belonged to the ancestral Rylands. She stood over Mr. Sempack like Venus in a semi-translucent mist. She spoke with a mingling of hostility and latent proprietorship in her manner.

"You will either blister or boil if you sit up here to-day," she said.

"I like it," said Mr. Sempack without disputing her statement, or showing any disposition to rearrange himself.

She remained standing over him. She knew that her level-browed face, looked-up-to and a little foreshortened, was at its bravest and most splendid. "We seem able to talk of nothing down here but the things you said the other night."

Mr. Sempack considered this remark without emotion. "The Mathisons?"

"They never talk. They gibber sport and chewed *Daily Mail*. But the others——"

"Mrs. Bullace?"

"She's a little hostile to you. You don't mind?"

"I like her. But still——"

"She thinks you've set our minds working and she doesn't like minds working. I suppose it's because the Colonel's makes such unpleasant noises when it works. She said—— How did she put it? That you had taken all the *chez-nouziness* out of Casa Terragena."

"You made me talk."

"I loved it."

"I didn't want to talk and disturb people."

"I wanted you to."

"I do go on, you know, when I'm started."

"You do. And you did it so well that almost you persuaded me to be a Utopian. But I've been thinking it over." The lady spoke lightly and paused, and only a sudden rotation of the large umbrella betrayed the deceptiveness of her apparent calm. "It's nonsense you know. It's all nonsense. I don't believe a word of it, this spreading web of science of yours, that will grow and grow until all our little affairs are caught by it and put in place like flies." She indicated a vast imaginary spider's web with the extended fingers of her large fine hand. She threw out after the rest, "Geometrical," a premeditated word that had somehow got itself left out of her premeditated speech. "You won't alter human life like that."

Mr. Sempack lifted one discursive eyebrow an inch or so and regarded her with a mixture of derision and admiration. "It won't affect *you* much," he said, "but life *will* alter as I have said."

"*No,*" said the lady firmly.

Mr. Sempack shrugged his face at the prickly pears.

Lady Catherine considered the locality and perched herself on a lump of rock so high that her legs extended straight in front of her. His note-making must stop for awhile. "It doesn't matter in the least what is going to happen on the other side of time," she said. "You make it seem to, but it doesn't."

"Things are happening now," said Mr. Sempack.

Lady Catherine decided to ignore that. She had prepared certain observations while she had been dressing that morning and she meant to make them. She was not going to be deflected by unexpected replies. "As I thought it over the fallacy of all you said became plain to me. The fallacy of it. It became ridiculous. I saw that life is going to be what it has *always* been, competition, struggle, strong people seizing opportunities, honest people keeping faith, some people being loyal and brave and fine—

and all that, and others mean and wicked. There will always be flags and kings and empires for people to be loyal to. Religion will always come back; we need it in our troubles. Life is always going to be an adventure. Always. For the brave. Nothing will change very much—in these permanent things. There will be only changes of fashion. What you said about people all becoming one was nonsense— becoming unified and forgetting themselves and even their own honour. I just woke up and saw it was nonsense."

"You just lost your grip on what I had been saying," said Mr. Sempack.

"It was an awakening."

"It was a relapse."

Lady Catherine reverted to her mental notes. "I shook it off. I looked at myself and I looked at the sunshine and I saw you had just been talking my world away. And leaving nothing in the place of it. I went downstairs and there on the terrace were those six Roman busts that have been dug up there, faces exactly like the faces of people one sees to-day, the silly one with the soft beard most of all, and I went out past that old tombstone, you know, the one with an inscription to the delightful Lucina, that Mrs. Rylands has just had put up again, and I thought of how there had been just such a party as we are, in the Roman villa that came before the Rylands. Perhaps Lucina was like Cynthia. I think she was. Very likely there was a Greek Sophist to anticipate you. All hairy and dogmatic but rather attractive. Talking wickedly about the Empire because he thought it really didn't matter. And hundreds and hundreds of years ahead, somebody will still be living in this delightful spot and people will be making love and eating and playing and hearing the latest news and talking about how different everything will be in the days to come. *Sur la Pierre Blanche.* There will still be a good Bombaccio keeping the servants in order and little maids slipping out to make love to the garden-boys under the trees when the fireflies dance. And there you are!"

"There am I *not*," said Mr. Sempack. "But there most evidently you are."

He waved his dispersed limbs about for some seconds, it reminded her of the octopus in the Monaco Aquarium, collected them and came to a sitting position, facing her.

"Talking of sane things to you is like talking to a swan," he said. "Or a bird of paradise."

She smiled her most queenly at him and waited for more.

"You seem to understand language," he said. "But unless it refers to *you*, in *your* world of acceptance and illusion, it means nothing to you at all."

"You mean that my healthy mind, being a thoroughly healthy mind, rejects nonsense."

"I admit its health. I regret its normality. But what it rejects is the unpalatable and the irrelevant. The truth is as irrelevant to you as a chemical balance to a butterfly."

"And to you?"

"I am disposed to make myself relevant to the truth. It is my peculiarity."

Lady Catherine had a giddy feeling that the talk was terribly high and intellectual. But she held on pluckily. "I don't admit that *your* truth *is* the truth. I stick to my own convictions. I believe in

76

the things that are, the *human* things." She gathered
herself for a great effort of expression. She let the
umbrella decline until it lay upturned at her side,
throwing up a green tone into her shadows. "I believe that the things that don't matter, *aren't*," she
announced triumphantly.

"Your world is flat?" he verified.

"It has its hills and valleys," she corrected.

"But as for its being a globe?"

She took the point magnificently. "Mere words,"
she said. "Just a complicated way of saying that you
can keep on going west and get home without a return ticket."

"An odd fact," he helped her, "but not one to
brood upon."

"But you brood on things like that."

"You have a philosophy."

"Common sense." And she restored the umbrella
to its duty.

"Suppose the world *is* a ball," she returned to the
charge, "that doesn't make it a pill that you can
swallow. It doesn't even make it a ball you can play
football with. But you go about believing that
because it is round, presently you will be able to
trundle it about."

"You have quite a good philosophy," he said.

"It works—anyhow," she retorted.

"I did not know that you ran your life on nearly
such a good road-bed. I think— I think your
philosophy is as good as mine. So far as your present
activities are concerned. I didn't imagine you had
thought it out to this extent."

"I thought it out last night and this morning because your talk had bothered me."

Mr. Sempack made no reply for some moments. He remained regarding her in silence with an expression on his face that she had seen before on other faces. And when he spoke, what he said was to begin with, similar to other speeches that had followed that expression in her previous experiences.

"I suppose that many people have told you that you are extraordinarily beautiful and young and proud and clever?"

She met his eyes with studied gravity, though she was really very much elated to have got this much from the great Mr. Sempack. "Shall I pretend I don't think I'm good looking?" she asked.

"You are and you are full of life, happy in yourself, sure of yourself and of your power, through us, over your universe. Naturally your time is the present. Naturally you are wholly in the drama, and you don't want even to think of the time before the curtain went up and still less of the time when the curtain will come down. You *are* Life, at the crest. Your philosophy expresses that. Your religion is just touching for luck and returning thanks. I wouldn't alter your philosophy. But most of us are not like you. What is life for you is 'Meanwhile' for most of us."

"There is too much meanwhile in the world," said Lady Catherine after a moment's reflection, and met his eyes more than ever.

"What would you have us do?"

"Believe as I do that things are here and now."

Mr. Sempack's eyes fell to her feet. His thoughts seemed to have sunken to great profundities. Still musing darkly he stood up and lifted his eyes to

78

her face. "Well," he said, with the shadow of a sigh in his voice; "here goes."

And taking her by the elbow of the arm that held the umbrella and by the opposite shoulder, in his own extensive hands, he drew her into a standing position and kissed her very seriously and thoroughly on the mouth. She received his salutation with an almost imperceptible acquiescence. It was a very good serious kiss. He kissed her without either unseemly haste or excessive delay. But his body was quivering, which was as it should be. They stood close together for some moments while the kiss continued. His hands fell from her. Then, as if it explained everything, he said: "I wanted to do that."

"And I hope you are satisfied?" she said with the laugh of one who protests astonishment.

"Not satisfied but—assuaged. Shall we sit down again? You will find it much more comfortable if you sit beside me here."

"You are the most remarkable man I have ever met," she said, and obeyed his suggestion.

§ 8

"I RARELY do things of this sort," said Mr. Sempack, as though he was saying that the weather was fine. He adjusted his hat, his respectable, almost clerical hat, which showed a disposition to retire from his brazen brow altogether.

"You are a *really* wonderful man," said Lady Catherine, leaning towards him, and her expression was simple and sincere.

"You are a *really* wonderful man," she repeated before he could reply, "and now I feel I can talk to

79

you plainly. I have never met any one for a long time who has impressed me as you have done. You are—an astonishing discovery."

Mr. Sempack had half turned towards her so that they sat side by side and face to face with their glowing faces quite close together. It was extraordinary that a man who was so ungainly a week and a room's breath away should become quite attractive and exciting and with the nicest, warmest eyes at a distance of a few inches. But it was so. "It is rare," he said, "that I come back so completely to the present as you have made me do."

"Come back to the present and reality," she urged. "For good. That is what I wanted to say to you. I have been watching you all these days and wondering about you. You are the most exciting thing here. Much the most exciting thing. You have a force and an effect. You have a tremendous effect of personality. I never met any one with so much personality. And you go so straight for things. I know all the political people at home who matter in the least. And not one of them matters in the least. There is not one who has your quality of strength and conviction; not one. Why do you keep out of things? Instead of talking and writing of what is coming; why don't you *make it come?*"

"Oh!" said Mr. Sempack and recoiled a little.

"You could dominate," she said.

"I wasn't thinking of politics or dominating just then," he explained. "I was thinking of—you."

"That's thrown in. But there has to be a setting. You seem to be masterful and yet you decline to be masterful. I am excited by you and I want you masterful. I want to see you—mastering things.

The world is waiting for confident and masterful men. See how Italy has snatched at Mussolini. See how everything at home waits for a decisive voice and a firm hand. It wants a man who is sure as you are sure to grip all this sedition and discontent and feeble mindedness. All parties the same. I'm not taking sides. Philip doesn't seem to know his own mind for five minutes together. And he owns coal galore."

Mr. Sempack had gradually turned from her during this speech. "Philip?" he questioned himself in a whisper. He drooped perceptibly.

His tone when he spoke was calmly elucidatory.

"When we were talking about those things the other night," he remarked, "I did my best to explain just why it was that one could not do anything very much of a positive sort now. Perhaps what I said wasn't clear. The thing that has to happen before anything real can crystallise out in the way of a new state of affairs is a great change in the ideas of people at large. That is the real job in hand at present. Reconstructing people's ideas. To the best of my ability I am making my contribution to that now. I don't see what else can be done."

He was looking at her no longer. He gave her his profile. The glow seemed to have gone out of him.

"But that is not living," she said, with a faint flavour of vexation in her voice. "Meanwhile you must have a life of your own, a life that hurts and excites."

He regarded her gravely. "That I suppose is why I kissed you."

She met his eyes and perceived that the glow had not vanished beyond recall.

"Live now—instead of all this *theorising*," she whispered. "You are so strange a person— You could make an extraordinary figure."

He turned from her, pulled up a great knee with his long hands, slanted his head on one side, considered the proposition.

"You think"; he weighed it; "I should project myself upon the world, flapping and gesticulating, making a great noise. It wouldn't you know be a lucid statement, but it would no doubt have an air. A prophetic raven. Something between Peter the Hermit, William Jennings Bryan and the great Mr. Gladstone on campaign? Leading people stupendously into unthought-of ditches. And leaving them." He turned an eye on her and it occurred to her to ask herself, though she could not wait for the answer, whether he was laughing either at her or at himself. He shook his head slowly from side to side. "No," he concluded.

"We have to learn from the men of science," he supplemented, "that the way to be effective in life is to avoid being personally great—or any such glories and excitements."

"But how can a woman enter into the life of a man who just sits about and thinks and tries it over in talk and writes it down?"

"My dear—you *are* my dear, you know—she can't. But do you dream that some day you and I perhaps might ride together into a conquered city? Beauty and the Highbrow."

"You could do great things."

"After the election, our carriage, horses taken out,

dragged by the shouting populace to the Parliament House."

"You caricature."

"Not so very much. You are, my dear, the loveliest thing alive. I can't imagine anything more sweet and strong—and translucent. I am altogether in love with you. My blood runs through my veins, babbling about you and setting every part of me afire. You stir me like great music. You fill me with inappeasable regrets. But— Between us there is a great gulf fixed. I live to create a world and you are the present triumph of created things."

She said nothing but she willed herself to be magnetic and intoxicating.

Mr. Sempack however was carried past her siren radiations by the current of his thoughts.

"I doubt," he reflected, "if life has very much more use for a perfect thing, for finished grace and beauty, than an artist has for his last year's masterpiece. Life grows the glorious fruit—and parts from it. The essential fact about life is imperfection. Life that ceases to struggle away from whatever it is towards something that it isn't, is ceasing to be life."

"Just as if I were inactive!" she remarked.

"You're splendidly active," he said with a smile like sunlight breaking over rugged scenery: "but it's all in a set and defined drama. Which is nearing the end of its run."

"You mean—I am no positive good in the world at all. A back number."

"Good! You're necessary. For the excitement, disappointment, and humiliation of the people who will attack the real creative tasks. Consider what you are doing! Out of whim. Out of curiosity.

You shine upon me, you dazzle me, you are suddenly friendly to me and tender to me. I forget my self-forgetfulness. I dare to kiss you. It seems almost incredible to me but you— You make it seem possible that I might go far with your loveliness. You bring me near to forgetting what I am, a thing like an intellectual Megatherium, slow but sturdy, mixed up with joints like a rockfall and a style like St. Simeon Stylites—and infinite tedious toil of the spirit—and you make me dream of the pride of a lover."

"*Dream*," she whispered, and radiated a complete Aurora Borealis.

But the mental inertia of Mr. Sempack was very great. Certain things were in his mind to say and he went on saying them.

"I don't want to be brought back to this sort of thing. After I have so painfully—got away from it. I don't want to have my illusions restored. It unmakes one. It is necessary before one can do one solitary good thing in life that one should be humiliated and totally disillusioned about oneself. One isn't born to any living reality until one has escaped from one's prepossession with the personal life. The personal life branches off from the stem to die. The reality of life is to contribute. . . ."

His expression ceased to be indifferent and became obstinate. He was beginning to feel and struggle against her nearness. But he held on for a time.

"All the things in human life that are worth while have been done by clumsy and inelegant people, by people in violent conflict with themselves, by people who blundered and who remain blundering people. They hurt themselves and awake. You know nothing of the inner life of the ungracious. You know nothing of being born as a soul. The bitterness. The reluctant search for compensations. The acceptance of the fact that service must be our beauty. But now this freak of yours brings back to me the renunciations, the suppressions and stifling of desire, that began in my boyhood and darkened my adolescence. I thought I had built myself up above all these things."

"You are—majestic," she whispered.

"Oh, *nonsense!*" He groaned it and, wavering for a moment, turned upon her hungrily and drew her to him.

No soundly beautiful woman has ever doubted that a man is better than a mirror for the realisation of her delight in herself, and it was with the profoundest gratification that Lady Catherine sensed the immense appreciations of his embrace. Her kiss, her rewarding and approving kiss, was no ordinary kiss, for she meant to plant an ineffaceable memory.

§ 9

THE triumphant self-absorption of Lady Catherine, a mood that comprehended not merely self-absorption but the absorption therewith of this immense and exciting and unprecedented Mr. Sempack, gave place abruptly to an entirely different state of mind, to astonishment and even a certain consternation. Central to this new phase of consciousness, was the vividly sunlit figure of little Mrs. Rylands, agape. Agape she was, dismayed, as though she had that instant been suddenly and horribly stung. A sound between the "Oo-er" of an infantile astonishment and a cry of acute pain had proclaimed her.

She stood in the blaze of the Caatinga, flushed and distressed, altogether at a loss in the presence of her surprising guests. She was bareheaded and she carried no sunshade. Her loose-robed figure had the effect of a small child astray.

A swift automatic disentanglement of Lady Catherine and Mr. Sempack had occurred. By rapid gradations all three recovered their social consciousness. In a moment they were grouped like actors who have momentarily forgotten their cues, but are about to pick them up again. Mr. Sempack stood up belatedly.

It was Lady Catherine who was first restored to speech.

"I have been telling Mr. Sempack that he ought to come into public life," she said. "He is too great a man to remain aloof writing books."

Mrs. Rylands' expression was enigmatical. She seemed to be listening and trying to remember the meaning of the sounds she heard. It dawned upon Lady Catherine that her eyes were red with recent weeping. What had happened? Was this some mood of her condition?

Then Mrs. Rylands took control of herself. In another moment she was the hostess of Casa Terragena again, with the edge of her speech restored. "You've been persuading him very delightfully, I'm sure, dearest," she smiled, the smile of a charming hostess—if a little wet about the eyes. "Is he going to?"

"No," said Mr. Sempack, speaking down with large tranquil decision. But his mind was upon Mrs. Rylands.

A different line of treatment had occurred to Lady Catherine. She snatched at it hastily. She abandoned the topic of Mr. Sempack and his career. "But, my dear!" she cried. "What are you doing in this blazing sun? You ought to be tucked away in a hammock in the shade!"

Mrs. Rylands evidently thought this sudden turn of topic disconcerting. She stared at this new remark as if she disliked it extremely and did not know what to do with it.

Then she broke down. "Everybody seems to think I ought to be tucked away somewhere," she said, and fairly sobbed. "I've done the unexpected. I've put everybody out."

She stood weeping like a child. Consternation fell upon Lady Catherine. Mutely she consulted Mr. Sempack and a slight but masterly movement indicated that he would be better left alone with Mrs. Rylands. His wish marched with Lady Catherine's own impulse to fly.

"I've got letters, lots of letters," she said. "I'm forgetting them. I was talking. To post in Monte Carlo this afternoon. If we go, that is."

Mrs. Rylands seemed to approve of this suggestion of a retreat and Lady Catherine became a receding umbrella that halted in the rocky archway for a vague undecided retrospect and then disappeared.

Mrs. Rylands remained standing, looking at the archway. She had an air of standing there because she had nowhere else in the whole world to go, and looking at the archway because there was nothing else on earth to look at. She might have been left on a platform by a train, the only possible train, she had intended to take.

"I thought I would talk to you," she said, not looking at Mr. Sempack, but still contemplating the vanished back of Lady Catherine.

"It *is* too hot for us to be here," said Mr. Sempack, taking hold of the situation. "Quite close round the corner beyond the stone pines, there is shade and running water and a seat."

"It was absurd, but I thought I would talk to you." Her intonation implied that this was no longer a possibility.

Mr. Sempack made no immediate reply.

The first thing to do he perceived was to get Mrs. Rylands out of the blaze of the sun. Then more was required of him. Evidently she had been assailed by some sudden, violent, and nearly unbearable trouble. Something had struck her, some passionate shocking blow, that had detached her spinning giddily from everything about her. And she had thought of him as large, intelligent, immobile, neutral—above all and in every sense neutral, as indeed a convenient bulk, a sympathetic disinterested bulk, to which one might cling in a torrent of dismay, and which might even have understanding to hold one on if at any time one's clinging relaxed. He had been the only possible father confessor. Sexlessness was a primary necessity to that. In this particular case. For he knew, the thought emerged with unchallenged assurance, that her trouble concerned Philip and Philip's fidelity. And instead of finding a priest, she had, just at this phase when the idea of embraces was altogether revolting to her, caught him embracing.

He glimpsed her present vision of the whole world as lying, betraying, and steamily, illicitly intertwined. And since his instincts and his habits of mind were all

88

for resolving the problems of others and extracting whatever was helpful in the solution, since he liked his little hostess immensely and was ready not only to help in general but anxious to help her in particular, he did his best to push the still glowing image of Lady Catherine into the background of his mind and set himself to efface the bad impression their so intimate grouping had made upon Mrs. Rylands.

With an entirely mechanical submission to his initiative she was walking beside him towards the shade when he spoke.

"I was talking about myself to Lady Catherine," he said, and paused to help his silent companion down a stepway. "I think I betrayed a certain sense of my ungainliness. . . . I *am* ungainly. . . . Lady Catherine is full of generous impulsive helpfulness and her method of reassuring me was—dramatic and—tangible."

Mrs. Rylands made no immediate reply.

A score or so of paces and they were in the chequered shade of the stone pines and then a zigzag had taken them out of the Caatinga altogether and down to a gully, with a trickle of water and abundant ferns and horse-tails and there in a cool cavernous place, that opened to them like a blessing, was a long seat of wood. Mrs. Rylands sat down. Mr. Sempack stood over her, a little at a loss.

"I thought I might talk to you," she repeated. "I thought I might be able to talk to you."

"And now—something has spoilt me," he said. "Perhaps I know how you feel. . . . I wish . . . If you cannot talk to me, perhaps you will let me sit down here and even, it may be, presently say a word or so to you."

He sat down slowly beside her and became quite still.

"The world has gone ugly," she said.

He stirred, a rustle of interrogation.

"It is all cruel and ugly," she burst out. "Ugly! I wish I were dead."

Mr. Sempack did not look at her. She swallowed her tears unobserved. "I was afraid this would happen to you," he said, "from the very moment I saw you. Afraid! I knew it had to happen to you."

She looked at him in astonishment. "But how do you know what has happened?"

"I don't. That is—I know no particulars. But I know you thought of a life, subtle and fine as Venetian glass, and I know that is all shattered."

"I thought life could be clean and fine."

Mr. Sempack made no answer for a moment. Then he said: "And how do you know it isn't clean and fine?"

"He told me lies. At least he acted lies. He pretended she was nothing—"

Mr. Sempack considered that. "Has it ever occurred to you that your husband is a very young man? Sensitive minded and fine."

"*He!*"

"Yes. In spite of everything. And telling a harsh truth is one of the last things we learn to do. Most of us never do. He hasn't told all sorts of hard truths even to himself."

"Hard truths and harsh truths!" said the lady, as though she did her best to apprehend Mr. Sempack's indications. "You don't know—the brutality . . ."

She choked.

"And she is nothing to him," said Mr. Sempack serenely.

"You don't understand what has happened. There they were. In the little bathing chalet. . . ."

Her woe deepened. "Any one might have come upon them!"

"Perhaps they had accounted for everybody but you."

"My fault then."

"They saw you?"

"Oh! they *saw* me."

"And he stayed with her?"

"No. He came after me almost at once."

"You told him to go back to her."

"How do you know?"

"It was the first thing to say. And he didn't go back."

"He tried to excuse himself?"

"That was difficult."

"He said horrible things. Oh, horrible!"

Mr. Sempack's silence was an invincible question and moreover Mrs. Rylands was driven by an irresistible impulse to tell the dreadful things that threatened to become destructive and unspeakable monstrosities if they were not thrust out while they still had some communicable form. Even now she told them with a shadow of doubt in her mind.

"He said, 'I can't live this life of milk and water. I must get excited somehow—or I shall burst!' "

"That stated a case," said Mr. Sempack with deliberation. "That stated a case."

She weighed this for some moments as though she felt it ought to mean something. Then she seemed

91

to feel about in her mind for a lost thread and resumed: "I said nothing. I hurried on."

"He asked you to listen?"

"I couldn't. Not then."

"You went on and he followed—that extremely inarticulate young man, trying to express things that he felt but could not understand. And you were in blind flight from something you did not wish to understand."

"He caught hold of me and I dragged myself away."

Mr. Sempack waited patiently.

"He shouted out 'Oh, *hell*' very loudly and dropped behind. I don't know where he went. He is somewhere down there. Perhaps he went back to her."

"And that was how it happened?"

"Yes," she said, "it happened like that."

She stared in front of her for a long time, and Mr. Sempack had so much to say that he found himself unable to say anything. To meet this case a whole philosophy was needed. The silence unrolled.

"My Philip!" she whispered at last.

It was clear that whatever idea she had had of talking to Mr. Sempack had evaporated from her mind. "I don't know why I have told you of this," she said at last with the slightest turn of her head towards him. "The heat. . . . I shall go back to bed. Put myself away."

She stood up.

"I will come back with you as far as the house if I may," said Mr. Sempack.

They walked in the completest silence. Not even a consolatory word came to him.

He watched her vanish between the white pillars into the deep cool shadows of the hall. "Poor young people! What a mess it is!" he said, and entirely oblivious of Lady Catherine, standing splendidly at the great staircase window and ready to descend at a word, he walked, downcast and thoughtful, along an aisle of arum lilies towards a great basin full of nuphar. He clasped his hands behind him and humped one shoulder higher than the other. His shambling legs supported him anyhow.

Here was something that it was immensely necessary to think out, and to think out into serviceable conclusions soon. He could not attend to the outlying parts of his person.

§ 10

TO Bombaccio, the first intimation that something had gone wrong in the house party of Terragena was brought by Miss Puppy Clarges. He had been putting out the English papers on the hall table and touching and patting the inkpots and pens and blotting-pads on the writing-tables in the southern recess of the hall and meditating on the just position of the various waste-paper baskets, and blessing and confirming all such minor amenities, when she came in. He wore a diamond ring, not one with an exceptional diamond like Mr. Plantagenet-Buchan's, but just a diamond ring, and as he did things he exercised himself in a rather nice attitude with the hand upheld, that Mr. Plantagenet-Buchan affected. It seemed to Bombaccio a desirable attitude. She came in from the terrace towards the sea while he was posed in this way. She gave his hand a passing unintelligent glance and spoke brusquely. "Bombaccio," she said, "I have to clear out at once. I've had a telegram that my half-sister in Nice is very ill."

"But," said Bombaccio, "I did not know the Signorina had had a telegram."

"Nor any one else. Wonderful how it got to me; isn't it? But it did—and don't you forget it. Don't you give way to any weakening on that point. I've had a telegram that my half-sister in Nice is very ill and now I've told you—you know I've had it."

Bombaccio bowed with grave submission.

"Off I go to pack and down I come to go. What car, Bombaccio?"

"I'll ask Mrs. Rylands."

"Don't. Just get me that old Fiat in the village and I'll clatter down to the station at Mentone right away. As soon as poss. It's a case of life and death."

"The next train for Nice," reflected Bombaccio, "does not depart—"

"Don't go into figures," said Miss Clarges. "Telephone and get that auto now."

She reflected, knuckle to lip. "Wait a moment," she said. "I'll write a note—two notes."

She went to a writing-table, placed a sheet before her, chose a pen and meditated briefly. Bombaccio waited. Then her pen flew. One note she addressed to her hostess. It was a note of exceptional brevity and it was unsigned. *"Sorry,"* wrote Miss Clarges. *"I'm gone and I won't worry you again."*

"Sorry I got caught," Miss Clarges remarked to herself, and licked the envelope. *"Fools* we were."

Then she directed a more elaborate epistle to Mr.

Geoffrey Rylands. *"Dear Geoff,"* she scribbled. *"That Limitless Field Preacher has got on my nerves. Another meal of talk with him and Mr. Pantaloon Buchan and I shall scream. I've fled to the Superba at Dear Old Monty. Where my friends can find me, bless 'em. A rividerci, Puppy."*

That got its swift lick also and a whack to stick it down.

"Here's the documents!" she said.

Bombaccio was left developing a series of bows and gestures to express that all things in the world would be as the Signorina wished, while Miss Puppy vanished upstairs. Then he went slowly and thoughtfully to the telephone.

But he did not telephone. He hated the man who owned the old Fiat and there were two cars in the garage. One of them was booked for Monte Carlo after lunch, but that was no reason why Signorina Clarges should not have the other. In the well-known Terragena car she'd go through the French douane like a bird; in the hired car she wouldn't. He would consult Signora Rylands. Or Signor Rylands.

And on reflection it became more and more distinctly unusual that a guest should depart in this fashion without some intimation from either host or hostess. There was something wrong in that. The fact of Signorina Clarges' swift passage upstairs, originally a bare fact, became encrusted with interrogations; the brow of Bombaccio was troubled. She was giving all the orders. What should a perfect major-domo do?

Signora Rylands, he believed, was still in bed and inaccessible. Signor Rylands? Signor Rylands?

But—? Consider—? He had gone off with Signorina Clarges to swim. Yes. Something must have happened. Where was Mr. Rylands now? Why was he not ordering the car for the Signorina Clarges? Had he by any chance insulted her—and was she departing insulted?

But then, was it possible to insult the Signorina Clarges?

Perhaps the best thing would be to consult Frant, Mrs. Rylands' maid, a stupid English person who mistook secretiveness for discretion, but still the only possible source of indications just at present. . . .

These questionings were abruptly interrupted by the appearance of Mr. Plantagenet-Buchan coming through the front hall, with the vague, prowling air of a guest who has found nothing to do with his morning. He was wearing a new suit of tussore silk and wasting much neatness upon solitude. The wave in his hair was in perfect condition.

He brightened at the sight of Bombaccio. *"Dove e tutto?"* he asked. He liked to address every man in his own language, as a good European should, and this was his way of saying "Where's everybody?"

Bombaccio replied with the most carefully perfect English intonation, "Colonel Bullace, Saire, is at the tennis."

"E l'altri?"

Bombaccio expressed extreme dispersal by an expansive gesture and disowned special knowledge by a deprecatory smile. "Others are at the tennis," he said.

"Lady Catherine?" asked Mr. Plantagenet-Buchan, trying to be quite casual in his tone.

"She loves the garden!" said Bombaccio and began a respectful retreat.

Mr. Plantagenet-Buchan hovered vaguely for a moment and then turned his face towards the front entrance. Abruptly the retreat of Bombaccio was accelerated and Mr. Plantagenet-Buchan looking round for a cause, became aware of Miss Clarges, clothed now with unusual decorum, at the bend of the staircase.

"How about that car, Bombaccio?" cried Miss Clarges.

Bombaccio, not hearing with all his might, disappeared, and the door that led to the domestic mysteries clicked behind him. "Damn!" said Miss Clarges. "Hullo, Mr. Plantagenet-Buchan!"

Mr. Plantagenet-Buchan moved to show that he was hullo all right.

"I've got a half-sister dangerously ill—in Monaco, and I want a car. I'm all packed up and ready to go. Leastways I shall be in ten minutes."

"Can I be of any assistance?" said Mr. Plantagenet-Buchan unhelpfully.

"Naturally," said Miss Puppy. "I want some sort of car got and some of the minions to carry my bags up to the gates. Every one seems to be out of the way."

"Anything I can *do*," said Mr. Plantagenet-Buchan, looking entirely ornamental.

"If you'd just warm Bombaccio's ear a bit," said Miss Clarges. "What's wanted is movement. Getting a move on."

Mr. Plantagenet-Buchan felt the reproach in her tone. "I will stir things up. I do hope your half-sister—"

But Puppy had vanished upstairs again.

Mr. Plantagenet-Buchan reflected. He would go to the bell and ring and when somebody came he would say in a gentle masterful way: *"La Signorina Clarges e nervosa da la sua automobiglia. Prega de l'accelerato prestissimo."*

But he would have much preferred to have gone on straight into the garden to look for Lady Catherine. He felt they went better together.

He found some difficulty in putting matters right with the minion who responded to his ring. The fellow did not seem to understand his own language and evidently missed the purport of Mr. Plantagenet-Buchan's communication altogether. He seemed to think Mr. Plantagenet-Buchan was complaining of the manner in which Mrs. Rylands' English chauffeur discharged his duties and expressed himself, with some vivid and entertaining pantomime, as being in the completest agreement. He repeated the expression "molto periculoso" several times with empressement. Now the Italian driver was a model of discretion. Mr. Plantagenet-Buchan was still trying, without too complete an admission of a linguistic breakdown, to mould the conversation nearer to Miss Clarges' heart's desire, when Lady Catherine appeared in the low oblong blaze of sunshine beyond the dark pillars of the portico. He dismissed the minion with a gesture and walked forward to meet her.

The hall behind him was left for a moment in silence and shadow, and then its ceiling and central parts resonated to the rich voice of Miss Clarges. "What the hell?" the voice of Miss Clarges inquired, passionately but incompletely, and her door slammed.

She must have been listening on the landing. A few moments later, the muffled wheeze of a distant electric bell was audible from the servants' quarters, a bell that kept on ringing persistently. Miss Clarges was ringing.

Before Lady Catherine became aware of Mr. Plantagenet-Buchan in the dim coolness of the entrance, her face betrayed a certain perturbation and she was hurrying. At the sight of him, she slackened her gait and became a sauntering queen, ruddy in the halo of the green umbrella.

"So hot," she said, chin up and smiling. "Too hot! I'm coming in to write letters. Are you for Monte Carlo this afternoon?"

"In this blaze?" he doubted and shrugged his shoulders.

She hovered over him for a moment, not quite sure what to do with him.

"Lucky man!" she said. "You've got nothing to do but read the English papers and keep cool."

She made her way round him to the staircase, smiling him down.

Mr. Plantagenet-Buchan was left in the silent hall. He went to the table on the terrace side where the freshly-opened newspapers were displayed. He threw them about almost petulantly. He felt he had never seen less attractive newspapers. Even the head-lines of the *Daily Express* seemed dull. He sat down at last to the *Times*, to learn who had died and who had gone abroad.

Then came an interruption of Geoffrey, very hot, moist and open-necked, in search of Bombaccio and drinks and ice for the tennis court. At his appear-

99

ance on the terrace Mr. Plantagenet-Buchan shrank deeper into his arm-chair beside the pillar.

"Hullo!" said Geoffrey. "Papers come?"

Mr. Plantagenet-Buchan made a gesture of his newspaper to express anything Geoffrey liked except an inclination to talk, and Geoffrey passed on. He came back presently, followed by Bombaccio with a jingling tray, and passed across the terrace and down the marble steps towards the tennis court. Then after a large interval of silence, came footsteps on the staircase. He turned hopefully and saw Miss Clarges in travelling dress. He stood up in spite of a faint disappointment. At any rate she was going.

"I'm off," she said. "No chance of saying ta-ta all round. You'll have to do it for me."

"I hope it's all right about the automobile."

"God knows," she said. "I'm going up the garden after my bags to see. Have to fuss round up there if it isn't. Extraordinary they don't bring a motor road right down to the house. Sacrificing comfort to gardening, I call it."

She smiled conventionally and turned towards the entrance. Then she stopped short and became rigid. She had seen something outside there that as yet Mr. Plantagenet-Buchan could not see. "*Glory!*" she gasped.

She had forgotten Mr. Plantagenet-Buchan for an instant. Then she turned to him and saw his inquiring face. "I've left something in my room," she explained, and turned tail and fled upstairs. The next moment the feet of two people became visible and then the all of them in the sunlit space uphill beyond the portico. Mrs. Rylands was approaching, and she walked like a woman in a trance and beside her in silence, looking very large and awkward and uncomfortable, was Mr. Sempack. Before the entrance, they parted without a word; Mr. Sempack stood irresolute and Mrs. Rylands came on in.

She did not seem to see Mr. Plantagenet-Buchan standing still beside the newspaper table.

She walked to the staircase and then, after a momentary pause, made her way up it, helping herself with a hand upon the bannister.

For some seconds Mr. Plantagenet-Buchan remained lost in thought, and then, still thinking, he seated himself upon the newspaper table. Presently Miss Clarges appeared descending the staircase with an unwonted softness. She looked as though she might say almost anything to Mr. Plantagenet-Buchan, but what she did say simply and almost confidentially was, "So long." Then she went out into the sun-glare and vanished up the hill towards the gates upon the road.

Mr. Plantagenet-Buchan shook his head slowly from side to side, disapprovingly, took counsel with his diamond ring, struggled off the table, and made his way, still thinking deeply, to his own room in the turret.

He paced his floor obliquely. It had become plain to him what had happened.

He was glad to have a little time to himself to consider the situation before facing the world. What exactly ought a fine-minded, thoroughly Europeanised American gentleman to do? Not simply that. He was really fond of his hostess. Fond enough to put his pose into a secondary place. What could he do for her?

The turret room had four windows that looked

east and west and north and south and as Mr. Plantagenet-Buchan paced up and down from corner to
corner, he would ever and again lift his downcast
eyes, first to this pretty sunlit picture and then to
that. And presently he became aware of something
white, minute in perspective, something moving, far
off, among the red sun-scorched rocks of the headland to the west that came out like a scenery wing to
frame the distant view of Mentone. He took a
pocket monocular that lay upon his toilet table out of
its case, focussed it and scrutinised this distant object.
It was a man in flannels scrambling along a little precipitous path that led round the cape. He moved
with every symptom of haste and irritation. He
slipped and recovered himself, and stood still for a
moment in profile looking up at the shiny rocks, with
an expression of reproachful inquiry. Unmistakably
it was Philip Rylands.

He was making off. To nowhere in particular.

§ 11

IT was evening and Mrs. Rylands lay in bed in
her unlit room. The windows were wide open
but the blue serenities without were seen through
a silken haze of mosquito curtain. And Mrs. Rylands was thinking.

Before lunch she had summoned Lady Catherine
to her bedside and thrust most of her duties as a
hostess upon her. "I'm ill," she said. "I've had a
shock, never mind what, dearest, don't say a word
about it, but it's made me ill. I want to be alone, and
there's all this party!"

All Lady Catherine's better self came uppermost.

She kissed her friend. "I'll see they get their lunch," she said; "I and Bombaccio. It's your privilege to be ill now, just as you please and whenever you please. And afterwards shall I pack some of them off?"

"They do very little harm," said Mrs. Rylands. "I shall get on all right—in a bit. Get the bridge and tennis Stupids out of the house if you can—if they have somewhere to go. But don't *chase* them out. They amuse each other. . . . Don't make them uncomfortable. . . . I like to have Mr. Sempack about. I like him. When they have gone I will come down again."

"And Mr. Plantagenet-Buchan?"

"He doesn't matter. Just take hold of things, Kitty. I can't arrange."

Lady Catherine took hold of things. "Don't you bother, Cynthia. Bombaccio and I could run four such parties."

"Don't want to see any one. Just want to think."

"I *quite* understand."

A last murmur from the bed. "Don't want to be told or asked about anything just now."

A kiss in response and Lady Catherine had gone.

The head on the pillow snuggled under the sheet with an affectation of profound fatigue until Lady Catherine was surely out of the room, and then it was raised and looked round cautiously. Slowly, wearily, Mrs. Rylands sat up again and became still, staring in front of her. The protective mask of the rather pathetic dear little thing had vanished. A very grave, very sad human being was revealed.

For a long time her mind remained stagnant. And when at last it did revive it did not so much move forward from thought to thought as sit down and contemplate her world unveiled.

She had been living in a dream, she realised, and only such a shock as this could have awakened her. She had been living in a dream wilfully. In spite of a thousand hints and intimations, she had clung to her beautiful illusions about Philip and herself and the quality of life. Now that she had not so much let go of her dream as had it torn from her hand, it began forthwith to seem incredible and remote. It was plain to her that for weeks and months she had understood Philip's real quality—and refused to understand. She was already amazed to remember how steadfastly she had refused to understand.

When at last, late in the afternoon, a letter came from Philip, a note rather than a letter, written in pencil, it did but confirm the hard outlines of her realisations.

"My darling Cynthia," wrote Philip. *"What can I say to you, except ask you to forgive me? I suppose you think I'm an utter beast and I suppose I am an utter beast. Yet these things take one in a way you can't understand and one finds out what seems just a lark isn't. I do hope anyhow that whatever you say or do to me you won't be too hard on old Puppy. It's my fault first and foremost and all the time. It is dead against all Puppy's code to go back on the hostess with whom she is staying in that fashion. But one thing led to another. I over-persuaded her and really we had not planned or arranged what happened. On my honour. It just came upon us. It may have been brewing in the air*

position and opportunities he may yet play a quite considerable part in the world's affairs."

"That is what I had dreamt," she said, and her eyes went back to that pencil scrawl.

"What has happened does nothing to change that. There are points material to this issue which I do not think you apprehend. I do not see how they can have entered into your consciousness. I will try to put them to you—if you will be patient with me. Let me repeat, I think enormous things of your Philip. I don't think that you made a mistake when you loved him and gave your life to him. And for you—you might be my daughter—I have that feeling, that only people who have been schooled to disinterested affection can have. I have watched you both. I care for you both deeply. I care doubly. I care for you also on account of him. I care for him also on account of you. Two fine lives are yours; two hopeful lives."

"And then *this!*" she whispered, and for some moments read no more.

"I want you to consider your differences. I don't think you have ever thought about your differences. Everything has disposed you to ignore them. You are a finer thing than Philip but you are—slighter. You are completer but slighter. He is still unformed but larger and more powerful. He has the makings of a far bigger and stronger and more effective person than you can ever be. You must grant me that. I think you will grant me that. We human things; what are we? Channels through which physical energy flows into decision and act and creative achievement. There is a pitiless pressure to *do*.

107

Living is doing. Life is an engine, a trap, to catch blind force and turn it into more life and build it up into greater and more powerful forms. That is how I see life. That is how you are disposed to see life. We are all under that pressure—in varying degrees. The chief business of every one of us, every one who has a consciousness of such things, is to master and direct and utilise his pressure. Most of us spend the better part of our lives trying to solve the problem of how that is to be done before all pressure of vitality is exhausted. And your Philip is under pressures, blind pressures, ten, twenty times as powerful as all the driving force in you. I hope this does not offend you?"

"There is a sort of truth in that," said Mrs. Rylands.

"And now let me assure you he loves you. It is you he loves, have no doubt of it. And he loves you for endless things of course, but among them, chief among them, because of this, that you have self-control, you seemed to him, as you are, serene, wise, balanced, delicately poised."

"Not now," said Mrs. Rylands.

"He thinks, no! he realises, that you have *direction*, which is just what he lacks. That brought him to you perhaps first. That does and can continue to hold him to you. But that does not prevent old Nature, who has made us all out of the dust and the hot damp and the slime, pressing upon him and pressing him. He is living here in this warmth, in this abundance, far off from the business life and political life that might engage him; he came here— that is the irony of it—to be with you, to wait upon you here in the loveliest, most perfect setting. You know that was his intention. You know he has treated you sweetly and delicately. Until, as you think, you found him out."

She nodded assent and turned the page quickly.

"But he wasn't deceiving you. You haven't found him out so much as he has found himself out. He meant all that devotion. If only some Angel above could have turned off the tap of his energy to a mere trickle, then this would really have been the paradise you thought it was, until to-day. But all he could do here, to be the perfect lover of your dreams, he could have done with one twentieth part of the energy that drives through his nerves and blood. You knew he was restless?"

"I thought it was this Coal Strike," said Mrs. Rylands.

"Any voice that called to him, he had activity released to hear. And dear old Nature, horrible old Nature, has only one channel for the release of pent-up energy."

"Horrible old Nature," Mrs. Rylands agreed and seemed to recall some impression. Nature! So gross and yet with a queer power in her grossness, so revolting in an ugliness that sometimes became suddenly and disconcertingly holy and terribly beautiful! But what was Mr. Sempack saying?

"With you— A man may show his love by a delicate restraint. Must indeed be very delicate and restrained. And here he was in this fermenting blaze with nothing else to do—nothing. He didn't want to make love to any other woman. He loves nobody but you. If he had wanted to make love— consider! Lady Catherine here is being driven towards trouble also by our tyrannous old Grandmother. There is no comparison in the loveliness of these two women. But Lady Catherine is an equal, a personality. He wouldn't look at her, wouldn't dream of her. Because that would be a real infringement of you. That would be a real division of love. But on the other hand there was this Miss Clarges, who disavows all the accessories of sex—and is simply sexual. She is good company in the open air. She swims well and one can swim with her. Things change their emotional quality away from the house. Wet skin and sunburnt skin, movement and sunlight and a smiling face. Comes a flare-up, a desire, and a consoling and refreshing physical release. Nervous release. It can seem such a simple thing. My dear Mrs. Rylands, you may choose to think of it as horrible, you may be compelled to think of it as horrible, but indeed, I can assure you, at times it can be as healthy a thing physically as breathing mountain air. That is outside your quality, your experience, but not outside your understanding. If you care to understand; if you have the generosity to understand. But of course you have the generosity to understand. There is a case for them both. What concerns me most is the case for him."

She put down the letter again. She had come to the end of a sheet.

"But I loved him," she said. "This is asking too much."

She lay still a long time. "It is asking too much," she whispered.

She glanced again at what she had read. "Nervous release," she re-tasted—and it tasted disgustingly.

What was wrong with Mr. Sempack—or what was wrong with her?

What were these different tunes that were being played simultaneously upon their two temperaments by the same world?

"It isn't right," she thought. "But I'm not clever enough, my head is not clear enough, to see where it is wrong. . . . I'm wrong too. I see I'm wrong. . . . Perhaps he's righter than I am. . . .

"My poor little wits!"

It seemed to her that Sempack put things with a sort of reasonableness, but in a light that was strange, like the light in the tanks of Monaco Aquarium. It was as if the sun had suddenly gone green. Everything had very much the same shape but nothing had its proper colour. Everything had become *deep*. This man's mind was as large and unusual as his body. She took up the next sheet and the light of Mr. Sempack's mind seemed greener and colder and the things it illuminated deeper than ever.

"If he is to stay here centring his life wholly upon you, what is to be done with the nineteen-twentieths of his vitality that will be left over? It is not merely physical vitality we are dealing with. That might be devoted to swimming, climbing, tennis. But you cannot separate bodily and imaginative energy so completely; the one drags at the other. There is no such thing as purely physical vitality. The accumulation of energy amidst this warmth and beauty and leisure affects the imagination, demands not simply an effort but a thrill."

There was a blank space of half a sheet.

"I am trying to expose the real Philip to you, this soul struggling with the mysteries of a body as a man struggles with an unbroken horse. And some one else also, I want to expose to you, whom perhaps you do not yet completely know, the real Cynthia Rylands. You see, I am not going to ask you to forgive him. That is the danger ahead for both of you. He will ask that, but I know better than he does in this matter, about him and about you. I want you to realise that there is nothing to forgive."

She stopped to think that over and then read on.

"Philip is your job," the resolute writing continued. "I see no other job in the world for you to compare with it or to replace it. Children? People overrate what a modern mother has to do for her children, as they underrate what she can do for her man. Women are for men and children are a by-product. You have given your life to Philip for better or worse, and nothing can ever take it altogether back. Try to take it back and you will leave a previous part of you to die.

"Is this true of all husbands and all wives? you may ask. No. Nothing is true of all husbands and all wives. Half the men in the world are nincompoops, and an unknown proportion of women idiots. I do not see that they and their horrid, sloppy relationships come into this discussion. Let them slop and squabble in their own way. I am thinking of two people of very fine quality and unequal energy. I am thinking of you and Philip. You can supply a protection, a charity, a help, a stability to that young man, without which he will just make the sort of mess of life natural to his type. And he is worth what you can give him. He has quality. He is worth saving from his temperamental fate. But your first sacrifice has to be, the sacrifice of your instinctive sexual resentments. Your first effort has to be an enormous patience and charity. Your first feat has to be your realisation that much may be clean or cleansable in him, that would be, well—a little disgusting to you. I must make myself quite plain. It is not a question of your forgiving him this affair with Miss Clarges, after due repentance on his part, and going on again on your old lines with the understanding that nothing of the sort is ever going to happen again. What is before you is something much harder than that. It is a matter of bracing yourself up to the new idea that this sort of thing is likely to happen again in your lives, and that it may happen repeatedly, and however often it may happen, it has never to make the slightest diminution of your support of him or of his respect and confidence in you. While you stand over his life, you unbroken and resolute, no affair of this sort will ever wreck it. He will come back to you. You will be his fastness, his safe place. Every time more and more. But talk and think of offending and forgiving, put yourself on a level with Miss Puppy Clarges, fight her for him, peck the other hen, and shut yourself against him—in any way, in any way, and down he goes and down you go, and your two lives will dribble through a tangle of commonplace sexual quarrels and estrangements to some sort of muddling divorce or separation or compromise. . . .

"I don't know why I write all this to you. Your brain is as fine as mine and you must know all that I am writing. As you read it it will come to your mind not as a new conviction but as the illumination of something that has always been there.

"You are Philip Rylands' wife. In the fullest

sense and to the last possible shade of meaning, you are his wife; you are a wife by nature, and the rôle of a wife is not to compete and be jealous, but to understand and serve and by understanding and serving rule. Wives are rare things in life, but you are surely one. You cannot possibly give yourself the airs of the ordinary married mistress. You have wedded yourself to your Philip—beyond jealousy—except for his sake. I can see you in no other part."

Again came a sort of break in the writing. "That is really all that I have to say to you. Perhaps I may add—rest assured that unless I am no judge of a man, when at last he comes to his full stature—through your protection and your help and stimulation—Rylands will be worth while. Through him you may do great things in the world and in no other way will you personally ever do great things. Because you are reflective; because your initiatives are too delicate for the weight and strains of life."

Mr. Sempack had not signed this letter. There it ended.

After re-reading this communication Mrs. Rylands turned out her bedside lamp and lay quite motionless in the deepening twilight, and thought. Far away Mentone returned out of the evening blue that had drowned it and became a little necklace of minute lights flung upon the deep azure darkness.

"He will be worth while." Was that written to comfort her?

Worth while? Was that true? Would Phil really become that strong competent man laying a determining hand on human affairs she had once dreamt of, or were not both she and Mr. Sempack a little carried away by his good looks, by his occasional high gravity and by something generous and naïve in his quality? . . . And also . . . Something dear about him? . . . Something very dear?

Mrs. Rylands found that she was weeping.

After all, she asked with an abrupt mental collapse, did it matter in the least if he was worth while?

"Sometimes such a dear," she whispered.

She had thought and perhaps feared that a repulsion, a physical dislike might have crept between herself and Philip, but suddenly she realised that he was just as magnetic for her as he had ever been. She found herself longing for him to come to her, longing, irrationally, monstrously.

She would not send for him. She could not send for him. That would be too much. But she longed for him to come to her.

§ 12

DOWNSTAIRS an attenuated house party sat at dinner. The Mathisons and Geoffrey Rylands had departed for Monte Carlo, moved and encouraged to do so by their host. Mr. Haulbowline had gone with them, making up his mind at the last moment when he realised that there might be no bridge in the evening. Unprotected by a bridge group he might have to be visible, audible and distinctive. And the Bullaces were away, dining with a dear old friend of the wife's at Diano Marino, the widow of an army chaplain who had been killed and partially eaten, no doubt at Bolshevik instigation, by an ill-disposed panther in Bengal. To-morrow the Bullaces were going back to England. The coal situation in Britain was becoming more threatening every day and the chance of social disturbance greater. The Colonel felt that his place was in the field of danger there, and that at any moment his peculiar gifts might be in request for the taming of insurgent labour.

Miss Fenimore and Lady Grieswold were both present. In spite of some very suggestive talk from Lady Catherine their movements were uncertain. Lady Catherine had perhaps exaggerated the gravity of Mrs. Rylands' health and her need for peace, and Miss Fenimore had felt not that she ought to go but that she ought to stay "in case some one was wanted." Lady Grieswold held on firmly without any explanation, but Lady Catherine had reason for hoping that when it was manifest a bridge famine was inevitable her grip would relax. Though of course there was the possibility of a break away into patience. However that was to be seen.

The Tamars were due at Geneva in three days' time and so Lady Catherine did nothing to dislodge them. They were very harmless; they had spent the day together in a long walk up the hills, had taken their lunch and she had done a water-colour sketch of the little chapel in the upper valley; they had returned just in time for dinner and heard of Mrs. Rylands' collapse only in the drawing-room. They were quietly happy and tired and their sympathy was pleasantly free from any note of distress.

The table talk was for a time disconnected and desultory, with long pauses, and then it broke into a loose debate between Stoicism and Epicureanism, in which Mr. Sempack and Mr. Plantagenet-Buchan said nearly everything. Mr. Sempack started with a panegyric of the Stoic; it seemed to be there in his mind and it was almost as if he thought aloud. He addressed what he had to say away from Lady Catherine, markedly. His discourse seemed by its very nature to turn its back on her. Mr. Plantagenet-Buchan talked rather at Lady Catherine and Miss Fenimore, appealing to them for support by the direction of his head and smiles and gestures. The Tamars were mildly interested and ever and again at some of the flatter passages they smiled mysteriously at one another, as though, if they cared, they could put quite a different complexion on things. Philip was unaffectedly lost in thought. He did not pretend even to listen.

Lady Grieswold said little but became visibly uneasy as the discussion soared and refused to descend. She was wondering if the Tamars would like to play bridge and still more how she might give this very difficult conversation a turn that would enable her to suggest this. Perhaps they did not know how to play yet and might like to be shown—of course for quite nominal stakes. It was wonderful the things these intellectual people did not know. She never contrived to get her suggestion out for all her alertness and she went up to a bridgeless drawing-room and sat apart and felt she was a widow more acutely than she had done for many years, and retired quite early to bed showing, Lady Catherine noted with satisfaction, no disposition whatever for the consolations of the patience spread.

Mr. Sempack began in a pause, almost or altogether out of nothing. If anything could be regarded as releasing the topic its connexion was so remote that it vanished from the mind as soon as it had served its purpose. "It is remarkable," he began, "how silently and steadily Stoicism returns to the world."

"Stoicism!" said Mr. Plantagenet-Buchan and raised his fine eyebrows.

"Consolation without rewards or punishments, a pure worship of right and austerity. It came too soon into the world; it had to give place to Mithraism and Isis worship and the Christianities for two thousand years. *Now*—it returns to a world more prepared for it."

"But *does* it return?" said Mr. Plantagenet-Buchan with a disarming smile.

Mr. Sempack pursued his own train of thought. "The simple consolations needed by life in an under-civilised world, the craving for exemplary punishments, rewards and compensations; those Christianity could give. And a substitutional love to make up for human unkindnesses—and failures of loyalty. . . . Not to be despised. By no means to be despised. . . . But in the cold light of to-day these consolations fade. In the cold clear light of our increasing knowledge. We cannot keep them even if we would. We strain to believe and we cannot do it. We are left terribly to the human affections in all their incompleteness—and behind them what remains for us? Endurance. The strength of our own souls."

His voice sank so beautifully that for a moment or so Lady Catherine knew what it was to be wholly in love. What a great rock he was! What tranquil power there was in him! He divested himself of all beliefs and was not in the least afraid. He was withdrawing to his fastness from her. So far as he was able. He would not be able to do it, but it was magnificent how evidently he thought he could. Almost unconsciously she began to radiate herself at him and continued to do so for the rest of the evening whenever opportunity offered.

"But need it be *Stoicism?*" said Mr. Plantagenet-Buchan.

"What else?"

"For my part I do not feel Christianity is dead," young Lord Tamar interpolated before Mr. Plantagenet-Buchan could reply. "Not in the least dead. It changes form but it lives."

Lady Tamar nodded in confirmation. "It changes form," she admitted.

Lady Grieswold made confirmatory noises, rather like the noises a very old judge might make in confirming a decision, and she took some more stuffed aubergine as if that act was in some way sacramental.

Mr. Sempack did not attend at once to these three confessions. He stared before him at the marble wall over Miss Fenimore's head. He had an air of explaining something carefully to himself. "Christianity has prevailed," he assured himself, "but indeed Christianity passes. Passes!—it has gone! It has littered the beaches of life with churches, cathedrals, shrines and crucifixes, prejudices and intolerances, like the sea urchins and starfish and empty shells and lumps of stinging jelly upon the sands here after a tide. A tidal wave out of Egypt. And it has left a multitude of little wriggling theologians and confessors and apologists hopping and burrowing in the warm nutritious sand. But in the hearts of living men, what remains of it now? Doubtful scraps of Arianism. Phrases. Sentiments. Habits."

He turned his large eye on Lady Tamar and took up her neglected remark. "If Christianity changes form, it becomes something else."

Lord Tamar gave a little cough and spoke apologetically. "*Love*," said Lord Tamar, "remains. The spirit. Christianity is love. It is distinctively the religion of love. All the rest—is excrescence. There was no such religion before."

Lady Tamar wanted to say "God is Love," but her courage failed and so she blushed instead. Evidently both the Tamars felt their own remarks acutely.

"Christianity can only be a *form* of love," said Mr. Sempack. "I doubt if it is that. And I doubt still more if any one can argue that love is the highest thing in life. Is it? . . . Is it? . . ." Lady Catherine watched him. Far over her head to things beyond, Mr. Sempack said, "No." He developed his disavowals. "There are nobler things for the soul—the conquest of the limited self, for example, at heights and in visions and apprehensions altogether above passion. There are, I am convinced, great mountains above the little village of the affections, high and lonely places. There lies the Stoic domain. There we can camp and harbour. Stoicism, which was too great for the world when first it dawned upon men's thoughts, comes back into life. Changed very little in essentials, but enlarged, because our vision of time and space has enlarged. It has returned so inevitably that it has returned imperceptibly. We have all become Stoics nowadays without knowing it. We have not been persuaded and convinced and converted; we just find ourselves there. We fall back by a sort of general necessity upon the dignity of renunciation and upon our subordination to a greater life. Perhaps we do not want to do it but we have to do it. What else can we do unless we play tricks with our intelligence and degrade ourselves to 'acts of faith'? What gymnastics this century has seen since its beginning! We abandon the Christian exaggeration of the ego and its preposterous claims for an everlasting distinctiveness—perforce. We give up craving for individual recognition because we must. Loneliness. Perhaps. In a sense we are all increasingly alone. But then, since nowadays we are all increasingly something more and something less than ourselves, that loneliness is no longer overwhelming."

This was in effect soliloquy. It may have been soundly reasoned but it had been difficult to follow. The desolate figure of little Mrs. Rylands was so vivid in his mind that he was still able to remain unresponsive to the glow he had evoked in Lady Catherine. He was talking neither to his hearers nor himself, but in imagination to that little lady upstairs against the disturbance of the lovely lady at the end of the table. He was making Cynthia his talisman against Catherine. By behaving like a wise man for Mrs. Rylands he might yet be able to arrest the deep warm currents about him and within him that were threatening to make a fool of him for Lady Catherine. The problem of that fine soul, so clear in its apprehensions and so fatally gentle in its will, flung so suddenly into a realisation of its immense unaided confrontation of the universe, was good enough to grip him. After he had written and sent her that letter he wanted to take it all back and begin all over again. Or to begin a second one and a longer. But the gong had arrested the latter impulse at the source and saved some of the material for this present allocution.

The rest of the dinner party were variously affected by his declarations. "But is one ever really alone?" asked Lord Tamar, carrying on the talk, and began to reflect upon what he was saying as he said it. What, asked a chilling voice within, what would stand by him in an ultimate isolation? If for example—but that was too horrible to think even. He glanced across the table at his wife and saw that she was longing to look at him in reply and could not do so. What Stoicism, he asked himself, could help if *that* were stripped from him? But then, his warmer self hastened to interpolate, it could not be stripped from him because love makes things immortal! Yet what did that mean?

There came a silence. Miss Fenimore felt she had rarely enjoyed so deep and subtle a conversation. She did not understand a bit of it, but it swept her mind onward intoxicatingly. Her glasses flashed round the table for the next speaker.

This was Mr. Plantagenet-Buchan. He fingered the stem of his glass. "Now *that,*" he said, speaking slowly and thoughtfully, "is a point of view."

Every one else was relieved to find there was some one competent to take up Mr. Sempack. What Mr. Sempack had been talking about was a point of view. That was really very helpful. Attention, embodied particularly in Miss Fenimore, focussed itself consciously on Mr. Plantagenet-Buchan.

"That," Mr. Plantagenet-Buchan improved, "is a method of apprehension. I admit the decay of Christian certitude. It has gone. And I admit the dignity and greatness of the Stoic vision. Yes. But it is, after all, only one of several possible visions." He paused and extended a fine index finger at Mr. Sempack. "Equally well you may look through the glass of another philosophy and see the world as a *glad* spectacle, as a winepress of sensation and happiness and sympathetic feeling and beautiful experiences. . . ."

He was launched.

He lifted a glance to Lady Catherine. "*Loneliness* is a fact," he said; "yes. But *loveliness* also is a fact. Which fact do you care to make the most important, which shall be the focus of attention? You are free to choose, it seems to me, to go out of yourself if you will, rather than retreat to the innermost. Why take the loneliness of the soul rather than the loveliness of circumambient things?"

"Loneliness and Loveliness!" It was a long way from such silly talk to sound and sensible bridge, thought poor Lady Grieswold. People who had the sense to play bridge didn't bother about such things. Awful stuff! And flouting Christianity too! Florence or Mentone? It would have to come to that. The nice people had gone.

"Against your Neo-Stoic," said Mr. Plantagenet-Buchan, still using his finger a little, "I set the Neo-Epicurean. I set such an attitude to the universe that a man may lament that he knows no God to thank for the infinitude of delicious things and marvellous possibilities wrapped up in the fabric of life."

And so forth. . . .

Thus was issue joined downstairs and a long rather rambling and cloudy discussion between Stoicism and Epicureanism began. Miss Fenimore followed it from first to last with an enraptured incomprehension, while Philip brooded on his secret preoccupations and Mrs. Rylands lay upstairs on her great bed, preparing the things she had to say when at last Philip should come to her.

It was an entirely inconclusive discussion. Except that Lady Catherine, converted it would seem on the spot, presently announced herself a Stoic, to Mr. Plantagenet-Buchan's visible surprise and distress.

Now why should she do that?

"But my *dear* Lady!" said Mr. Plantagenet-Buchan.

"Life should be *stern*," said Lady Catherine triumphantly. . . .

After a time Philip, regardless of his formal duties as a host, got up and very quietly slipped away.

§ 13

IT seemed ever so late in the night when Philip came upstairs. He made a scarcely perceptible noise, but she was alert. "Phil dear!" she cried. "Are you there? Phil!"

He came softly out of the shadows, stood aloof for a moment, black, mysterious and silent against the blue night, and then was at the bedside. "I hoped you were asleep," he said.

She clicked on her shaded light and the two regarded each other in a sorrowful scrutiny, perplexed with themselves and life.

"Cynthia," he whispered. "Cynthia, my darling; can you forgive?"

"Perhaps," she panted and paused. "Perhaps there is nothing to forgive."

"But—?"

"Nothing that matters."

"She's cleared out."

"It doesn't matter. Don't trouble about her. . . . You I think of."

"I've been such a beast."

"No. It happened. It had to happen. Something had to happen. You couldn't help yourself. You've nothing to do here. You've been a prisoner here, waiting on me."

"Oh! don't say that. I meant to be so dear to you—my dear. But there's something rotten in me."

"No, no. Rotten! Dear, Phil dear, you're not even ripe. But I've let you stay here. . . ." She put out her hand and he sat himself on the bed beside her. He kissed her. "My dear," he said. "Dear! Dear!"

"Listen," she said, and kept her hand upon him. She whispered. Both spoke in whispers. "Go to England, dear one. Things are happening there. Trouble and muddle. Men—men ought to work. You—you ought to find out. You ought to understand. You so rich and—responsible. Things have to be done. I can stay here. . . ."

"You banish me?"

"No. *This* is banishment. *Here*. Here I can't help you—to grow into the man you have to be. Not now. I've got to be three parts vegetable for a bit now—and then a sort of cow. No fit companion for a growing man. I don't mind, dear. It's worth it. It's what I'm for. It had to be. But you—*you* go home to England *now*. *You* can't stand idleness. *You* can't stand these long empty days."

He released her and sat thinking it out.

After a long pause he said, "I think you are right. I ought to go."

"Yes—*go*."

"We've got all the Red Valley property. All that Yorkshire stretch. The Vale of Edensoke. A third perhaps of the Rylands millions is in coal. I ought to know about it. I've let the older men, Uncle Robert and the others, do what they pleased."

Now that was a man!

"Go for *that*," she said. "Go for the sake of that."

He turned his eyes to her. She did her best to look at him with a grave, quiet, convincing face and her strength was not enough. Suddenly the calm of her countenance broke under her distress and she wept like a struck child.

"Oh, my dear!" he cried in an agony of helplessness; "that I should hurt you now! What have I done to you?" and threw his arms about her and drew her up close to him, very close to him, and kissed the salt tears.

"Poor Phil!" she clung to him weeping, smoothing his hair with one hand. "Dear Phil!"

END OF BOOK ONE

BOOK THE SECOND

ADVENT

ADVENT

THE SECTIONS

Advent

§ 1

FOR a brief interval it seemed probable that the dispersal of the party would be even more thorough than Mrs. Rylands and Lady Catherine had contemplated. Mr. Sempack, after what would appear to have been a troubled night, proclaimed his intention of going back to Nice forthwith to get some books and carry them off with him to Corsica.

His explanations lacked lucidity. He was not a good enough liar to invent a valid reason for going to Corsica. Lady Catherine, very subtly, left him to Mrs. Rylands; who summoned him secretly to the little sitting-room next her bedroom and received him in a beautiful flowery Chinese silk wrapper, and told him how she had looked forward to talking to him when the others had gone. She reduced him to the avowal that his motive in going was "mere restlessness," contrived to convert the Corsican project into a few days' walking from some centre upon the Route des Alpes, and made him promise to come back so soon as he had walked himself calm.

Neither she nor he made the slightest attempt to account for his restlessness. She accepted it as a matter of course. So with a slightly baffled air, carrying a knapsack and a small valise and leaving his more serious luggage as it were in pawn, Mr. Sempack took the local train for Nice.

Mr. Plantagenet-Buchan was also affected by the general dislodgment. He discovered or invented a friend—Mrs. Rylands was in doubt which—a friend he had not met for years at that jolly hotel with the convex landlord at Torre Pellice up above Turin, and remained oscillating on the point of departure for some days—without actually going, keeping the friend in reserve.

The only irremovable visitor indeed was dear Miss Fenimore, who made it apparent, quietly but clearly, that she had never yet been in at the birth of a baby and this time nothing whatever would induce her to abandon her place in the queue. She was resolved to be useful and devoted and on the spot, and nothing but two or three carbinieri seemed likely to dislodge her. Lady Grieswold after circling vaguely about the ideas of Mentone or even Florence was drawn down by the centripetal force of the green tables to a not too expensive pension at Beausoleil.

The Tamars went off a day earlier than they had intended, they were taking a night at Cannes en route to stay with the Jex-Hiltons and talk to a distinguished refugee from Fascism whose house had been burnt, whose favourite dog had been skinned alive, and who had been twice seriously injured with loaded canes and sandbags on account of some mild criticism of the current régime. Lord Tamar had hitherto been too diplomatic to express even a private opinion of Mussolini, but he felt that possibly it might give pause to that energetic person's dictatorial tendencies to learn that one or two English people of the very best sort were not in the very least afraid to meet his victims and make pertinent enquiries about him.

Colonel and Mrs. Bullace had some difficulties about their wagon-lit and went a day later than they had proposed. The Colonel threw a tremendous flavour of having been recalled over his departure. The vague suggestion that some sort of social struggle of a definitive sort was brewing in England grew stronger and stronger as his farewells came nearer. Philip came down to find him discoursing to his wife and Miss Fenimore and Lady Grieswold, who was going with the Bullaces as far as Monte Carlo.

"This coal difficulty is neither the beginning nor the end of the business," he was saying. "Rest assured. We know. It is just the thin end of the Moscow wedge. They've been watched. They've been watched. Intelligence against intelligence."

He would have preferred not to have had Philip join his audience, but he stuck to his discourse. Bombaccio brought his master his coffee and Philip sat back, hands in his trouser pockets, staring deeply at his guest.

"You really think," said Miss Fenimore. "You really think—?"

"We know," said the Colonel. "We know."

"Is this the social revolution again?" asked Philip.

"It would be, if we were not prepared."

"But what are you prepared for?" asked Philip. "What do you think is going to happen? To need you at home?"

"The British working man, Sir, has to take smaller wages and work longer hours—and he won't. Ever since the war and Lloyd George's nonsense, he's been too uppish. And he has to climb down. He's got to climb down before he topples things over. That's

133

the present situation. And behind it—the Red Flag. Moscow."

"Surely this coal business is a question in itself. We have the Coal Commission Report. The owners have haggled a bit about things and the men are inclined to be stiff, but there's nothing that can't be got over, so far as I can see. It's a case of give and take. Baldwin is doing his utmost to bring the parties together and arrange a settlement and a fresh start. Won't he get it? I don't see where your social conflict is to come in."

"I will explain," said Colonel Bullace, and cleared his throat. He turned and rapped the table. "There will be no coal settlement."

"Why?"

"Neither the miners nor the coal-owners will agree to anything."

"Well."

"Then there will be a lock-out and then—we know what they are up to all right—and then there will be a strike—of *all* the workers—yes, of all the workers in the country, a new sort of strike, Sir, a general strike, a political strike, an attempt at—" The Colonel paused and then gave the words as it were in italics—"Red Revolution!"

"In England!"

Philip's voice betrayed his unfathomable faith in British institutions.

"We know it. We know it from men like Thomas, sensible men. Too sensible for the riff-raff behind 'em. The hotheads, the Moscow crew, have had this brewing for some time. Don't think we're not informed. It has been their dream—for years. This coal trouble won't be settled, rest assured, and I for one, don't want to see it settled. No, Sir. The fight has to come and it may as well come now while we have men, real red-blooded men like Churchill and Joynson-Hicks and Birkenhead, to fight it through.

"Thrice is he armed who hath his quarrel just—yes.

"But Thricer he who gets his blow in fust."

Colonel Bullace pronounced these words in ringing tones, nodded his head, and gave his host a stern grimly masticating profile until he caught his wife's eye. His wife's eye had been seeking capture for some time, and now, assisted by an almost imperceptible pantomime it said, "egg—moustache." Colonel Bullace made the necessary corrections with as little loss of fierceness as possible.

"You mean," said Philip, "that when Baldwin calls the conference of owners and men and tells them to make peace on the lines of the coal commission, he is, in plain English, humbugging—marking time for something else to happen? Something else about which he cannot be altogether unaware."

"Mr. Baldwin is a good man," said the Colonel. "But he does not fully realise what we are up against."

Mrs. Bullace nodded. "He doesn't know."

"We do," said the Colonel. "The General Strike, the Social Revolution in England is timed for the first of May, this first of May. The attack is as certain as the invasion of Belgium was in August 1914."

A diversion was made by the appearance of Mr. Plantagenet-Buchan in the beautiful tussore suit. He hovered in the doorway. "Don't tell me," he expostulated, "that you are talking *coal*, in the midst of this delicious heat!"

He sauntered to the open terrace, rubbing the faultless hands, and returned to confide—with just one greenish glint of the diamond—his need of a plentifully sugared grape-fruit to Bombaccio's satellite. He indicated the exact height of the sugar. "Zucchero. Allo montano. Come questa."

Philip got up, hesitated towards the terrace and then went into the hall and upstairs to his wife's room.

§ 2

BOTH Philip and Cynthia had a feeling that they had much to communicate to each other and neither knew how to set about communicating. She even thought of writing him a long, carefully weighed letter; it was a trick her father had in moments of crisis, retreat to his study, statements, documentation, distribution; her brain kept coining statements and formulæ, but it seemed useless to write a long letter to some one who was so soon to depart and make letters the only means of intercourse. Moreover he kept drifting in and out of her sitting-room and sitting beside her couch, so that she had no time for any consecutive composition. He would pat her and caress her gently, sit about her room, fiddle with things on her dressing-table or take up and open books and then put them down again, and he would sometimes sit still and keep silence for five minutes together. He had a way of getting up when he had anything to say and walking about while he said it, and he seemed never to expect her to answer at once to anything he said. And if they were walking in the garden then on the contrary he would stop to deliver himself, and afterwards pick a flower or throw a pebble at a tree. As soon as Lady Grieswold and the Bullaces and Tamars were well out of the way, and the weekly visiting-day when the chars-à-bancs poured their polyglot freight through the garden was past, she came down out of her seclusion and walked about the paths and stairways with him and sat and talked here and there. They never seemed to thresh anything out and yet when at last he too had gone, she began to realise that they had, in phrases and fragments, achieved quite considerable exchanges. Three separate times he had said: "You've never looked so lovely as you do now," which did not at all help matters forward but still seemed somehow to make for understanding.

She detected in herself a disposition to prelude rather heavily, to say often and too impressively: "Philip, dear; there is something I want to say——" She hated herself every time she found that this preluding tendency had got her again, and had foisted itself upon her in some new, not instantly avoidable variation.

Yes, things were said and there were answers and acceptances. In the retrospect things fell into place and the remark of the late afternoon linked itself to the neglected suggestion of the morning. He had attended to her observations more than she had supposed, and expressed himself she realised with a fragmentary completeness.

Among the things she thought had been got over between herself and Philip was the recognition of their personal difference. They had to understand that their minds worked differently. Mr. Sempack had made that very plain to her, plainer even than he had intended, and she meant to make it very plain to Philip. Philip would have to make allowances for her in the days ahead. It was not only she who had to make allowances for Philip. They had to see each other plain. Illusions were all very well for lovers but not for the love of man and wife.

"I worry more with my mind over things than you do," she had struggled with it. "Your mind bites and swallows; you hardly know what has happened, but mine grinds round and round. I'm an intellectualiser."

"You're damned intelligent," said Philip loyally.

"That's not so certain, Phil. I not only think a thing but I've got to think I'm thinking it. I've got to join things on one to the other. I've got to get out my principles and look at them before I judge anything. Philip, has it ever dawned on you that I'm a bit of a prig?"

"*You!*" cried Philip. "My God!"

He was so horrified; she had to laugh. "Dear, I am," she said. "I don't forget myself in things. You do. But I'm always there, with my set of principles complete, in the foreground—or the frame if you like—of what I'm thinking about. You can't get away from it, if you are like that."

"You're no *prig*," said Philip. "What has put that into your head?"

"And so far as I can see," she said, "it's no good making up your mind not to be a prig if you are a prig. That's only going one depth deeper into priggishness."

Philip had one of his flashes. "Still that's not so bad as making up your mind that you won't make up your mind not to be a prig, you little darling. This —all this is adorable and just like you. You are growing up in your own fashion, and so perhaps am I. I've always loved your judgments and your balance. . . . How little we've talked since our marriage! How little we've talked! And I always dreamt of talking to you. Before we married I used to think of us sitting and talking—just like this."

That was a good phase of their time to recall. And she recalled it, with a number of little things he said later, little things that came back again and again to this question of some method, some reasoned substance, in their relationship that she had broached in this fashion. At times he would say things that amounted to the endorsement and acceptance of her own gently hinted criticisms. It was queer how he gave them back to her, enlarged, rather strengthened.

"Of course," said Philip, half a day later; "all this taking things for granted is Rot—sheer Rot. Every one ought to think things out for himself. Every one. Coal strike. Everything. How lazy—in our minds I mean—people of our sort are! We seem to take it all out of ourselves keeping fit. . . . Fit for nothing."

And: "Empty-minded. I suppose that people never have been so empty-minded as our sort of people are now. Always before, they had their religion. They had their intentions to live in a certain way that they thought was right. Not simply just jazzing about. . . ."

It was extraordinary with what completeness he

grasped and accepted her long latent criticisms of their life in common. "Puppy," he remarked, "only put the lid on. I see I must get clear. The damned thing of it, wasn't *that* at all. It was the drift. The day after day. The tennis. Just anything that happened."

He had seized upon her timid and shadowy intimations to make a definite project for their intercourse while he was away. "Prig or no prig," they were to explain their beliefs to each other, clear up their ideas, "stop the drift." They were to write as fully and clearly as possible to each other. "God and all that," he said. It didn't matter.

"I've never written a letter, a real letter, I mean about serious things, in my life. I shall try and write about 'em now to you. Just as I see them over there. I shan't write love-letters to you—except every now and then. Lill' nonsense, just in passin'. I shall write about every blessed thing. Every blessed thing.

"You mustn't laugh at the stuff I shall send you. It will clear my mind. People of our sort ought to be *made* to write things down that we believe. Just to make sure we aren't fudding."

Walking up and down with her in the broad path beyond the stone of the sweet Lucina, he remarked at large, loudly and with no sequence: "Prig be damned!"

And also he said: "A woman is a man's keeper. A wife is a man's conscience. If he can't bring his thoughts to her—she's no good at all.

"No real good."

Then a confession. "I always thought of talking

about things with you. When first I met you. We did talk rather. For a bit."

Her fullest memory was of him late at night on the balcony outside her sitting-room. She was lying on a long deck-chair and he stood leaning against the parapet, jerking things at her, going from topic to topic, lighting, smoking, throwing away cigarettes.

"Cynthia," he asked abruptly, "what do you think about Socialism and all that sort of thing?"

So comprehensive a question found her unprepared. One was trained at school, he went on, to think "that sort of thing" Rot and not think any more about it. But it wasn't Rot. There was such a thing as social injustice. Most people didn't get a fair deal. They didn't get a dog's chance of a fair deal.

He stepped to another aspect.

"Have you ever thought of our sort of life as being mean, Cynthia?"

Latterly she had. But she wanted him to lead the talking and so she answered: "I've always assumed we gave something back."

"Yes. And what do we give back?"

"We ought to give back——" She paused.

"More than we do."

"Considering what *they* get," he said. *"Rather!*

"F'r instance," he began, and paused.

The moon with an imperceptible swiftness was gliding clear of the black trees and he stood now, a dim outline against a world of misty silver, taut and earnest, leaning against her balustrade. "I've been trying to make out this coal story for myself," he said. "Rather late in the day seeing how deep in coal we are. But I've always left things to Uncle

Robert and the partners. I grew up to the idea of leaving things to Uncle Robert."

The face of Uncle Robert, Lord Edensoke, the head of the Rylands clan, came before her eyes, a hard handsome face, rather like Philip, rather like Geoffrey; she could never determine in her own mind which he was most like. He was the autocrat of the Rylands world and she fancied a little hostile to her marriage. It was very easy to understand how Philip had grown up to the idea of leaving things to Uncle Robert.

"I don't like the story," Philip was saying.

"You know, Cynthia; it's a greedy history, on our part.

"I wish old Sempack hadn't trotted off in the way he did. I'd have liked to have had a lot of this out with him. That old boy has a kind of grip of things. I'm getting his books. I suppose it was just his tact took him off. He noticed something. Of that trouble. Thought we might want a bit of time together. We did. But I'd have liked to have had his point of view of a lot of things. We coal-owners f'r instance.

"You know, Cynthia, in the coal trouble, we coal-owners don't seem to have done a single decent thing. I mean to say a generous thing. I mean we just stick to our royalties. We get in the way and ask to be bought off. I think you ought to read a bit of this Royal Commission Report. It's in the file of the *Manchester Guardian* downstairs. I'll mark you some papers. There's the Commission's report and the Labour Plan and various schemes and they're all worth reading. These are things we *ought* to read. It's a Tory Commission, this last one. The other wasn't. The Justice Sankey one. But the things this

Report is kind of obliged to say of us. Ever so gently, but it gets them said. The way we hang on. And get. I never saw it before. I suppose because I've never looked. Been afraid of being called a prig perhaps. Taking life too seriously and all that. But when you look straight at it, and read those papers—which aren't Bolshevik, which aren't even Labourite, mind you—you see things."

He faced the socialist proposition. "*Are* we parasites?" he asked.

Out of something he called their "net production" of coal, Rylands and Cokeson got in royalties and profits seventeen per cent. "Royalties by right and profits by habit," he said. She made a mental note to find out about net production.

He laughed abruptly. "I'm talking to-night. I seem to be doing all the talking. Just outpouring."

"Oh! I've wanted you to talk," she said. "For all our life together I've been wondering— What does he think? What does he feel? I mean about these things—these things that really matter. And this is how you feel. It's so true, my dear, we don't give enough. We're not good enough. We take and we don't repay."

"But even if we did all we could, how could we repay?"

"We could at least do all we could."

He stood quite still for a time and then came over to her. He bent down over her and sat down beside her, he kissed her face, cool and infinitely delicate in the moonlight, and crumpled up beside her chaise-longue, a dark heap with a pale clear profile, and his ear against her hand. She loved the feel of his ear.

"My dear, it's so *amazing!*" he whispered.

"When we begin to look at ourselves. To see how near we may be to the things they say of us in Hyde Park."

He brooded. "Getting all we do out of the country and doing nothing for it. A bit of soldiering in the war—but it was the Tommies got the mud and the short commons. And things like that. . . . What else have I done for—this?"

This in his whispered voice was all the beauty in their lives, this warm globe of silver and ebony in which they nestled darkly together.

"Presently I am expected to sit for Sealholme—just to make sure nobody gets busy with our royalties. . . .

"Suppose I stood for Sealholme on the other side!

"It is funny to wake up, so to speak, and find myself with all this socialism running about in my head."

He rubbed his ear and cheek against her hand as a cat might do. "Is it you has given me this socialism? I must have caught it from you."

She pinched his ear softly. "You've been thinking."

"If it isn't you, it's—"

He paused for her to fall into his trap.

"Sempack," she guessed.

"Bullace," he said. "Queer beast. Something between an ass and a walrus. Egg on his moustache. But he gave the show away. All his talk about labour—and keeping labour down. So utterly mean. Bluster and meanness. Yes. But how does Bullace stand to Uncle Robert? . . .

"Where does Uncle Robert come in?"

Long silence.

"You are the rightest thing in the world, Cynthia. I've not given you a fair chance with me. I've never given us a fair chance with ourselves. We have to think things out. All this stuff. Where we are and what we are."

He sighed.

"And then I suppose what we have to do."

He went off at a tangent. "My Cynthia. I love you."

"My *dear*," she whispered and drew his head into the crook of her arm against her crescent breast and kissed his hair.

"Two kids. That's been the pose. Pretty dears! Lovely to see how happy they are. Uncle Robert will see to things. But not such kids. Not such kids that we can't spend twenty-two thousand a year on ourselves and bring a child into the world. What am I? Twenty-nine! . . . Too much of this darling kid business. We're man and woman, caught unprepared. . . ."

He had a flash of imagination. "Suppose I went and looked over this balcony and down there in the black shadows under the palm trees I saw the miners who pay for this house, with their lanterns, cramped as they are in the mine, creeping forward, step by step, picking and sweating through the shadows, eh? Chaps younger than me. Boys some of 'em. And suppose one or two of 'em looked up! . . .

"God! the things I don't know! The things I've never thought about! The hours of perfect health I've spent on that cursed tennis court while all this trouble was brewing! . . . When you and I might have been talking and learning to understand!"

Astounding this burst of pent-up radicalism! How long had it been accumulating?

Brooding, reading, thinking; how *silent* he had been! And then these ideas, these very decisive ideas—for all their inchoate expressiveness.

§ 3

SO soon as Philip had departed it was Mrs. Rylands' intention to begin a great clearing and tidying-up of her mind. She was delighted but also she was a little alarmed at her husband's fall into violent self-criticism and his manifest resolve to think things out for himself. She felt that he might very easily outrun her in mental thoroughness, once he set his face in that direction, and so she would get as far along the road as she could before he could overtake her. She condemned other people for Stupidity, perhaps too readily, but what if she were put to the question? How far from the indefensibly Stupid were the philosophical and religious assumptions upon which she rested? What really could she say she believed about the world? What did she think she was living for, if so comprehensive a question chanced to be put to her? And if she could so far accept that question as to imagine it put to her, wasn't she in conscience bound to set about preparing her answer?

One of her Oxford cousins, some years ago, had made her a very pleasant and tantalising present of three books of blank paper, very good hand-made paper, gilt edged along the top and bound in green leather. She had resolved at once to write all sorts of things in these books, so many sorts of things, that still the pages remained virgin. But now was a great occasion. She had brought them with her to Italy. She looked for them and found them and took out one of these little volumes and handled it and turned its pages over. In this new phase of existence she had entered, she found her pleasure in the sense of touch much increased and it seemed to her that her delight in fine and pretty things was greater than it had ever been before. She almost caressed the little book and stood before her window holding it with both hands, dreaming of the things she would put into it. She saw, though not very distinctly, pregnant aphorisms and a kind of index to her knowledge and beliefs spreading over those nice pages. The binding was quite beautifully tooled, the leather had a faint, exquisite smell and the end paper was creamy, powdered with gold stars, all held together by a diamond mesh.

She mused a great deal about what she would write first, but for a time she could not sit down to think out anything to the writing stage because Catherine would insist on talking to her. Hitherto she and Catherine had got on very well together but without any excesses of directness or intimacy. She had always accepted the view of her husband and his set that Catherine was "all right" and more sinned against than sinning, but she had never been disposed to wander imaginatively in those romantic tangles which made Catherine's passions, it would seem, so different from her own.

Catherine's rôle was to be a gallant and splendid beauty, a summoner and a tester of men. Men who were going east turned west at her passing and, for better or worse, were never quite the same men again.

She had summoned and tested her wealthy husband until he had become an almost willing respondent, with a co-respondent of no importance, and left her the freest woman in the world. What she did was right; the essential purity of her character was not so much accepted as waved before the world like a flag. She did quite a lot of things. Cynthia had shirked her confidences because among other reasons she felt that it would make her own relations to Philip seem too abject. But the confidences came.

"I'd like to take you in the car along the upper Corniche and up to Puget-Théniers or Annot to-day," she said. "It would do us both good. Everybody going has left me—jangling."

"We might run against your Mr. Sempack," said Cynthia. "Annot? Aren't the Verdon gorges somewhere there?"

"I don't see why all the blue mountains of France should be closed to us because Mr. Sempack is wandering about with a knapsack in a bad temper trying to remember something he has never as a matter of fact forgotten."

Mrs. Rylands made no effort to understand. "We'd have to ask Mr. Plantagenet-Buchan to come," she remarked.

Lady Catherine by a beautiful grimace expressed an extreme aversion to Mr. Plantagenet-Buchan. "This little sitting-room of yours is the only refuge. . . . 'Dear Lady,' he says. . . . Why doesn't he go off to that other cultivated American of his at Torre Pellice?"

She became derogatory of Mr. Plantagenet-Buchan.

"I saw him from my window. He was walking

along the path to the marble faun and he was waving that hand of his and bowing. All to himself. I suppose he was rehearsing some new remark."

Her mind went off at a tangent. "Cynthia," she said. "Do you think a man like Mr. Plantagenet-Buchan ever makes love to women—I mean, really makes love—actually?"

Mrs. Rylands declined to take up the speculation. Meanwhile Lady Catherine threw out material. "He may be seventy. Of course he's *pickled* for fifty-five. He'd say things. Elegant things. Gallantry's in the man. He'd say everything there had to be said perfectly—but then? . . ." She brooded malignantly on possible situations.

"I suppose men go on with the forms of love-making right to the end of their lives—just like a hen runs about when its head's chopped off."

She came round through such speculations to what was evidently her disturbing preoccupation. "Now Mr. Sempack *talks*," she said.

She plunged. "What do you think of Mr. Sempack, Cynthia? What do you think of him? What do you think of a man like that? There's an effect of strength and greatness about him. And yet what does he *do*? Is he a snare and a delusion?"

She seated herself on the end of the sofa, side-saddle fashion with one foot on the floor, and regarded her friend expectantly.

"What are you up to with Mr. Sempack?" said Cynthia.

"Quarrelling."

Mrs. Rylands would not take that as an answer. She remained quietly interrogative.

"He exasperates me," said Lady Catherine.

"Every one," she went on, "seems to look up to him and respect him. Every one, that is, who's heard of him. Why? He's tremendously big and I suppose there's something big about the way he looks at the world and talks about progress, and treats all we are doing as something that will be all over in no time and that cannot matter in the least, but, after all, what does all this towering precipice sort of business amount to? He isn't *really* a precipice. I suppose if some one up there in the mountains held him up and demanded his pocket-book, he'd do something about it. He couldn't just try to pass it off with the remark that robbers would be out-of-date in quite a few centuries' time and so it didn't matter. Especially if they hit him or something."

Mrs. Rylands was smilingly unhelpful.

"I believe he'd hit back," said Lady Catherine.

"I don't see why he shouldn't," said Mrs. Rylands.

"He'd be clumsy but he might hit hard. He's one of those queer men who seem to keep strong without exercise. Unless walking is exercise."

Mrs. Rylands offered no contributions.

"He seems to think women are like raspberries in a garden. You pick one as you go past, but you don't go out of your way for her."

"I can't imagine a Mrs. Sempack."

"It's a bit of an exercise," said Lady Catherine. "Rather like that awful hat of his, she'd be. Or his valise. Put up on the luggage rack, left in the consigne, covered with rags of old labels, jammed down and locked violently with everything inside higgledy piggledy. And yet— What is it, Cynthia? There's something attractive about that man."

"One or two little things I've observed," reflected

Cynthia absently, looking down at the dear green leather book in her hand. Then she regarded her friend.

Lady Catherine coloured slightly. "I admit it," she said. "I suppose it's just because he's so wanting in visible delicacy. It gives him an effect of being tremendously male. He *is* that. Don't you think that's it, Cynthia? And something about him—as though there were immense forces still to be awakened. His voice; it's a good voice. And something that smoulders deep in his eyes."

Mrs. Rylands suddenly resolved to become aggressive.

"Catherine! Tell me; why did he go away from here?"

"That's exactly what I want to know. He meant to go for good."

"That's why you made me see him."

"I thought it was your place to see him."

Mrs. Rylands put her head on one side and regarded her friend critically. "Did you make love to him—*much?*"

Lady Catherine's colour became quite bright. "I want to see, my dear, what that man is like *awake*. I am curious. Like most women. And he hesitates and then runs away—to walk about Gorges! He did—hesitate. But this flight! . . . And here am I—left—with nothing in the world to do! . . . Except of course look after dear little you. Who're perfectly able to look after yourself."

Mrs. Rylands smiled with a perfect understanding at her friend. "And talk about him."

"Well, he interests me."

"You made love to him—and startled and amazed

him. Why did you do it? You didn't want to be Lady Catherine Sempack?"

"I want to make that man realise his position in the world. Making love—isn't matrimony. One can be interested."

It occurred to Lady Catherine that, in view of recent events, she might be wandering near a sore point. But Mrs. Rylands' next remark showed her fully able to cover any sore point that might be endangered.

"Catherine—I don't want to know about things I'm not supposed to know about—but isn't there some one in England called Sir Harry Fearon-Owen? Who always goes about with his hyphen? Hasn't he some sort of connexion—?"

Lady Catherine concealed considerable annoyance rather imperfectly. She took a moment or so before she replied compactly.

"He's in England. And he's busy. Too busy even to write to his friends."

"He's preparing to save England from the Communist revolution, isn't he? He's one of Colonel Bullace's great idols. The colonel talked about him."

Lady Catherine allowed herself to be reluctantly drawn off the Sempack scent.

"It's amazing the things men will take seriously. Do *you* believe there is any sense in this talk about a revolution? Harry's great stunt is the National Service League. As you probably know. Plans for doing without the workers in all the public services and that sort of thing—if it comes to a fight. I liked him. For a time. He's a very good sort. And handsome. With a voice. Opera tenor blood perhaps—it saves him from being dull. But I can't go on being in love with a man who's in love with a Civil War, that nobody in his senses believes will happen."

Lady Catherine wriggled off her sofa end and went to the window. She felt that Cynthia by dragging in Sir Harry had deliberately spoilt a good conversation. She still had a lot of speculative matter about Sempack in her mind that she would have liked to turn over. She had hardly begun. And the Fearon-Owen affair had got itself a little disjointed and wasn't any good for talking about.

"These glorious empty days!" she said without any apparent perception of the trees and flowering terraces and sapphire sea below.

She stood against the blue for a time quite still.

She came back into the room and hung a shadowy loveliness over her recumbent hostess.

"If I thought there was a word of truth in this Great Rebellion of the Proletariat I'd be off to England by the night train."

§ 4

MRS. RYLANDS found herself at last at peace and with nothing between her and her green leather book. Catherine had hardly gone from the room before she was forgotten.

The couch on which Mrs. Rylands was lying was a very comfortable couch and the jambs of the tall window, the lower border of the orange sun-blind and the parapet of her balcony framed a still picture of the crowning fronds of three palm trees, a single more distant cypress and the light-flood of the sky. The day outside was intensely bright and real and everything within cool, faint-coloured and unsubstantial. Mrs. Rylands' sensations floated on a great restfulness and contentment; she was sustained by this deep life stream that had entered into her and taken control of her once uneasy self, a self in the profoundest contrast now to Lady Catherine's restless activity. She had never felt so little disposed to hurry or so serene. This high resolve to think out all her world for Phil and have it clear and plain was quite unruffled by any fret of urgency.

To begin with, she asked herself, "What do I know? What have I that is fundamental?"

"Nothing," she told herself, with perfect calm.

"Do I believe anything?"

That she thought over. God? Nothing that would have passed for a God in any time but this. No trace of that old gentleman, the God of our Fathers. At the dinner table of the Warwickshire rectory she had been allowed to listen to much modern theology and it had left her with phrases about the Absolute and Comprehensive Love that were hardly more human than the square root of minus one. Yet as her father used to say, the most impossible hypothesis of all was a universe ruled by blind chance. And the most incredible, an evil world. It was something to believe that if one could see it whole, as one never could, and if one could see it through, the everything, was all right. She did believe that. Or was her conviction deeper than belief?

It might be the mere mental reflection of the physical well-being that had succeeded the first resistances of her body to her surrender to destiny. But in a mirror can there ever be any truth more profound than reflection? That floated in her mind like some noiseless moth and soared and passed beyond her.

Should she write this for the first entry in her book: "There is no need to hurry. There is nothing in the whole world to justify fear."

So far from believing in nothing, this was a tremendous act of faith.

She lay criticising these projected first propositions, indolently and yet clearly. Was this act of faith of hers just then the purring of a well-fed cat upon its cushions? No insect grub was ever cradled in so silky and secure a cocoon as she. For her indeed there might be no hurry and no fear, but what of the general case, the common experience? Wasn't all the world hurrying, all the world driven by fear? But one hurried to make a speedy end to hurrying, and fear was just an emotional phase in the search for security. A man running from a tiger might be mentally nothing but a passion of fear but, one way or the other, that passion ended. A man running from a tiger was in no fit circumstances to apprehend fundamental truth; a woman caught up for a little while from the intenser stresses of life seemed more happily posed. Fear was an unendurable reality but it was incidental. It was a condition of travel. Just as haste and all struggle were incidental. The final rightness of things was wider; you might only see it incidentally in resting moments, but it was always there. Faith could be more than incidental and was more than incidental. While the water was troubled it couldn't reflect the sky, but that didn't prevent the sky being there to await reflection. All religions and philosophies since the world began had insisted that one must get out of the turmoil, somehow, to catch any vision of true realities. And as soon as you got that vision—serenity.

That should be the first entry then, so soon as she got up and could sit down to write it: "There is no need to hurry. There is nothing in the whole world to justify fear."

After that the Thinker on the sofa rested for a while.

Presently she found a queer little aphorism drifting through her mind with an air of wanting to get into the green leather book: "Faith in good, Faith in God." Just as easy to believe as deny that there was something directive and friendly and sure of itself, above all the contradictions and behind all the screens. Immense, incomprehensible, stupendous, silent, something that smiled in the starry sky. . . .

Then her mind drifted to the idea that every one was too *troubled* about life, so very largely because they had no faith in good. They hurried. Every one was hurrying. If there was nothing whatever to hurry about then they hurried about games, about politics, about personal disputes. They invented complications to trouble themselves. They accepted conventions and would not look thoroughly into anything because of this uncontrollable hurry. If only they would take longer views and larger views, they would escape from all this stress. It was just there that the importance of Mr. Sempack came in. He did take longer views and larger views and help other people to take them. He presented Progress as large and easy, swift and yet leisurely, sweeping forward by and through and in spite of all the disputations and hasty settlements and patchings up and running to and fro. He conveyed his conviction

of a vast forward drive carrying the ordinary scurry-
ings of life upon its surface, great and worth while,
that comprehended a larger human life, a finer individual life, a happier life than at present we permitted ourselves to realise. His vision of mankind
working its way, albeit still blindly and with tragic
blunderings, to a world civilisation and the attain-
ment of ever increasing creative power, gave a standard by which all the happenings of to-day, that
swirled us about so confusedly and filled the newspapers so blindingly, could be judged and measured.
He must come back to Casa Terragena and he must
talk some more; and into the frame of progress he
would evoke, his hostess, with her green leather book
close at hand and receptive for all the finer phrases,
would fit her interpretation of the coal question and
the strike question and all the riddles and conflicts
of the arena into which Philip had gone down. And
Philip would begin writing those letters he had promised and she would get books and read. . . .

At this point Mrs. Rylands' mind was pervaded by
a feeling that work time was over and that it ought
to be let out to play. It went off at once like a
monkey and ran up and down and about the still
palm fronds outside. They were like large feathers,
except that the leaflets did not lock together. Was
there any reason why they should be so like feathers?
Next the stem the leaflets were extraordinarily narrow; she wondered why? Each frond curved over
to its end harmoniously and evenly, so that to follow it was like hearing a long cadence, and the leaflets
stood up at the arch of the curve and then slanted
and each was just the least little bit in the world
smaller and slanted the fraction of an inch more

steeply than the one below it. Each had a twist so that it was bright, bright green and then came round to catch the light and became dazzling silver to its point. Each frond was a keyboard along which the roving eye made visual music. Each played a witty variation on the common theme.

§ 5

MRS. RYLANDS came down out of her privacies in time for lunch, but lunch was a little delayed by the absence of Lady Catherine and Mr. Plantagenet-Buchan. Catherine had flitted off to Ventimiglia. A telegram and some letters had awaited her in the hall, Bombaccio explained, something had excited her very much and off she had gone forthwith in the second car, sweeping up Mr. Plantagenet-Buchan on her way. She had been given the second car because in defiance of all instructions to the contrary, Bombaccio kept the first car for his mistress. He would always do that to the end of things. Lady Catherine was coming back, she was sure to come back, said Bombaccio, but Mrs. Rylands was not to wait lunch.

Mrs. Rylands found Miss Fenimore all alone in the hall reading Saturday's English newspapers. "Nothing seems settled about the miners," said Miss Fenimore, handing over *The Times,* and neither lady glanced at the French and Italian papers at all. Mrs. Rylands found the name of an old school friend among the marriages.

Miss Fenimore said she had been studying botany all the morning. Her hostess asked what book she had been using. "Oh! I haven't got a *book* yet," said

Miss Fenimore. "I've just been walking about the garden, you know, and reading some of the labels, so as to get a General Idea first. One can get books anywhere. . . . I've always wanted to know something about botany."

Then with an immense éclat Lady Catherine returned from Ventimiglia to proclaim the Social Revolution in England. She came in trailing sunlight and conflict with her, a beautiful voice, rich gestures and billowing streamers, Mr. Plantagenet-Buchan holding his own, such as it was, on her outskirts.

"My dear," she cried. "It's come! The Impossible has happened. I must go to England to-night —if the Channel boats are still running."

"What has come?" asked Mrs. Rylands.

"The General Strike. Proclaimed at midnight. They've dared to fight us! Haven't you seen the papers?"

"There's nothing in the English papers," said Mrs. Rylands and became aware of Miss Fenimore rustling the French sheets behind her. "Grève générale," came Miss Fenimore in confirmation. "And a long leader all in italics, I see; *Nos pauvres voisins!* Now the turn of England has come."

Bombaccio appeared and took Mr. Plantagenet-Buchan's hat and cane.

"Don't wait lunch for me," said Lady Catherine, sweeping across the hall to the staircase. "I'll be down in a minute. I'll have to tell Soames to pack. This has stirred me like great music."

"Lunch in five minutes," said Mrs. Rylands to Bombaccio's enquiring pause and turned to the Italian papers. The General Strike? Because of the miners. But Mr. Baldwin had been quite determined to settle it, and the owners and the government and the miners' representatives had been holding conference after conference. In the most friendly spirit. Was her picture of it all wrong? What was Philip doing away there? And Colonel Bullace and his braves? And all the people one knew? How skimpy the news in these foreign papers was, the important news, the English news!

Mrs. Rylands was still dazed by the sudden change in the aspect of things in general and of Lady Catherine in particular when the party had assembled at the lunch table. Lady Catherine dominated the situation. "Letters of mine went astray. To Rapallo. Or I should have known before. How amazing it is! How wonderful and stirring!"

"One thing I observe," began Mr. Plantagenet-Buchan, but Lady Catherine was following her own thoughts and submerged him.

"To think that they have *dared!*" she cried. "I shall go back as a volunteer—to serve as a nurse, a helper, anything. Captain Fearon-Owen says——"

"You have heard from him?" asked Mrs. Rylands.

"Two letters. They came together. From Rapallo. And a summons—by wire. Every one is wanted now, every sort of help. The printers have struck. There are no papers. The railwaymen are out! Not an omnibus in London. For all we know, while we sit here, all the Russians and Yids in Whitechapel may be marching under the red flag to Westminster!"

"You really think so?" said Mrs. Rylands and tried to imagine it.

"There is one thing I think about this business," Mr. Plantagenet-Buchan tried.

"I wonder if they have machine-guns," the lady

160

flowed over him. "Three months ago Captain Fearon-Owen wanted a search through the East End for munitions. But nobody would listen to him. And he always said the Royal Mint was much too far to the east for safety. There are always grenadiers there—just a few. They go along the Embankment every morning. A mere handful. Against hundreds of thousands."

"Like the poor dear Swiss Guard in Paris," Miss Fenimore shivered. "The Lion of Lucerne."

"Months ago, Captain Fearon-Owen made a plan. I read it and laughed at it. I thought it was extravagant. I suppose every one thought it was extravagant. But he had foreseen all this."

"Foreseen *what*, my dear?" asked Mrs. Rylands.

"This rising. He was for evacuating the Mint. And having naval forces ready to throw into the Docks right away."

"Rough on the naval forces," Mr. Plantagenet-Buchan allowed himself to murmur to some new potatoes.

"The Docks are full of food," said Lady Catherine, pursuing her strategic meditations.

"There is *one* aspect of this business," Mr. Plantagenet-Buchan tried again softly, addressing himself to a freshly acquired potato.

But Lady Catherine was too intent on battle to heed his attempted interpolation. The poor little potato never learnt that *one* aspect of the business before it vanished from the world. Its end was silence. Did it meet truth and knowledge in those warm darknesses? Who can tell?

"The main danger," Lady Catherine had to explain, "is the North. Captain Fearon-Owen does not think very much of the Midlands. Labour there is too diversified for unity and too soundly English for insurrection. But the Tyne is a black spot. And the Clyde. Red as it can be. And there's no reckoning with South Wales. A Welsh mob could be a very ugly mob, excitable and cruel. Especially *when* it sings. If they chanced on some song like the Marseillaise! Nothing could stop them."

"You talk as though there was an insurrection, Catherine," said Mrs. Rylands. "But the French papers speak only of a strike. Isn't that rather a more *passive* thing?"

"A General Strike," said Lady Catherine informingly, and there were trumpets in her voice. She looked like Britannia after putting on her helmet and drawing her sword. "A General Strike *is* an insurrection."

It was plain that in the absence of the other patriots, lunch was going to be a solo. A cowed feeling came over Mrs. Rylands. She had always felt that some day Catherine would up and cow her and now that day had come. Bombaccio too looked cowed, as cowed as Bombaccio could look. There was no checking Lady Catherine by offering her vegetables. One had a feeling all through the lunch as though one was eating in church. One could not fight it down. But what a marvel Catherine was, what a chameleon! For days she had been a shadow and echo of Mr. Sempack, a goad in that excellent man's loins. Now it was as if a record had been whisked off a gramophone and replaced by another, of an entirely different character. One heard the British patriot marching to battle and saw a forest of waving Union Jacks, one heard the lumbering artillery, the jingle-jangle of cavalry, the loud purring of tanks defiling into industrial towns at dawn. One heard the threatening whirr of aeroplanes dispersing dangerous meetings in public squares. And amidst the storm, and over the storm and through the storm one heard of Captain Fearon-Owen.

"Captain Fearon-Owen says there must be no weakness. There must be no faltering. Not even in the highest quarters."

"But *surely*—!" protested Miss Fenimore.

"The King is too kind," said Lady Catherine.

Then reflectively: "Of course I must fly from Paris. At Dover there will be no trains. I shall telegraph from Mentone to Le Bourget to keep a place.

"Flying over England in revolt. Watching them striking and striking—far below. Dreadful!—but exciting!"

Afterwards Mrs. Rylands tried to gather together and preserve some of the handsomer thistles that thrust themselves up through the jungle heat of Lady Catherine's mood. But she found much of it was lost for ever, gone like tropical vegetation in the moment of its flourishing.

The government she learnt might falter—or some of it. Mr. Baldwin was an *ineffective* man. Captain Fearon-Owen was not sure of Worthington Evans; he would have far preferred Winston at the War Office. Jix at the Home Office was a godsend however. He was truly strong. He never reprieved. Quiet, almost nervous in appearance, a slender man with a round *boyish* face—but he never, never reprieved. Practically. Well—impatient at what seemed detraction of her idol—"once perhaps." But vigorous action he was sure to support. Occasions might arise, said Captain Fearon-Owen, when it would be necessary to "take over" initiative from "falterers in positions of responsibility."

"You cannot always be sending back for instructions," said Lady Catherine darkly.

"Now it has come," said Lady Catherine, "I am glad it has come," and sat still for some moments with a quiet smile on her handsome animated face.

"There is a little point I have noticed," Mr. Plantagenet-Buchan reflected, with the nutcrackers in his hand—for by that time they had got to dessert. "I have observed—"

Lady Catherine was not heeding him. "It makes one feel frightfully Nietzschean," she said. "Suppose England too has to fall back on a dictatorship!"

"I suppose," said Mrs. Rylands with an innocence that seemed almost too obvious to her, "that would *have* to be Captain Fearon-Owen?"

But Lady Catherine was exalted above all ridicule. "Anyhow it was he who saw it clearest," she said and bestirred herself for the chasing of Soames.

"Mr. Sempack," Mrs. Rylands began, but her guest did not heed that once so interesting name.

"Leadership," said Lady Catherine, standing up splendidly, "is the supreme gift of the gods."

She went off to pack for civil warfare like a child going to be dressed for a treat.

§ 6

LADY CATHERINE and her maid departed in the late afternoon after a flurried and unconsoling tea and left an atmosphere of crisis and dismay behind them. After lunch Mrs. Rylands tried to sleep according to her régime, but the gaunt spectacle of dear old England, the unimaginable spectacle of dear old England torn by a monstrous civil conflict, with a massacre of the sentinels at the Royal Mint and a sinister rabble marching upon Westminster; Scotland Yard more like the Bastille than ever and machine-guns making a last harvest of resistance down the Mall before the sack of Buckingham Palace began, kept her awake. These were preposterous notions, but failing any other images it was difficult to keep them off the screen of her mind. What could this strike of a whole people be like in reality and why had no one realised the advent of this frightful clash of classes in time?

She just lay awake and stared at the blank of her imagination as some gravelled author destitute of detail might stare painfully at a sheet of paper.

When at last Lady Catherine had truly gone, it was as if earth and silence had suddenly swallowed a Primrose League fair with five large roundabouts and a brass band. She turned round to find Mr. Plantagenet-Buchan behind her appreciating the calm.

"Marvellous energy," he said.

"She will be a great help," said Cynthia with unusual asperity.

"There is one thing I observe," said Mr. Plantagenet-Buchan.

"Let us have some fresh tea," said Mrs. Rylands, "and sit down and try to restore our minds to order."

Then his words awakened a familiar echo in her mind. Surely he had said them before—as far as that! Several times. And several times been interrupted.

Of course he had! He had been trying to make

this remark ever since he and Lady Catherine had come back from Ventimiglia. Perhaps he had been trying to make it even in Ventimiglia. It was a shame! Mrs. Rylands turned to him brightly. "You were saying, Mr. Plantagenet-Buchan?"

He laughed deprecatingly. "Well," he preluded.

"There is one little thing about this crisis, dear lady," he said, and made the diamond glitter; "one small consoling thing. If you will consult those French and Italian papers. You will see that while on the one hand they proclaim the outbreak of the social war and the probable end of the British Empire, they note, less conspicuously but I think more convincingly, that the franc is still falling and the pound sterling still holding its own even against our own more than golden dollar."

"And that means?"

"That every one does not take this crisis quite so seriously as Lady Catherine. Suppose we wait a day more before we despair of England. I can quite believe that even now—Westminster is not in flames. I am convinced even that dinner will be served quite normally in Buckingham Palace to-night."

"And meanwhile," smiled his hostess, "unless Bombaccio has heard the call of his union, we might have a little fresh tea."

Miss Fenimore leapt to the bell.

They moved into the lower part of the hall and Mr. Plantagenet-Buchan yielded himself to the largest armchair with a sigh of contentment that it was difficult to disconnect altogether from the recent departure of their lovely friend.

There were some moments of silence.

"This man at Torre Pellice," began Mr. Plantagenet-Buchan in a reflective voice, "this man I am proposing to visit, has a very fine taste indeed. He collects. He has a curiosity and a liveliness of mind that I find most enviable. In these times of conflict and dispersal it is rather nice to think of a collector—and of a few minor things anyhow being put out of immediate danger of breakage."

He paused. Miss Fenimore made a purr of approval and Mrs. Rylands instructed Bombaccio about the fresh tea. Mr. Plantagenet-Buchan continued meditatively.

"One sort of thing he collected for a time were those prostrate trumpets of coloured glass in which the early Victorians put flowers. 'Cornucopias,' I fancy they were called. Typically there was a solid, heavy slab of alabaster-like substance and on this the cornucopia reposed and often by a pretty fancy its lower end was finished off by an elegant hand of metal and the cornucopia became a sleeve. These cornucopias may have interbred a little with those cups they call rhytons which end in a head below. There must have been a great abundance of them at one time in early Victorian England, and they are still to be found in considerable variety, in purple and blue and coloured glass and in dead white glass with spangles and in imitation marble. At one time no dinner table could have been complete without a pair, probably matching a glass epergne. My friend discovered one in a little back street shop in Pimlico. At first he knew so little about these things that he accumulated single ones and only realised later that they must go in pairs. He was happy for a time. Until he began to detect the tracks of some abler seeker in this field. Another—others perhaps—were collecting. He came upon articles—in the *Connoisseur*, in other art magazines. The situation became plainer. The harvest had been gathered in. Mr. Frank Galsworthy, the painter who has that beautiful cottage garden in Surrey, had got so far ahead with them, that my friend could not hope to do more than glean after him. So my friend turned his attention to Welsh love spoons.

"Do you know of them? Do you know what they are? They are wonderful exploits in carving. (Thank you, that is exactly as I like it. One lump only.) They used to be made—perhaps some are still made—by Welsh lovers when they were courting. They were carved all out of one chosen piece of good oak. There would be a spoon and then at the end of its short handle a chain of links and it would all end in a hook or a whistle. The links would be free and there would be perhaps an extra bit, a barred cage with little balls running about inside; the whole contraption made out of one solid piece of timber. I never imagined the Welsh were such artists at wood carving. I suppose Mr. Jones would sit at the side of the beloved while he did it. Love spoons. What an answer to Caradoc Evans! You have heard the mysterious word 'spooning.' It is said to come from that."

Miss Fenimore was greatly delighted at this unexpected etymology. Her pleasure cried aloud.

Her sudden nervous laughter, a certain glow, might have led a careless observer to suppose her an adept at spooning. She slaked her excitement by attention to the teapot. There was a brief interval of cake-offering. Miss Fenimore offered cake to Mr. Plantagenet-Buchan and Mr. Plantagenet-Buchan offered cake to Mrs. Rylands and Miss Fenimore and Mrs. Rylands offered cake to Mr. Plantagenet-

Buchan and Mr. Plantagenet-Buchan took some cake.

"I am afraid," said Mr. Plantagenet-Buchan biting his cake, "that I am too hopelessly indolent and inconsecutive ever to make a good collector or else I think I should have devoted myself to bergamotes."

"I thought they were a kind of pear," said Mrs. Rylands.

"A kind of orange, primarily. But the name is also used for a delicious silly sort of little leather box made years ago in the country round about Grasse. You may have seen one by chance. They still lurk, looking rather depressed and dirty, in those queer corners of old curiosity shops where one finds little bits of silver and impossible rings. It is a box of leather, yes, but the skin of which the leather is made is orange skin and it is polished and faintly stained and has a dainty little flower or so painted upon it. The boxes are oval or heart-shaped; you know the delicate insinuations of that age. These bergamotes must be, most of them, a hundred years old or more and yet when you open them and snuff inside you can persuade yourself that the faint flavour of orange clings to them yet, scent that was brewed in the sunshine when Louis Philippe was King."

Mr. Plantagenet-Buchan could not have chosen a better theme to exorcise the flare of unrest and alarm that had blown about the Casa Terragena household for the past three hours.

§ 7

MR. PLANTAGENET-BUCHAN was quite charming that night. It was to be his last night, he intimated ever so gently, and tomorrow he would make his devious way by local trains to Torre Pellice and his collector friend. For it really seemed there was a friend.

After dinner there was a luminous peacefulness in the world outside and an unusual warmth, the rising moon had pervaded heaven with an intense blue and long slanting bars of dreamy light lifted themselves from the horizontal towards the vertical, slowly and indolently amidst the terraces and trees and bushes. At two or three in the morning when every one was asleep they would stand erect like sentinel spears.

"I think I could walk a little," said Mrs. Rylands and they went outside upon the terrace and down the steps to the path that led through the close garden with the tombstone of Amoena Lucina to the broad way that ended at last in a tall jungle of subtly scented nocturnal white flowers. They were tall responsible looking flowers. The moonlight among their petals armed them with little scimitars and bucklers of silver. Among these flowers were moths, great white moths, so that it seemed as if ever and again a couple of blossoms became detached and pirouetted together. Hostess and guest—for Miss Fenimore, with her instinctive tact, did not join them —promenaded this broad dim path, to and fro, and Mr. Plantagenet-Buchan spread his Epicurean philosophy unchallenged before Mrs. Rylands' enquiring intelligence.

He had been much struck by his own impromptu antithesis of Loveliness to Loneliness and this he now developed as a choice between the sense of beauty and the sense of self. He began apropos of Lady Catherine and her excited interest in present things. "How strange it is that she should incessantly want to do, when all that need be asked of her more than of any one else is surely that she should simply *be*."

He passed easily into personal exposition.

"I treat myself," he said, "as a piece of bric-à-brac in this wonderful collection, the universe, a piece that differs from the other odd, quaint and amusing pieces, simply because my eye happens to be set in it. Here in this lovely garden, which is so irrelevant to all the needless haste and turmoil of life, I can be perfectly happy. I am perfectly happy—to-night. My chief complaint against existence is that it *happens* too much and keeps on hurrying by. Before you can appreciate it in the least. I seem always to be trying to pick up exquisite things it drops, with all the crowding next things jostling and thrusting my poor stooping back. Get out of the way there! Eager to trample my treasure before I can even make it a treasure. Like trying to pick up a lost pearl in the middle of the Place de la Concorde. If I could plan my own fate, I would like to live five hundred years in a world in which nothing of any importance ever happened at all. A world like a Chinese plate. I should have a little sinecure perhaps or I should perform some graceful functions in the ceremonies of a religion that had completely lost whatever reality it ever had."

Mrs. Rylands was not unmindful of her duty to the little green leather book that waited in her sitting-room.

"You do not believe in God?" she asked, to be perfectly clear.

"In loveliness, I believe. And I delight in gods. But in God— How it would spoil this perfect night, this crystal sky, this silver peace, if one thought it was not precisely the pure loveliness it is! Without an *arrière pensée*. If one had to turn it all into allegory and guess what it meant! If one even began to suspect that it was just a way of signalling something to us, on the part of a Supreme Personage!"

"But if one took it simply as a present from him?"

"That would be better. Then the only duty in life would be to accept and enjoy. And God would sit over us like some great golden Buddha, smiling, blessing and not minding in the least. Not signifying in the least."

"That is all very well for happy and pampered people like ourselves, living in houses and gardens like this one."

"One can start in search of beauty from any starting point and one is still a pilgrim even if one dies by the way."

"But most human beings start from such frightful starting points. They hardly get a glimpse of beauty."

"Not sunlight? Not the evening compositions of clouds and sun? The sunsets in Mr. Bennett's Five Towns are the loveliest in the world. I assure you. The beauty of London Docks again? Or it may be music heard by chance from an open window in the street? Or flowers?"

He shook his head gravely, almost regretfully. "Every one can find beauty. Think of the beauty of sunlight at the end of a tunnel."

"I am afraid the world is full of crippled and driven lives. They're hungry and afraid. What chance of seeing beauty have most poor people— anywhere? Even when it is under their noses. You can't see beauty with miserable eyes. Beauty does not make happiness; it only comes to the happy. Latterly that has begun to haunt me dreadfully."

"No," said Mr. Plantagenet-Buchan. "That is wrong. Don't *spoil* to-night."

"But they pay for this! Haven't we a duty to them?"

"Surely as much duty to this night, to leave it serene."

"I can't feel like that. I can't forget this dismal coal strike, the trouble of it, the people out of work, the anxiety, the need in millions of poor worried brains."

"My dear lady! they chose it. They need not have been born."

Came a pause as the great modern topic of restriction was faced.

"But it is rather difficult for a child, which doesn't exist, and isn't perhaps going to exist for some time, to weigh all the pros and cons and decide——"

"Its parents and guardians, its godfathers and godmothers wherein it was made, could act for it. It isn't consulted as a whole so to speak, its constituents are consulted—tacitly. And it has at any rate its own blind Will to Live. Most parentage is inadvertent. What a precious relief is the thought of birth control! The time is coming when it will be practically impossible to tempt any one to get born except under the most hopeful and favourable circumstances."

"But meanwhile?"

"I am like the great Mr. Sempack; I refuse to be eaten up by meanwhile."

"Meanwhile one must live."

"As calmly as possible. As inactively appreciative as possible. It is just because one must live that one tries to give oneself wholly to a night like this. How rarely do even such favoured ones as we are get an hour so smooth and crystalline as this! The stillness! The chief fault I have with living is the way life rushes us about. Rushes every one about. What a hurry, what a scurry is history! Think of all the hosts and armies and individuals that have thrust and shoved and whacked their mules and horses along this very Via Aurelia in your garden. Which to-night is just a deep black pit smothered in ivy. Grave of innumerable memories. If we went down there to-night to that old paved track I wonder if we should see their ghosts! Romans and Carthaginians, Milanese and Burgundians, French and Italians, kings and bishops and conquerors and fugitives. It would be a fit punishment for all their hurry and violence to find them there. It would serve them right for all their wicked inattention to loveliness, to put them back again upon their paces and make them repeat them over and over, over and over, night after night, century after century. . . ."

Mr. Plantagenet-Buchan was smitten by a bright idea. "Perhaps some day some later Einstein will take out patents and contrive a way of slowing down time. Without affecting our perceptions. Then we shall not be everlastingly hurried on by strikes and wars and passions and meal-times and bed-times. With the newspapers rustling and flying through the air like witches in a storm.

"But I chatter on and on, my dear Mrs. Rylands. You set me talking. And I am trying to forget the Social Revolution now in progress and how we are all to be swept away. Or else saved by Captain

Fearon-Owen, was it? and Lady Catherine. Whichever is the worse.

"Before we go in, may we just walk up that path above the house to the little bridge over the gorge beyond the herbarium and the laboratory? Do you know it? By night? There the hillside goes up very steeply and everything, the trees and even the rocks, seems to be drawn up too in a kind of magical unanimity. You must see it by moonlight. An immense flamboyance of black and white. Stupendous shadows. I discovered it last night as I prowled about the garden before turning in. It streams up and up and up, and over it brood the wet black precipices of the mountains, endlessly vertical, with little threads of silver. The eye follows it up. It is like all the Gothic in the world multiplied by ten. It is like listening to some tremendous crescendo. Farther than this he cannot go, you say, and he goes farther. At the top the precipices fairly overhang. One stands on the bridge at the foot of it, minute, insignificant, overawed. . . .

"By daylight it is nothing very wonderful. Hardly anything at all."

§ 8

M R. PLANTAGENET-BUCHAN had scarcely gone from Casa Terragena before Mr. Sempack reappeared. Mrs. Rylands had walked part of the way up to the road gate with Mr. Plantagenet-Buchan and after wishing him farewell she had turned off to a seat beneath some Japanese medlars where there were long orderly beds of

violets like the planche of a Grasse violet grower,
and a level path of pebble mosaic that led round the
headland towards the rocky portals of the Caatinga.
She had brought the green leather book with her, because his talk overnight had set her thinking. She
found herself in the closest sympathy and the completest intellectual disagreement with the things he
had said.

Just as she felt that at the core of things was
courage, so she had an irrational conviction that,
properly seen, the general substance of things was
beauty. To Mr. Plantagenet-Buchan's craving to
lead a life of pure appreciation she found a temperamental response. She could quite easily relax into
that pose. But also she perceived something selec-
tive, deliberate and narrowing in his attitude. He
reminded her of those people, now happily becoming
old-fashioned, who will not look at a lovely landscape except through a rolled-up newspaper or some
such frame. Or of people who cannot admire flowers
without picking them. He seemed to think that the
appreciation of beauty was a kind of rescue work; to
take the lovely thing and trim it up and carry it off.
But she thought it was a matter of recognition and
acceptance. So while in practice he was for sealing
up himself and his sensations in a museum case as it
were with beauty, she was for lying open to the four
winds of heaven, sure that beauty would come and
remain. And while he posed as a partisan of beauty
even against the idea of God; her idea of an ever
deepening and intensifying realisation of the beauty
in things was inseparably mingled with the conception of discovering God. He and she could perceive
the poignant delight of a star suddenly flashing

through forest leaves with a complete identity of pleasure and a complete divergence of thought. And so while art for him was quintessence, for her it was only a guide.

But while she was still struggling with this difficult disentanglement of assents and dissents that her analysis of Mr. Plantagenet-Buchan required, and before she had made a single entry in the green leather book as a result of these exercises, she became aware of Mr. Sempack descending the winding path that was the main route of communication between the gates and the house. Beside him a requisitioned under-gardener bore his knapsack and valise and answered such questions and agreed with such opinions as the great Utopologist's Italian permitted him to make.

It was Mr. Sempack. And he was changed.

Recognition was followed by astonishment. He was greatly changed. He was different altogether. More erect—rampant. No longer had he the quality of rocky scenery; he had the quality of rocky scenery that had arisen and tossed its mane and marched. "Tossing its mane" mixed oddly with rocky scenery, but that was how it came to her. His hair had all been thrust and combed back from his forehead, violently, so that the effect of his head, considered largely, had become leonine; he lifted his roughly handsome profile and seemed to snuff the air. He had no hat! Hitherto he and his hat had been inseparable out of doors, but now he neither wore nor carried one. What could he have done with his hat? Moreover his cravat had suffered some exchange, had become large and loose and as it were, it was too far off to be certain, black silk, tied with the extravagance natural to a Latin man of genius, but otherwise remarkable and improper. And he walked erect with a certain conscious rectitude and large confident strides and assisted himself with a bold stout walking stick. Mrs. Rylands could not remember that stick; she had an impression he had gone off with an umbrella. At any rate he had gone off with the appearance of having an umbrella. She became eager to scrutinise this renascent Sempack closelier. She stood up for the moment to give her voice play and make herself more conspicuous. "Mr. Sempack," she cried, "Mr. Sem-pack!"

He heard. He turned eagerly. Just for a moment a shade of disappointment may have betrayed itself in his bearing. He hesitated, waved his stick, glanced down towards the house and then after a word or so with his garden man, submitted to his obvious fate and ascended the steps to her.

"You've come back to us," she said, so giving him the very latest news as he approached.

"I've had a splendid time among the hills," he answered in that fine large voice of his. "How endlessly beautiful and unexpected France can be! And what lonely places! How are you?"

He was now standing in front of her.

"I'm better and happier, thanks to some good advice I had."

"If it was of service," he said. "Yes, you look ever so much better. Indeed you look radiantly well. How are the others?"

"Scattered for the most part."

He did not seem to mind about that. "Where is Lady Catherine?" he asked.

As he spoke he looked at the cypresses and magnolias that masked most of the house from him and then up and down the slopes about them for the lovely figure he sought. How easy a thing, Mrs. Rylands reflected, it was to make a man over confident. He'd gone off to make up his mind about Lady Catherine, it was only too evident, and here he was back with his mind made up, made up indeed altogether, and quite oblivious to the fact that Lady Catherine had gone on living at her own natural pace, during his interval of indecision. He became aware of a pause in answering his enquiry. His eyes came back to the face of his hostess. (Surely he had not been clipping those once too discursive eyebrows! But he had!) She tried to impart her information as though it was of no deep interest to either of them.

"Lady Catherine," she said, "has gone to England."

Mr. Sempack was a child when it came to concealing his feelings. "Gone to England!" he cried. "I was *convinced* she would stay here."

"She was restless," said Mrs. Rylands.

"But *I* was restless!" protested Mr. Sempack, opening vast gulfs of implication.

"She went yesterday."

"But why has she gone? Why should she go to England?"

"When the news of the strike came it lit her up like a rocket and off she went fiz-bang," said Mrs. Rylands.

"But why?"

"To save the country."

"But this strike," said Mr. Sempack, "is nothing at all. Just political nonsense. Why should she go to England?"

She found her respect for Mr. Sempack collapsing like a snowman before a bonfire. She ceased to scrutinise his improvements. "I'm not responsible for Lady Catherine," she said and smoothed the nice back of the green leather book. "She's gone."

It seemed to dawn upon Mr. Sempack that he was forgetting his manners. He had stood in front of her without the slightest intention of staying beside her. Now he gave one last reproachful glance down the hill towards the paths, terraces, lawns, windows and turrets where Lady Catherine ought to have been waiting for him, and then came slowly and sat down beside his hostess. The first exhilaration of his bearing had already to a large extent evaporated.

"Forgive me," he said. "I quite expected to find Lady Catherine here. We had a sort of argument together. It had excited me. But, as you say, she has gone. And the American gentleman with the hyphenated name? Who had an effect of being manicured all over. What was he called? Mr. Plantagenet-Buchan?"

"Went this morning. To Torre Pellice above Turin."

"And Miss Fenimore?"

"Is with us still."

"I'm so surprised she's gone. You see I don't attach any great importance to this General Strike in England. So that I can't imagine any one going off—a woman particularly. . . . I may be mistaken. . . ."

"It has stopped all the English newspapers," said Mrs. Rylands. "And most of the English trains. It has thrown millions of people out of employment. There is talk of famine through the interruption of food supplies."

"An acute attack of Sundays in the place of the usual week. But why should it affect Lady Catherine?"

It was not Mrs. Rylands' business to answer that.

"Are you *sure* she went on account of the General Strike?"

Mrs. Rylands had serious thoughts of losing her temper. "That was the reason she gave," she said, in the tone of one who loses interest in a topic. But Mr. Sempack had a habit of pursuing his own line of thought with a certain regardlessness for other people.

"She may have gone to demonstrate her point of view in our argument," he surmised. Mrs. Rylands, being in better possession of the facts, thought it a very foolish surmise but she offered no comment.

"The matter at issue between us," said Mr. Sempack, prodding up the pathway with the stout stick, "had of course, extraordinarily far-reaching implications. Reduced to its simplest terms it was this, Is the current surface of things a rational reality?"

Mrs. Rylands wanted to laugh. She regarded Mr. Sempack's profile, gravely intent on spoiling her excellent path. She was filled with woman's instinctive pity for man. Every man is a moody child, she thought, every man in the world. But the children must not be spoilt. "So that was why you went off for a walking tour?" she remarked, intelligently.

"I thought we both needed to think over our differences," he said.

"And you still don't think—what is it?—that the current surface of things is—whatever it is?"

"No," he said and excavated a quite large chunk of earth and smashed it to sandy fragments in front of his boots. "But I suppose this flight to England is to show me that the issues between us are not false issues but real, and that while I dream and theorise, she can play a part. . . . I wish she hadn't gone. There is nothing happening in England at all that is not perfectly preposterous. Utterly preposterous. Political life in England becomes more and more like Carnival."

He shrugged his shoulders. The large tie became a little askew. "Carnival without a police. Well— that is political life everywhere nowadays. . . ."

As this was manifestly not the subject under discussion between them a silence of perhaps half a minute supervened. Then Mr. Sempack bestirred himself.

"She has gone," he said, "just because she likes Carnival. And that is the truth of the matter."

He glanced sideways at his hostess as if he hoped she would contradict him.

But she did nothing of the sort. She reflected and bore her witness with a considered effect. "Mr. Sempack," she said, "I know Catherine. And that *is* the truth of the matter."

"I thought it was."

His bones *did* move about under his skin, because they were doing so now. He dug industriously at the path through another long silence. "Forgive my moodiness and my rudeness. And my confidences. My almost involuntary confidences. As you know perfectly well already, I am in the ridiculous position of having fallen in love with Lady Catherine; and it isn't any the less disorganising for being utterly absurd. It has made me, I perceive, absurd. To fall in love, as I have done, is—to reverberate melodrama. It is as unreal as an opium dream and one knows it is unreal. Yet one clings with a certain obstinacy. . . . I expected— Heaven knows what I expected! But that is no reason, is it? why I should come and set myself down here and interrupt your writing in that extremely pretty book of yours and dig large holes in your path."

"The paths were made for man and not man for the paths," said Mrs. Rylands. "I wish all my gardeners worked as you have done for the last few minutes. I am sorry for what has happened. Catherine is one of those people who ought not to be allowed about loose."

"I may go to England," he said after he had digested that. "I am preposterously dislocated. I do not know what to do."

"But in England, won't the melodrama lie in wait for you?"

"Perhaps, I wish it would. At present, my mind and my thoughts—are just swirling about. I can't go on writing. I might of course go into Italy."

"Meanwhile stay here. For a day or so anyhow. There are all sorts of things I would like to hear you talk about. If you could talk about them. And this garden has a place for almost any mood. No one shall worry you. If I dared I would ask you about a score of things that perplex me."

"You are very kind to suffer me," he said.

She shook her head and smiled and then stood up.

"I think you have done enough to my path this morning," she said. "Look at it!"

He made some clumsy and ineffective attempts to repair the mischief of his immense hands with his immense feet, and then came hurrying after her down the steps.

§9

THAT evening after dinner they sat in the great room upstairs before a fire of logs in the Italianate fire-place, and Mr. Sempack without any allusion whatever to Lady Catherine talked about Thought and Action and the change of tempo as well as of scale that was coming upon human concerns. Mrs. Rylands lay on the big sofa and Mr. Sempack occupied an armchair beside her. Miss Fenimore assisted at the conversation on the other side of the fire-place. She played also a slow difficult patterning patience on a card table with two packs of cards, a patience that kept her lips moving, not always inaudibly with, "Black Knave goes on Queen and red ten on Knave, but what then? All these come up, nine, eight, seven, but does that free a space? Won't do. Won't do."

She had excused herself for her patience. "I can hear just as well," she said, "and it seems to steady my attention. I don't think I miss the least little thing you say."

Sometimes her patience kept her quite busy and sometimes she would leave it alone and just sit back with the residue of her deck in hand and take a long deep swig of whatever Mr. Sempack was saying. Then she would sigh and resume her attack on her cards, visibly refreshed.

Although Mr. Sempack never made the ghost of an allusion to Lady Catherine, it was quite plain to Mrs. Rylands that the gist of his talks with that lady lay under the rambling discourse like bones beneath the contours of a limb. When he talked of the greater importance of the man of science to the politician, he was really exonerating himself from her charge of political impotence and insignificance, and when he declared that with the abolition of distance through the increasing ease of communication in the world, there had come such an enlargement and complication of political issues that they could no longer be dealt with dramatically in a day or a week, she felt that he was still trying to disabuse Lady Catherine from her delusion that decisive incidents at elections, scenes in the House and displays of "personality" at Cabinet meetings could have any real influence any longer upon the course of human affairs. He talked casually and indolently as things came into his head, but Mrs. Rylands perceived that the green leather book would profit considerably by the things he was saying.

His remarks joined on very directly to that earlier talk, that successful social evening, that had so pleased her, that renewal of the legendary glories of the Souls—and it was still not a fortnight ago! He revived the vision of a greater civilisation ahead, a world civilisation, in which the pursuit of science would be the chief industry and increasing power an annual crop. That vision had a little faded from Mrs. Rylands' mind. He restored it to probability and even to imminence. It became reality again and all the social and political conflicts of to-day mere temporary disorders, like battles and contests of hobbledehoys amidst advertisement-covered hoardings on the vacant site of some great building. War became a declining habit that mankind was shaking off. And those troubles in England were no more than a legacy of barbaric methods that would still win coal by hand labour and make a private profit out of a common necessity. Some day we should win our coal out of the earth in so different a fashion that there would be neither myriads of dingy toilers nor groups of owners concerned with it at all, and from the point of view of the larger issue therefore, the dispute between them was a false issue that led nowhere and settled nothing at all. Even as they disputed the grounds of the differences were dissolving under their feet.

But there were certain things that the green leather book would want to know to-morrow morning and Mrs. Rylands sought elucidation.

"I see the world could be changed, ought to be changed, from all its present confusions," she agreed. "Things do not change themselves. Much of this progress so far has taken people by surprise. Now the surprise is over and we see the steps, the enormous steps that have to be made, if we are to pass from this—this complex muddle of affairs—to the world civilisation. You speak as though that would certainly be brought about. But who are the people who are bringing it about?"

"The scientific minded people," said Mr. Sempack. "The people who think ahead."

"I see that people of that sort are adding to the vision of the great age coming, filling in details, helping our imaginations to smooth over difficulties. You alone have done wonderful things to make the prospectus credible. But it is still only a prospectus. Are people taking shares? Are any of these people who talk and wish so well, doing anything to bring the World Utopia about?"

"I think, *yes*," said Mr. Sempack after a slight pause.

She felt she was pressing him, but she wanted to know. "How?" she asked.

"By making it increasingly evident that it is possible and bringing people to realise that it is desirable—a refuge from the vast dangers that threaten us all, while with the immensely powerful weapons of to-day we stick to antiquated moral and social traditions."

"Yes, but——" said Mrs. Rylands.

She gathered all her forces. She wasn't trying to argue with him but she did want to be able to face the candid pages of the green leather book to-morrow without any inconvenient queries arising—finished and sure in what she had to write. She had to write it as plainly as she could and then she had to copy out her exercise and send it to her fellow student Philip, who would be, she felt certain, quite wonderful at jabbing in destructive questions.

"You see, Mr. Sempack, this is my difficulty. I see the world abounding in projects for doing things better. People who write about that sort of thing write about it and we read it when we are in the reading mood and want our imaginations stirring. But the mass of people just go on. I suppose that if you told all that you are telling me to a miner and said that there were to be no miners at all in the new world, but only very clever boring machines, and ways of taking air into the pit to burn the coal and make power there instead of digging it out and so on, I doubt if he would be ready to bring the change about. He would think of himself and say that though it was bad enough to be an underpaid miner, perhaps not employed too regularly, but still getting a sort of living, it might be worse to be in a world where he wasn't wanted at all."

"He could be changed."

"Not all at once. He'd have his missus and the kids and his dog and his habits. Would he want to be changed? Changed I mean in his nature, as you would change him. More money perhaps he would like and a rather better house. But what more? And take the mine-owner: you can't expect him to welcome and help his own abolition."

"The new things will come gradually enough to smooth over that sort of thing."

"If somebody wants them. But who is going to want them? I'm asking, because I really want to know, Mr. Sempack, who is going to want them enough to take a lot of pains to bring them about? Many of us no doubt want them vaguely and generally but do any of us want them particularly and fiercely enough to get them past the awkward turns and difficult corners?"

"They involve the clear promise of an ampler life."

"I don't worry you with my persistent questions? They are silly questions, I know, but they puzzle me."

"Not a bit silly. You argue very closely. Go on."

"Well, this clear promise of an ampler life. Suppose you said to a cat, 'Come, I will teach you to swim and dive like a seal and fly like a bat,' and so on, 'if only you will stop catching the songbirds in my garden,' and suppose the cat were so say, 'Life is short. It is fun to think of such things and they make me yearn to leave the little birds alone and eat fish, but all the same this means a frightful change in my habits. I might prove less adaptable than you suppose. I might die before I adapted. I do get along fairly well as it is. Have you ever seen me go up a tree? Or jump and catch a young nestling in the air? Do you mind if I just go on being a cat?' "

Mr. Sempack nodded and smiled thoughtfully at the fire and left his hostess free to continue.

"All the sorts of people I see about me, all the soldiers we know for example; they are most liberal-minded about war I find and about the League of Nations and that sort of thing, provided there is no serious interference with soldiering."

"They will get most horribly gassed in the next war."

"They hope to gas first. But even if they think the outlook a little unpleasant in that way, they still have no idea of how they are going to change over. Or what they are going to change into. And mean-while—meanwhile they go on being soldiers."

"They will be changed over," said Mr. Sempack largely.

"But *who* will change them over? Directly one goes out of a talk like this back into one's everyday life, one finds every one more or less in the same position—doing something in the present system, hanging on to it, dreading dislocation, objecting to any improvement that really touches them. But otherwise quite liberal-minded and progressive."

"The forces of change will override them. Change of conditions is incessant."

"But change may go any way, Mr. Sempack. There is no one steering change. Why shouldn't it go hither and thither? It raises up; it may cast down."

"Why not?" asked Mr. Sempack of the flaring olive knots.

"We may 'meanwhile' for ever. People may be driven this way and that. Some may go down and some up. Old types may vanish and new ones come. Some of that may be progress but some of that may be loss. Nature gives no real guarantee. Change may go on until men are blue things three feet high and rats hunt them as we hunt rats and your great civilisation may never arrive—never arrive at all. It may have loomed up and receded and loomed up again and been talked about again as you talk about it, and then things may have slipped back and slipped back more and gone on slipping back. And the rats may have got bolder and the disease germs more dwarfing and crippling, and energy may have ebbed."

"Touché," said Mr. Sempack and paused tremendously.

Mrs. Rylands adjusted a cushion and regarded him expectantly before lying back more comfortably.

"It's come out," said Miss Fenimore and made a great triumphant scrabbling with her cards. "They don't *often* come out."

"That is precisely the question that occupies my mind nowadays—dominantly," said Mr. Sempack, disregarding Miss Fenimore. "My life has been so largely given to thought and the project. . . . After all, all this constructive Utopianism is a growth of very recent years. . . . But I do see that a time comes—and in the case of these matters the time may be here already—when these creative ideas must

come down into the market place, among the hawk-
ers and the cheats and the Carnival maskers, and
fight to impose themselves. Science can never be
really pure science. Science sprang from practical
curiosities and justifies and refreshes itself by practical applications. Yet it must go apart to work out
its riddles. There is a rhythm in these things.
Thought must be neither too close nor too aloof from
actuality. There has been a need in the past century to take social and economic generalisations a little way off from current politics and active business
and work them out into a new, broader, deeper, modern project. That in its main lines is done. Now,
we, who have gone apart, have to come back. We
have got clear to the conception of a possible world
peace, a world economic system, a common currency,
and unparalleled freedoms, growths and liberties. . . ."

"Yes?" said Mrs. Rylands.

"We have at last made it seem extremely credible
and possible."

"Yes?"

"And how to get there? remains still with hardly
the barest rudiments of an answer. A League of
Nations. Vague projects of social revolution. Pious
intentions. Practical futility."

"And *meanwhile?*" whispered Mrs. Rylands.

"I do not even know whether the same type of
mind that has mastered the first can work out the
second problem. Perhaps there is a difference of
personality needed, just as there is perhaps a difference between the pure scientific man and the scientific
commercial man. It may be because I am realising
that this business is entering upon a new phase that

I find I am writing freely no longer and that I am restless and attracted by unseasonable hankerings for experience and at last—I confess it—disposed to go back to look into these queer troubles in England. I have had a dream, a ridiculous dream, of being revitalised. The Sacred Fount—of passion."

He seemed to remember the presence of Miss Fenimore and abandoned what might have become a fresh confidence.

"I do not know. I do not know whether men of my kind have to turn into men of action or whether they have to turn over all they have thought-out and worked-out to men of action. A young man like your Philip attracts me, just because he seems to have all the vigour, flexibility and aggressiveness, that my type of withdrawn, persistently sceptical, habitually sceptical enquirer, does not possess. I do not know. I wish I did. And there you are! I am afraid I have left that question of yours, Mrs. Rylands, very largely open."

He seemed to have finished and then he resumed.

"It may be that this concrete conception of human progress awaits its philosophy and its religion. Idea must clothe itself in will. The new civilisation will call for devotion—something more than the devotion of thinking and writing at one's leisure. It may need martyrs—as well as recluses. And leaders as well as prophets. It will call for co-operative action, for wide disciplines. . . ."

He stood up before the fire, a great shambling figure that cast a huge caricature in shadow on the wall opposite.

"I think I will go back to England in a day or so—anyhow—if only to see why people can struggle with such courage and passion for ends that do not seem to me to have any real relation to the Civilisation of the World at all. Hitherto I have been thinking so much of what I am after myself that it may be good for me, for a change, just to find out what other people are after. And why none of them seem to be after the only thing that I think makes life worth living.

"Yes," he reflected, "*make* your World Civilisation. That is just what Lady Catherine told me. You, with your questions, repeat the challenge. . . . I wonder if at bottom, Mrs. Rylands, both the scientific investigator and the philosopher are not profoundly indolent men. They work—I admit they work—continuously—but how they fortify themselves against interruptions and counter strokes and irrelevant issues!"

His thoughts seemed to Mrs. Rylands to glance suddenly in a different direction. "*Essentially*," he said, "they must be celibate. . . ."

Mr. Sempack had come to the end of his meditations. His hostess and Miss Fenimore wished him good-night. He was left to consume two glasses of barley water and put out the lights.

§ 10

PHILIP'S "first real letter," so he called it, came on the day of Mr. Sempack's departure for England. There had been an "arrived safe" telegram from London and a pencil scrawl of affectionate "rubbidge," so he put it, with various endearments and secret and particular names, that he had posted in Paris. That was just carrying on.

But this she felt was something momentous. It came while she was resting on her bed, through sheer laziness, and she felt its importance so much that for a time she could not open it. It was a fat letter, a full letter, it was over the two ounces, fivepence ha'penny worth of letter, and inside there was going to be something—something she had never had before—Philip mentally, all out, according to his promise. She was going to learn fresh and important things about him. She was going to scrutinise his mental quality as she had never done before.

What sort of a letter was it going to be? She had a shadow of fear in her mind. Things said can be forgotten. Or you recall the manner and edit and rearrange the not too happy words. Things written hammer at the eye and repeat themselves inexorably. Written clumsiness becomes monstrous clumsy. So far she had never had anything more from Philip than a note. His notes were good, queer in their phrasing but with an odd way of conveying tenderness. . . . Philip would be Philip. She took courage and tore open the distended envelope.

She found half a dozen fascicles each pinned together. It was neither like a letter nor like a proper manuscript, but it was like Philip. The paper was of various sorts, some of it from their house in South Street, some from the Reform Club, some from Brooks' and some ruled foolscap of unknown origin carefully torn into half-sheets so as to pack comfortably with the spread out notepaper. Somewhere he had got hold of a blue pencil and numbered the fascicles with large numbers, one, two, three and so forth, emphasised by a circle. The fascicle numbered one, was

"General Instructions for a little Cynner to read these Lubrications."

Lucubrations?

Then this touching design and appeal:

"My dearest Cynthia, wife," it went on, "I find it pretty hard to set down all my impressions of things here. Which is all the more reason I suppose why I should begin to set down my impressions. It's hard to make it go, one, two, three, and away. I just can't make the stuff I have to tell you flow off my pen as trained chaps like old Sempack seems able to do. Whatever he has to say seems to begin at one place and go right through to an end, missing nothing by the way. I've been reading in some of his books. In fact I've been reading him no end. People talk about 'writing' and I've always thought before it meant purple patches and lovely words, but this sort of thing also is writing; driving ten topics in a team together—and getting somewhere, getting through doors and narrow places and home to where you want to go. I seem to begin at half a dozen places and it is only after a time that one finds that this joins up with that. I've made half a dozen starts and here most of them are.

"This is a sort of student's note-book. I've helped it out with diagrams and here and there pictures seem to have got themselves in when I wasn't looking. But it is a multiplex affair here. Here in England I mean—not in this letter. An imbrolio. It isn't a straight story. You take Part numbered Two and then Three and so on in the order of the numbers, and I think at the end you'll get the hang of what I'm thinking all right. Forgive some of the spelling, and all the heavy lumpish way of putting things. If I do much of this sort of thing I shall have to take lessons from Sempack and Bertrand Russell, how to be clear if complex. As you said, we've got to know each other—even if it hurts. So I've done my best. I don't think I've struck any attitudes.

"If you despise me over this stuff—well, it had to be. Better than not knowing each other. Better than that. Truly. Dear Cynthia, my Friend. All you said to me about being truly near, mind more than body, went to my heart. Both."

That was the substance of Part One. Followed a sort of index and a few remarks about each part, that were simply preparatory matter. Rather business-like preparatory matter. He must have written that index after all the rest was done.

She held Part One in her hand and thought for some moments. Queer! This wasn't her Philip; the Philip she had known for a wonderful year. But it was not inharmonious with her Philip. It was

196

an extension of him, the wider Philip. It was at once a little strange and more intimate. It was very honest; that was the first thing about it. And it had a quality of strength. It was extraordinary that a man who had been as close to her as he had been, with such warmth and laughter and delight, should still betray so plainly a maidenly bashfulness over the nakedness of his prose and the poverty of his spelling. Bodies one can strip in half a minute. Now—and he knew it—he was revealing his mind.

And then the drawing. She had never suspected him of skill, but there was skill in the way he got what he wanted to express over to her. The figure of himself, a little oafish and anxious. And herself. He didn't spare her littleness. And yet plainly he couldn't draw—as she judged drawing. There were several other drawings. . . .

She glanced at Part Three. But these looked more like the figures one scribbles on blotting paper. Perhaps it would be plainer when she came to them in order.

She took up Part Two which was entitled:

"General Observations on the General Strike.

"Firstly I am disposed to call this General Strike the Silliest Thing in the History of England. I don't know whether I would stick to that. What old Muzzleton used to get red in the nose working us up about, what he used to call 'Our Island Story,' is full of dam silly things. But this is a monstrous dam silly affair, my Cynthia. It is a tangle of false issues from beginning to end. So silly one can't take sides. One is left gibbering helplessly as the silly affair unrolls itself.

197

"Imagine a procession of armoured cars and tanks going through the dear old East End of London to protect vans of food-stuffs nobody has the least idea of touching. *After the strikers have guaranteed a food supply!* A sort of Lord Mayor's day crowd of sightseers and chaps like old Bullace in tin helmets —you know, helmets against shrapnel!! stern and solum. If presently they began to throw pots of shrapnel out of the East End top windows, old Bullace's little bit of brains will be as safe as safe.

"Then imagine a labour movement which imagines it is appealing to the general public against the goverment. Which nevertheless has called out all the printers and stopped the newspapers! As the goverment has seized its own one paper, I mean the labour paper, and monopolises, the goverment does, the wireless, the labour movement is making its appeal *inaudibly*. As a consequence that side of the dispute has become almost invisible. You see police and soldiers and all that, but all you see or hear of the strike side is that it isn't there. The engineers and the railway men and the printers aren't there. Just a bit of speaking at a corner or a handbill put in your hand. Pickets lurking. A gap. Silence."

Mrs. Rylands pulled up abruptly, went back from the beginnings of the next sentence, scrutinised a word. It was "goverment." And down the sheet and over, she found it repeated. And what did it matter if he did take the "n" out of government, so long as his head was clear?

"The strike stopped all the buses, trams, trains, etc., etc. The streets are full morning and evening of a quite cheerful (so far) crowd of clerks, shop

198

people and suchlike walking to business or walking home, getting casual pick-ups from passing motor cars. General disposition to treat it as a lark. Thanks chiefly to the weather. Most buses are off the streets. Some are being run by volunteers and they go anyhow, anywhere and anybody rides. They get their windows broken a bit and there is often a bobby by the driver. Some have wire over their windows and one or two I saw with a motor car full of special constables going in front of them. Convoy. There is a story of some being burnt but I can't find out if that is true. The voice of the gearbox is heard in the land and the young gentlemen volunteers don't bother much about collecting fares. For some unknown reason most of them have come to the job in plus fours. Pirate buses having the time of their lives. Disposition of crowds to collect at central positions and stand about and stare. Police and soldiers in quantity lurking darkly up back streets, ready aye ready for trouble that never comes, and feeling I think rather fools. They seem uneasy when you go and look at them. What are they all waiting for? They've sworn-in quantities of special constables and I've had a row with Uncle Robert on that score, because I won't be sworn-in and set an example. All his men-servants have been sworn-in and are on the streets with armlets and truncheons. The specials just walk about, trying to avoid being followed by little boys; harmless earnest middle-class chaps they are for the most part.

"As might be expected Winston has gone clean off his head. He hasn't been as happy since he crawled on his belly and helped snipe in Sidney

Street. Whatever any one else may think. Winston believes he is fighting a tremendous revolution and holding it down, fist and jaw. He careers about staring, inactive, gaping, crowded London, looking for barricades. I wish I could throw one up for him."

In the margin Mr. Philip had eked out his prose with a second illustration.

Winston doing anything

"The goverment has taken over the *Morning Post* office and machinery and made Winston edit a sort of emergency government rag called the *British Gazette*. Baldwin's idea seems to be to get the little devil as far away from machine guns as possible and keep him busy. Considerable task. His paper is the most lop-sided rag you ever. It would be a disgrace to any goverment. The first number is all for the suppression of Trade Unions, a most desperate attempt to provoke them to the fighting pitch.

"I met Mornington at the Club; he is mixed up with the *Morning Post* somehow and he says the office is simply congested with young Tories who have fancied themselves as writers for years. For them it's perfect Heaven. They've collared most of the *Morning Post* paper; they are grabbing all *The Times* paper *pro bono Winstono*. *The Times* still puts out a little sheet but they say it will have to stop in a week or ten days—in favour of Winston's splutter. That seems to me nearly the maddest thing of all. The Labour people have had their own *Daily Herald* suppressed. Instead they are trying and failing to go a peg below Winston with a sort of bulletin newsheet called the *British Worker*. But Winston has a scheme for stealing their paper supply, raiding their office and breaking them up in the name of the British Constitution. Like undergraduates at election time. Isn't it all bottomlessly silly? Most of the papers seem to be handing out something, a half-sheet or suchlike just to say 'Jack's alive,' and you happen upon it and buy it by chance. Fellows try and sell you typewritten stuff with the latest from the broadcasting for sixpence or a shilling, and here and there you see bulletins stuck up outside churches and town halls. In the west end they display Winston's *British Gazette* in the smart shop windows. I suppose their plate glass insurance covers risks like that. But perhaps they realise there isn't much risk.

"I just go along the streets talking to people in the character of an intelligent young man from New Zealand. I say I don't rightly understand what the strike is about and ask them to explain. I get a dif-

ferent story each time. *Who* is striking?' 'Oh!'
they say, 'It's a general strike!' 'Are you?' I ask.
'No fear!' Some of them say it is in sympathy with
the miners. But they never know the rights and
wrongs about the miners. Very few of them know
if the miners have struck or whether it is a lock-
out. They don't know which is the pig-headest, the
miners or the mine-owners, and yet you'd think they
would be curious about that. And the whole country
is disorganised, no papers, no trains, no trams, and,
this morning, no taxis. Post offices are still going on,
but the labour people talk of bringing out what they
call their second line. That will stop letters, telegrams, gas and electric light and power, it seems. If
the second line really comes out—which Hind says is
rather doubtful. So if I am swallowed up by silence
all of a sudden you will know it is the second line
you have to blame. Unless Winston happens to
have got hold of a machine gun and shot me suddenly in the back.

"But I don't think that will happen while he has
ink and paper. Don't you worry about that.

"Well, there's some features of this General
Strike. Not a bit like a revolution. Far more as if
a new sort of day not quite a weekday and not quite
a Good Friday had happened. I don't know whether
what I have told you will make any sort of picture
for you. There are foreign reporters in London and
probably you will get it in the French papers or
the Paris edition of the *New York Herald*. The es-
sence of it is, miners locked out, transport workers of
all sorts striking, printers striking, Winston probably certifiable but no doctors can get near him to do

it, soldiers and police going about with loaded guns
looking for a Revolution that isn't there, Jix incit-
ing the police to be violent at the least provocation,
and the general public, like me, agape. All London
agape. And over it all this for a Prime Minister:—

Trusty old Baldwin
keeps on doing naffin'

"Here endeth Part Two."
The third fascicle was headed:

"What Labour thinks it is doing.

"Here, my dear Cynthia, I am going to set down
what I can make out of how this strike came about.
It is a queer history, but you can check it back and
fill it out in details by the newspaper files I marked
for you before I left Casa Terragena. This muddle
has been tangling itself up for years. These are
matters the Rylands family, branch as well as root
(which is for current purposes Uncle Robert) ought
to have some ideas about.

"After the war, you must understand, to go back
to beginnings, Great Britain had a boom time for
coal. It had a little boom in 1919. Then there was
dislocation and trouble turning on de-control after
the war and bringing men back from the army,

problems of men taken on and so on. There was a Royal Commission and a very startling report called the Sankey Report, pointing out how wastefully British coal was won and proposing "Nationalisation," and that was followed by a strike—I think the year after. But it was possible to fix fairly good wages for the men just then. All Europe wanted coal, the French coal regions were all devastated area and Poincaré danced into the Ruhr and put that supply out of gear too. English coal prices mounted, wages mounted, we got in thousands of fresh miners from the agricultural workers over and above the war drift to the mines. There was a time when coal stood at £4 a ton. I mean *we* were selling it at that. Not for long of course. Even when it fell back below 40/- it was still a big price for us. Exports rose to huge figures. The miners and the coalowners purred together and nobody bothered about Sankey and nationalisation. Say the top of '23.

"Then we deflated the pound, and also continental coal-winning began to recover.

"By 1924 the slump was plain in the sight to all men. Coal prices couldn't be kept at the old level. There was trouble about wages in 1924 and a new arrangement which we owners dropped last year. Time, said the coal-owners, to take in sail. Naturally they kept mum about the stuff they'd put away during the boom years. Merely 'business' to do that. They just looked round for some one else to make up the current deficit, John Taxpayer was called upon, and Baldwin (a bit of a coal-owner himself) made him fork out the Coal Subsidy until he would stand it no longer. Then the coal-owners made what seemed to them the reasonable proposal that the miners should take lower wages—not a small reduction but a drop of twenty per cent., one shilling in five—work longer hours and (though this wasn't clearly stated) a lot of them become unemployed. Obviously longer hours means fewer men.

"The reply of the miners was a most emphatic No. I sympathise. Though as a rational creature I see that there are now more miners in Britain than can ever be employed at the boom rates or perhaps at any rates again, I see also how the miners who have settled down on the high rates feel about it. Their main representative is a man named Cook and he says 'Not a penny off the pay; not a second on the day.' If I had to live like a miner I should say the same. I'd rather die than come down below the present level. I have just happened upon a little book called *Easingden* by a man named Sinclair and it gives a flat, straightforward account of the life of a miner. I half suspect some connexion between Easingden and Edensoke, but never mind that. No frills about his story and to the best of my knowledge and belief dead true. It's a grimy nightmare of a life. I am going to send it to you. When you read it, you will agree with me that it is intolerable to think of Englishmen—many of whom fought in the Great War to save me and you among others from the Hun—having to go a single step lower than that cramped, sordid, hopeless drudgery. Let the coalowner, who didn't foresee, who failed to reorganise on modern lines in his boom days, who has got a tidy pile stowed away, let him pay the racket now and not take it out of the flesh and blood of the people.

"That's what the miner feels and partly thinks. The hoards of the successful, he thinks, ought to be the elastic pads we fall back upon in a squeeze; not the living bodies of the miners and their families.

"The miners never professed to organise business and make reserves, they thought the clever fellows were seeing to that. Their job was to hew coal. They say they didn't suppose the clever fellows were just out to get away with profits and leave them in the lurch. So that a lot of them now are feeling decidedly Communist and would like to go out and hew at the clever fellows. I should, Cynthia, if I were a miner.

"The new Coal Commission although it is all Herbert Samuels and business men and not a Justice Sankey upon it and no one to speak for the miners, admits a lot of reasonableness in the miners' case. But the coal-owners say in effect, 'Not a penny out of our hoards, not a shadow of sacrifice from *us*!' They propose to knock wages down to the tune of a shilling in five and practically don't offer to bear any equivalent hardship on their own part. I had it out —or partly had it out with Uncle Robert last night. 'Partly,' because he got so obviously cross that my natural respect for the head of the family made me shut up. He was all for the unreasonableness of the miners in not making any concessions. Stern and dignified and rude. Wouldn't say what was to be done with the miners who will have to be laid off whatever concessions the poor devils make. The more concessions they make in hours, the more will get laid off. He wouldn't say whether the shilling in five was his last word or not. And he got really vicious on the subject of Cook.

" 'At present,' said his lordship, 'all discussion is in abeyance. The whole social order has been struck

at—and has to be defended.' Repeated it. Raised
his hand with an air of finality.

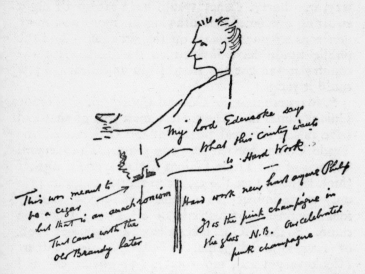

"Baldwin and Co just went from one party to the
other, pulling long faces or pretending to wring
their hands—I've got something to say about that
—and repeating, 'Do *please* be reasonable,' instead of
taking us coal-owners by the scruff of the neck as
they should have done and saying 'Share the loss like
decent men.' If the coal-owners won't give way,
said Baldwin and Co in effect, then the miners *must*.
Nothing was done. The coal-owners simply demanded lower wages and more work and prepared
for a general lock-out if the miners didn't knuckle
under. And that is how things were between the
coal-owners and the miners.

"In a country that had honest newspapers and
clear heads all this would have brought such a storm

about the ears of the coal-owners that they would have met the men half-way—three quarters of the way, in a hurry. They would have sat up all night sweating apologies and drawing up more and more generous schemes to ease off the situation. And the public would have insisted on the deal. But the country never got the story plain and clear. How could it judge?

"Now here it is the General Council of the Trade Unions comes in. The miners are a part of that and have raised this coal puzzle at the Congress of the Trade Unions for the last two years. The General Council of the Trade Unions declares, and I myself think rightly, that the attack to reduce the miners is only a preliminary to a general reduction, railway men, engineers, industrials of all sorts. Common cause. So the T.U.C. takes a hand and you get a sort of four-cornered game, (1) T.U.C., (2) miners (Cook very vocal, too vocal), (3) goverment and (4) owners. (1) and (2) are theoretically part-ners: (3) and (4) profess not to be—but I am afraid are. If the miners are locked out, if nothing is done, then says the T.U.C. we shall have to call out the railwaymen, transport workers, engineers, postal em-ployees and so forth and so on. 'That,' says the goverment, 'is a general strike. It isn't an industrial dispute; it's politics. It's an attack on the goverment of the land.' Says the T.U.C., 'Damn you! Why don't you *be* the goverment of the land? We aren't going to let the miners be downed in this fashion, politics or not. Something has to be done. We don't want a strike of this sort but if there is a miners' lock-out, some such strike there will have to be.'

"But the T.U.C. wasn't very resolute about all

that. That's a nasty point in my story. Not the only one. They backed up the miners but they didn't quite back them up. Several of the Labour Leaders, chaps of the court suit and evening dress type, were running about London, weeks and weeks ago, wringing their hands and saying, 'The extremists are forcing our hands. We don't *want* the general strike. We're perfectly peaceful snobs on the make. We are indeed. It's an attempt at revolution; we admit it. *Do* something—even if it only looks like something.' Mornington met two of them. Those were practically their words. They started out upon a series of conferences with the goverment. Conferences and more conferences. Suggestions, schemes. Running to and fro—T.U.C. at Downing Street. T.U.C. goes to the miners. To and fro. Talk about the Eleventh Hour. But in England nobody ever believes there is an Eleventh Hour until it comes. Like the war. Cook going on all the time like a musical box that can't leave off: 'Not a penny off the pay, not a second on the day.' Twenty speeches a day and still at it in his sleep.

"My dear, I don't know if you will make head or tail of this rigmarole so far. I set it down as well as I can. But try and get that situation clear—which brings things up to last week-end. Miners, inflexible; owners, inflexible; Goverment ambiguous, T.U.C. forcible feeble, rather warning about the General Strike than promising it. And doing nothing hard and strong to prepare for it. Under-prepared while the goverment was over-prepared.

"And here I must conclude by Part Three because I have already been writing about the next stage in Part Four. Go on to Part number Four."

Mrs. Rylands did.
Part Four was headed:

"The Goverment isn't playing straight."

"Here little Cynna comes the stuff that troubles
my mind most. I don't think Baldwin and his goverment have played a straight game. I don't think the
miners and the rank and file of the workers are getting a square deal. I think that Baldwin and Co are
consciously or subconsciously on the side of the coal-
owner and the profit extractor, and that they mean to
let the workers down. They are making an Asset of
Cook and his not listening to reason. I've had that
smell in my nose for some time. Even at Casa Terragena. Churchill's first number of the *British Gazette* stank of it. Gave the whole thing away.

"They didn't want to prevent a General Strike.
They wanted it to happen. They wanted it to happen so as to distract attention from the plain justice
of the case as between miners and coal-owners. And
between workers generally and employers and business speculators generally, in a world of relative
shrinkage. They wanted the chance of a false issue,
to readjust with labour nearer the poverty line.

"You may say that is a serious charge to make
against any goverment. But consider the facts.
Consider what happened last Sunday night. Probably you haven't got the facts of Sunday night over
there yet. It's the ugliest, most inexplicable night
in the record of our quiet little Baldwin. If after
all there does happen to be a Last Judgment, Master
Stanley will be put through it hard and good about
Sunday May 2nd. Or to be more exact, Monday
May 3rd. 'Put that pipe down Sir,' the great flaming
Angel will say, 'We want to see your face.'

"We shall all want to see his face.

"What happened was this. The Trade Union leaders were haggling and conferring between the miners and the cabinet all Sunday and they really seemed to be getting to a delaying compromise, and something like a deal. If the goverment really meant to make a deal. Late in the night the trade Union leaders at Downing Street, had hammered out some sort of reply to certain cabinet proposals. They went back to the conference room with it. And they found the room empty and dark and the lights out.

"The goverment had thrown down the negotiations. They came into a darkened room and were told that the goverment had gone away. Gone home!

"Bit dramatic that, anyhow.

"*Why?*

"My dear, you might guess at a thousand reasons. Some compositors at the *Daily Mail* had refused to set up an anti-labour leading article! The *Daily Mail!* I have never been able to understand how the *Daily Mail* is able to get compositors to set up *any* of its articles. But this thing I have a nasty feeling was foreseen. The coup was prepared. It was too clumsy, too out of proportion, to be a genuine thing. Forthwith the cabinet hear of the *Daily Mail* hitch. Remarkably quick. "It's come off,' I guess some one said. 'Get on with the break.' Like a shot the cabinet responded. Like an actor answering his cue. The goverment snatched at the excuse of that little *Daily Mail* printing-office strike to throw down the whole elaborate sham of negotiating for peace. They called the bluff of the poor old vacillating T.U.C. 'This is the general strike and we are ready,' said they. Off flew Winston and the heroic set to get busy, and Mr. Baldwin went to bed.

"The empty room. The lights put out. The labour leaders peering into it, astonished and not a little scared. Like sheep at the gate of a strange field. Don't forget that picture, Cynthia.

"And since then the goverment hasn't been a goverment. It's been like a party trying to win an election. By fair means or foul. It's stifled all discussion. It's made broadcasting its call boy. It is playing the most extraordinarily dirty tricks in shutting up people and concealing facts. I've just heard things—but these I'll tell you later. And all the rights and wrongs as between miners and coal-owners have vanished into thin air. Which is what the goverment wanted to happen. Q.E.F. as Mr. Euclid used to say.

"That ends my fourth section."

Mrs. Rylands reflected for a time. Philip had told his story well. It sounded—credible. For the first time she seemed to be realising what this queer business in England meant. And yet there were difficulties. She must think it over. Some of it startled her and much that he had to say sounded excessively uncompromising. His note was one of combatant excitement. But then he was not living in the soft air of a great Italian garden which makes everything seem large and gentle and intricate. She must read those marked papers downstairs. But now what else had he to say? Part Five was headed:—

"*Why did the Goverment want the Strike to happen?*

"And now, my dear wife, I want to write of something more difficult. But it's about the state of mind of the sort of people to which after all we belong. It's about more than the General Strike.

"I've been about at the Club; I lunched at the Carlton with Silverbaum; I spent an evening with Hind and Mornington and their crew at Hind's flat. And more particularly I've studied the words and proceedings of our esteemed uncle Lord Edensoke and of our honoured and trusted partner Sir Revel Cokeson, not to mention Mr. Gumm, the burly British Mr. Gumm. You remember them?

"Let me try and get it set down, as it has come to me. There is a feeling in the air that Britain is going down. I don't mean that there is any sort of crash in view, but that industrially and financially she is being passed and overshadowed. She is in for a time of relative if not of absolute shrinkage. We may never be able to employ the same mass of skilled and semi-skilled labour that we have done in the past.

"I am not telling you here what I believe. Never mind what I believe. I am telling you what is in the minds and not very far from openly showing upon the surface of the minds of a lot of these people. Uncle Robert practically said as much. One of those speeches of his that begin, 'My dear boy.' One of those speeches of his that seem to admit that so far he has been lying but that now we have really come to it. And one has been getting the same sort of thing for a long time between the lines of such a paper as the *Morning Post*. Well, here is my reading of hearts. They think that there is shrinkage and hard times ahead and they think that it is the mass of workers who will have to bear the burthen. Because otherwise it will fall on—ourselves. Labour in Great Britain has seen its sunniest days. That is what *they* think.

"I suppose one has to face a certain loss of pre-eminence in the world for England. I don't like it, but I suppose we have to. We were the boss country of the Nineteenth Century and the Nineteenth Century is over. Possibly there will not be a boss country in the Twentieth Century. Or it may be America. But it isn't going to be us and we have to face up to that. That I say has got into the minds of pretty nearly all the sort of *protected* people, established people, go-about-the-globe people, financial and business people, who support the present goverment. And it takes two forms in its expression just according as intelligent meanness or unintelligent prejudice prevails in their minds.

"*First Class;* The intelligent mean wealthy people of Great Britain want to shove the bigger part of the impoverishment due to our relative shrinkage in the world upon the workers. They want a scrap that will cripple and discredit the Trade Unions. Then they will reduce wages and at the same time cut down social services and popular education. So they will be able to go on for quite a long time as they are now and even recover some of their investments abroad and—to make these economies possible—we shall just breed and train cheaper and more miserable common English people.

"But they are not the majority of their sort, this class are not. They are just the mean left hand of Baldwin and Co. The right hand, which is heavier and lumpier, is able to be more honest because it is more stupid. Let us come to them.

"*Second Class;* The unintelligent wealthy people in Great Britain. The majority. On them too for some time the unpleasant realisation that Great Britain is shrinking in world importance has been growing. It seems to have grown with a rush since the coal trade began to look groggy after deflation. Perhaps it has grown too much. But this sort cannot accept it as the others do—clearly. All ideas turn to water and feelings in their minds. This is the sort that disputes the plainest facts if they are disagreeable. It is too horrible an idea for them. So it remains a foreign growth in their minds. *Their* Empire threatened! *Their* swagger and privileges going! Their air of patronage to all the rest of the world undermined! They refuse the fact.

"The more I hear our sort of people talk and see how they are behaving over this strike, the more I am reminded of some Gold Coast nigger who is suffering from the first intimations of old age and thinks he is bewitched and will get all right again if he only finds out and kills the witch. They lie awake at nights and hear the Empire, *their* Empire—for they've never given the working man a dog's chance in it—creaking. They think of China up, India up, Russia not caring a damn for them—and the Americans getting patronising to the *n*th degree. Foreign investments shrunken and no means of restoring them. These people here about me, the wealthy Tory sort of people, the chaps in the Clubs, the men and women in the boxes and stalls and restaurants and night clubs, the Ascot people and the gentle jazzers, are not thinking of the rights and wrongs of the miners and the trade union people at all, and of fair play and what's a straight deal with the men. Their attention will not rest on that. It seems unable to rest on that. The men are just a pawn in their game of foreign investment. The plain story

I have told to you about the mines and the strike has passed right under their noses and they have missed the substance of it altogether. They have something larger and vaguer in their minds; this shrinkage of their credit as a class; this arrest in growth and vigour of their Empire, the Empire of their class—because that is all it is; its loss of moral power, the steady evaporation of its world leadership in finance and industry; the realisation—and they have it now in their bones if not in their intelligences, even the stupidest of them—that new and greater things are dawning upon the world. They are too ill-educated and self-centred and consciously incompetent to accept these things fully and try to adapt themselves to new conditions. They become puzzled and frightened and quarrelsome at the bare thought of these new conditions—which threaten them—with extinction—or worse—with education. On no terms will they learn. That is too horrible. So they go frantic. They bristle up to fight. They want a great fight against time and fate. Before time and fate overtake them. They dream that perhaps if there was a tremendous scrap of some sort now, now while they are still fairly strong, somehow at the end of it this creeping rot, this loss of *go*, in all they value and of all that makes them swagger people, would be abolished and made an end to. It would be lost in the uproar and at the end they would find themselves back on the top of things, strong and hearty again without any doubts, without a single doubt, just as they used to be. Making decisions for every one, universally respected, America put back in its place, all the world at the salute again.

"That I am convinced is what the Winston-Bullace state of mind amounts to—as distinguished from the more cold-blooded types you find like our thin-lipped Uncle Robert. That is Class Two.

"But what is the enemy? *I* say it is time and fate, geography and necessity. Sempack I suppose would say it was the spread of scientific and mechanical progress about the world which is altering the proportions of every blessed thing in life, so that (Sempack is my witness) a world system has to come. But you can't fight time and fate and scientific and mechanical progress. You don't get a chap like Bullace grasping an idea like that. And Bullace is our class, Cynthia; he is the rule and we are the exceptions. For him therefore it has to be a conspiracy. If he finds his blessed Empire is losing the game, or to put it more exactly, if he finds the game is evaporating away from his blessed Empire, then there must be cheating. There is an enemy bewitching us and there ought to be a witch—smelling. (If only it was half as simple!)

"They call the witch Bolshevism. The Red Red Witch of the World. They pretend to themselves that there is a great special movement afoot to overthrow British trade, British prestige and the British Empire. Wicked men from Moscow are the real source of all our troubles. The miners are just their 'tools.' You remember old fool Bullace saying that. If it wasn't for Moscow the miners would *like* lower pay and longer hours. Ask for them. So you just take something that you call Bolshevism by the throat and kill it, and every one will be happy.

"You can call almost anything Bolshevism for this purpose. You tackle that something and kill it and then the dear old Nineteenth Century will be restored and go on for ever and ever and ever.

"This is what I mean when I say that this trouble

here is on a false issue. The miners and workers haven't the ghost of an idea of what they are up against. They are out because their lives are squalid and their prospects dismal. They object to carrying all the hardship of the shrinkage of England's overseas interests and investments. To them it is just the old story of the employer trying to screw them down. They don't connect it yet with the decline of Britain as a world market and a world bank or anything of the sort. The reactionary party in the goverment, the 'sojers' as we call it, on the other hand are prancing about saving the country from an imaginary Social Revolution. You see the miss?

"The goverment lot, both Class One and Class Two, *wants* a fight. Class One to shift their losses on to labour and Class Two to exorcise the phantom of decay. Class One just wants to win. But if Class Two gets the least chance to make it a real bloody fight it will. They want to bully and browbeat and shoot and confuse everything in wrath and hate. They will make silly arrests; they will provoke. If they get a chance of firing into a crowd, they will do it. If they can have an Amritsar in Trafalgar Square they will. They want to beat the Reds and then tie up the Trade Unions hand and foot—and trample. And that, my dear, is the dangerous side of the present situation.

"What adds to its danger is that the miners are being led too stiffly. I sympathise with them, but I see they aren't playing to win—anything solid. If Cook can, he will give our Bullaces an excuse. Cook is Bullace in reverse. Perhaps there *is* some Moscow about Cook. Or he shares a dream with Bullace. He dreams Bullace's nightmare as a paradise. Both dreamers.

"So far our patient, humorous, common English hasn't given the goverment a chance. But anywhere now, an accident might happen. Some silly provocation. An ugly crowd. Or pure misunderstanding. It's touch and go these days. I have said it is a silly situation, but also it is a dangerous one. And above all it is a game of false issues. Nothing fairly meeting anything else. Nothing being plainly put, the real world situation least of all. Two different things. Labour wanting to be comfortable in a time of slump and the old Empire lot wanting to feel as lordly as ever in a spell of decline. And the common man with his head spinning. This sort of thing:—"

Came a queer little drawing of which Mrs. Rylands only discovered the import after some moments of attention.

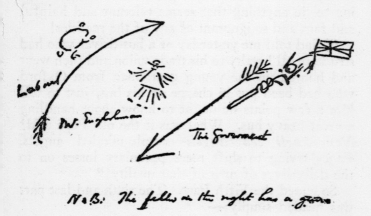

"There my dear Cynna is a long history, tediously told, but I think it gives the general shape of this business here in England up to date. On one hand workers striking wisely or not, against shrinkage and going down in the scale of life; on the other a goverment, a governing class, all of our sort, coal-owners, landowners, industrials and financiers, anticking about, believing or pretending to believe we are fighting Red Revolution, and setting out in good earnest under cover of that to kill or cripple trade unionism and labourism generally. Much good it will do their blessed Empire if they do. Against time and fate.

"But can you imagine the solemn glory of an owl like Jix, in the midst of all this? Can you imagine what I have to put up with at the club from the old fools and the young fools burning to 'give these Bolshevists a lesson'? And the tension in the air when I go to investigate Uncle Robert. Meanwhile the reasonable, kindly, unsuspicious English common public is so puzzled, so good-humoured, so willing to do anything that seems tolerant and helpful and fair, and so ignorant of any of the realities!

"Hind told me yesterday of a bus-driver who had struck, in all loyalty to his trade union and then went and hunted up the young gentleman from Oxford who had been put in charge of his bus, just to tell him a few points he ought to know about handling a great heavy bus. What was it the old Pope said? *Non Angli sed Angeli*—simple-minded angels. Fancy trying to shift mere pecuniary losses on to the daily lives of men of that quality!"

So ended the Fifth Part. The sixth and last part was headed simply:—

"About myself and Cynthia.

"And now lastly, my darling, what am *I* doing? Nothing. Going about with my mouth open in the wonderful spectacle of England paralysed by its own confusion of mind. Baiting Uncle Robert. Reading the dreams of Mr. Sempack and comparing them with the ideas of the *British Gazette*. Learning something perhaps about the way this extraordinary world of ours, as Sempack would call it, fumbles along. And writing to you.

"I don't know what to do, Cynthia? I don't know where to take hold. This is a world change being treated as a British political and social row. Its roots are away in world finance, gold and the exchanges, and all sorts of abstruse things. It isn't London or Yorkshire or New York or Moscow; it's everywhere. Part of everywhere. Where we all live nowadays. No. 1, The Universe, Time. I sympathise with the strikers but I don't really see what good this general strike is going to do, even if it does all it proposes to do. Throw everything out of gear, but what then? The goverment would have to resign. Who would come in if the goverment went out? Unheard of labour men? Snobs and spouters. Miscellaneous liberal leaders. What difference is there—except for the smell of tobacco—between Asquith and Baldwin? Lloyd George saving the country? Half the liberals and all the labour leaders would see the country in boiling pitch before they let it be saved by Lloyd George. Communism and start again? There aren't three thousand Communists in England and half of them aren't English.

"On the other hand, I won't do a hand's turn to break the strike.

"I feel most horribly no good at all. I have twenty-two thousand a year, I'm a pampered child of this England and I don't belong anywhere. Dear

Uncle Robert drives our great concerns and our fifth share, or thereabouts, is like a trunk tied behind an automobile. I'm an overpaid impostor. Nobody knows me. I've got no authority. If I said anything it wouldn't matter. It would be like some one shouting at the back of a meeting. And even if it did matter it wouldn't matter, because free speech is now suppressed. There are no newspapers and the broadcasting is given over to twaddle—there was a fellow gassing most improvingly about ants and grasshoppers yesterday—mixed up with slabs of biassed news and anti-strike propaganda. You see one is just carried along by the stream of events— and the stream is hopelessly silly.

"And that brings me round, Heart of my World, to all we were talking about before I left you. How good it was to talk like that just at the end and how good those talks were! People like us, as you said, ought to *do*. But what are we to do and how are we to do? Where do we come in? It is all very well for old prophet Sempack to lift his mighty nose and talk of the great progessive movements that will ultimately sweep all these things away, but will they? Are they sweeping them away? Even ultimately? This muddle, this dislocated leaderless country, finding its level in a new world so clumsily and dangerously, this crazy fight against a phantom revolution, is Reality. It is England 1926. Sempack isn't Reality; *this* is Reality. People smile about the streets and make dry jokes in our English way, but hundreds of thousands must be hiding worry almost beyond bearing. Anxiety untold, hardship and presently hunger. And the outlook—*bad*. At any time there may be shooting and killing. Sempack's great glowing golden happy world is only a dream. A remote dream. I cannot tell you how remote from this disorganised London here.

"All very well to talk of the ultimate reasonableness of mankind, but what chance has ultimate reasonableness when some avatism like Winston collars all the paper for his gibberings and leaves you with nothing to print your appeals to the ultimate reasonableness on; or when a lot of young roughs like your Italian Fascists break up every one who writes or speaks against their imbecile ideas about the universe and Italy?

"This ultimate reasonableness of Sempack's is a rare thing, a hothouse plant. It's the last fine distillation of human hope. It lives in just a few happy corners of the world, in libraries and liberal households. If you smash the greenhouse glass or turn off the hot water it will die. How is it ever coming into the open air, to face crowds and sway millions?

"If he is back there with you I wish you would ask him that. Drive him hard, Cynthia. He ought to come over here.

"Last night my mind was so puzzled and troubled I could not sleep. I turned out long after midnight and prowled down through Westminster and out along the Thames Embankment. There were not so many lights as usual and all those flaring advertisements about whisky and dental cream and suchlike helps to the soul weren't lit. Economy of power. It made the bridges seem browner and the little oily lights on barges and boats more significant and it gave the moon a chance on the steely black water. I thought you might be looking at the same old moon—

at that very moment. It looked hard and a bit cold over here but with you it must have been bigger and soft and kindly. There were very few people about and not a tram running. Cold. Such few people as did pass were for the most part hurrying —home I suppose. I looked at the moon and thought how you would presently be reading over the things I have been trying to tell you and how perplexing they were. I had a great heartache for you, to be with you. I wished I could talk to you instead of just writing to you. Do you remember—it isn't a week yet, how I sat beside you on your balcony above the old palm trees and talked to you? Not very much. How much I would say now that I couldn't say then!

"I wandered along the Embankment wondering what was brewing beneath all this frightful foolishness of the strike. Things are surely brewing that will affect all our lives, change all the prospects of that child of ours. A country that has been very proud and great and rather stupidly and easily great, learning its place in a new world. A finer world perhaps later—but bleak and harsh at present.

"London rather darkened, rather unusually quiet —in spite of its good humour—has something about it—

"Awe?

"It's like Bovril. I mean, so much of the world's life is still concentrated here. London is a very wonderful city. I don't think it is just because I am English that I think that.

"I stood and looked back at the Houses of Parliament and Big Ben and thought of the way the members must be going to and fro in that empty resounding maze of a place with its endless oak-lined passages, every one rather at a loss as to what was to happen next. Saying silly things to each other, little jokes and so on because they can't think of anything sensible to say. Futile lot they are at Westminster nowadays when anything real shows its teeth at them. There would probably be more people than usual, but trade union sort of people, standing about in the lobbies. No sight seers. Not the usual mixed crowd. . . .

"My mind ran on to all these riddles we have to guess together, you and I, if we are not to be lost in the general futility. If we are not to be swept along just as everything here is being swept along by forces, too misunderstood to be used or controlled. I thought of what a sterling thing you are so that you almost persuade me I can be sterling. And it came to me all over again that I wasn't nearly as good a thing as even I might be, nor making nearly enough of myself in spite of all my freedoms and money and position. Nor were any of the people who were wrapped up in the vast, ungracious, mean quarrel made up of fear and hot misunderstandings and the meanness and cowardice of comfortable wealth. Millions of strikers saying their life wasn't good enough—like some big thing talking in its sleep. And the anti-revolutionaries being firm and unflexible like an uneasy dream when your fist gets clenched. Why didn't *any* of these people seem able to wake up? Why was I only awake in gleams and moments like that moment?

"I got into a sort of exalted state out there on the Embankment in the cold moonlight.

" 'Good God!' I said to you—I said it to you; you

can't imagine how much I have talked to you lately, trying to explain things—'Can none of us get together in the world to make something of it better than such silly squabbling and conflict as this? Is it a lie that there ever were martyrs—that men have died for causes and set out upon crusades? Is religion over for ever and the soul of man gone dead? And if it isn't, why is there none of it here? Why are these people all jammed against each other like lumpish things against the grating of a drain? Why is there no league for clear-headedness? Why are there no Fascisti of the Light to balance the black Fascists? Why are none of us banded together to say "Stop!" all these politicians' tricks, these shams, to scrap all the old prejudices and timidities, to take thought—and face the puzzle of the British position and the real future of England and the world, face it generously, mightily—like men?'

"That much I said or some such thing. I seemed to have a gleam of something—not yet. It is too much to get put together yet. Now I am trying to get what I said and thought back again and to write it down and send it to you so that you can know what I said."

Abruptly it ended, "Philip."

§ 11

THAT apparently was all that Philip had intended to send, but in addition there was a loose sheet on which he had been thinking and which had evidently got itself among the fasciculi by mistake.

He had jotted down disconnected sentences.

"The common man," she read, "wants to do nothing with general affairs—wants to be left alone. Why not leave him alone?"

There was a sort of Debit and Credit account. On the credit side was written: "A man who doesn't think conserves energy. Parties of reaction like the Fascists, parties of dogma like the Communists, are full of energy. They get something done. They get the wrong thing done but it is done. Independent thought, critical thought, has no chance against them."

On the Debit side she read: "In the long run intelligence wins," and then: "does it?" and mere scribbling. Across the lower half of the sheet ran one word very slowly written in a large fair hand, "Organisation."

Much smaller: "Intelligence plus energy."

Then beginning very large and ending very small, a row of interrogation marks.

？ ？ ？ ？ ？ ？ ？ ？ ？

§ 12

MRS. RYLANDS read over her husband's letter and re-read her husband's letter a very great deal before she set herself to answer it. In many ways he had astonished her. His lucidity struck her as extraordinary. It was not as if he was learning to express himself; it was as if he had been released from some paralysing inhibition. Evidently he had been reading enormously as well as talking, and particularly he had been saturating himself in the wisdom of Mr. Sempack. At times he passed from pure colloquialism to phrases and ideas that instantly recalled Mr. Sempack's utterances. Perhaps it was better that he should learn to write from Mr. Sempack than from a schoolmaster, even though it was an Eton schoolmaster. The spirit of all he said was quite after her own heart. How could she ever have doubted that there was all this and more also beneath his darkness and his quiet?

To her his vision of affairs seemed fresh and powerful and broad. How much he knew that he had never spoken of before! His implicit knowledge of the sequence and meaning of strikes and Royal Commissions made her feel not only ignorant but unobservant. She must have read of all these things at the time—or failed to read of them. And she had led debates at Somerville and passed muster as a girl with an exceptional grasp of social questions!

Well, she must read again and read better. She had thought—before all her thoughts were submerged in her personal passion for him—of some such fellowship as this that was now beginning between them. In discovering Philip anew she was being restored to herself. He wrote of his futility, but in every page she found him feeling his way to action. Futility! She turned over that self-revealing sheet with the word "Organisation" upon it. Half his dreams he had not told her yet because as yet they were untellable.

She turned the sheets over again and again. He was a stronger beast then she was: it showed in every line. His handwriting had a certain weakness or immaturity; he spelt wildly ever and again, but these were such little things beside his steadfast march to judgments. He saw and thought and said it plain. "He's a man," she said and fell to thinking of what virility meant.

Comparatively she was all receptiveness. She perceived for the first time that there was initiative even in thought. For example, the things he said about Lord Edensoke were exactly the things she had always been disposed to think but she reflected with a startled and edified observation that she had never actually thought them. It was not merely that there was virility and decisiveness in action, there was virility and decisiveness even in mental recognition. To judge was an act. Always her judgments were timid and slow. He crouched and watched and leapt and behold! there was fact in his grip. Her rôle was circumspection until the lead was given her. And behind his judgments even in this first letter there was the suggestion of action gathering.

That afternoon and later and the next day she wrote him her own first real letter in reply to his. The conclusion of his came so near to the matter of Mr. Sempack's last talk that she thought she could do no better than write a description of that gentleman's return to Casa Terragena and of how he had argued with himself and her about the relations of thought to activity. She got all that she felt pretty clear. She hoped that he would look up Philip in London, for she was quite sure they would both be ready to meet again and exchange ideas amidst that conflict of witless realities. She tried to be very simple and earnest about Mr. Sempack and his views, but when she told of him and Lady Catherine, the humourist and novelist latent in every intelligent woman, found release. She thought she would write about his new tie and then she decided not to write about his new tie and finally she wrote about it rather amusingly at some length. And afterwards she was inclined to regret having written about that new tie. She felt she ought never to have noted his new tie. But the letter had gone before this last decision was made.

At the end of her letter she found herself beginning afresh after Philip's own manner.

"About what you say of getting together, of organisation, of sane organisation, I find my mind almost too excited to write. It is work in that way that has to be done now. Manifestly. 'Fascists of the Light' is a great phrase. Who would have thought of you my dear dear Man as a maker of phrases? Before we have done, perhaps we shall make many things. You and I, I hope, but I begin to see it will be mainly you. I am torn my dearest between the desire to do and a fear of vain gestures that we cannot justify. I send my heart to you. I wish I had you here just for a moment to kiss your ear and put my cheek against yours. I wish I could put my arm across your broad shoulders. I am very well, I am flourishing here, my dear Man. I glow. I grow. I am a water melon in the sun. A wonderful nurse from Ulster comes to-morrow. Stella Binny is bringing her. It is early to bring her yet, but she is free and must be secured. McManus her name is. In a little while, I gather, Casa Terragena will belong to Mrs. McManus and Bombaccio will do her reverence. Stella has given up Theosophy now, by the bye, and is a fully fledged R.C. She was 'received' in Rome. Much fuss over her, to judge by her letters. They always make a fuss at first. We shan't argue much. She will just drop the

McManus and pass on. Four long weeks more, my dear. When all this is over I will work for you, with you and for you, my dear. Philip, my darling, my Man, I love you and that is the beginning and the end and beginning over again of all I have to say to you."

§ 13

MRS. RYLANDS was agreeably interested in Mrs. McManus.

Stella Binny had never quite seemed to exist and now this Mrs. McManus intensified that quality. Stella arrived just like any one, exactly like any one. She might have been an item in big figures in statistics; visitor 3792, *normal*. But Mrs. Mc-Manus was exceptionally real. The only other thing that was equally real in her presence was the expectation of Mrs. Rylands. She stuck out from Stella in the car; and her one entirely masculine valise, painted with broad bands of white and blue, made all the rest of the joint luggage a mere et-cetera.

She was strong and rather tall, she got into a nurse's costume straight away upon her arrival, she presented a decided profile, a healthy complexion and lightish hair just shot with grey. It was not faded hair, it was either light brown or it was silver; it never hesitated. On her lips rested a smile and a look of modest assurance. One perceived at once that she knew every possible thing there was to be known about obstetrics and that it rather amused her. Partly that smile of hers was due to the fact that she had very fine large teeth and her lips had stood no nonsense with them and had agreed to meet pleasantly but firmly outside them. Her eyes were observant, ready and disposed (within reason) to be kind. Her speech was pervaded by a quality that made it rather more definite in outline and rather clearer in statement than normal English. Mrs. Rylands referred it to Ulster. She felt that this was confirmed when Mrs. McManus took an early opportunity to mention that she was a "Prodestant." Nowadays Protestants who call themselves Protestants are only to be found in Ulster and the backwoods of America. Mrs. McManus evidently did not come from the backwoods of America; her accent would have been entirely different if she had.

"Almost all my work is done in Italy and the south of France in Catholic families, and I shouldn't get half of it if I wasn't known to be a Prodestant out and out," she explained. "It gives them confidence. You see—"

Her expression conveyed an intense desire to be just and exact. "You can't make a really thorough nurse out of a Roman Catholic woman. It's known. There's holy, devoted women among these Roman Catholic nurses, mind you. I'm not denying it. Some of them are saints, real saints. It is a privilege to meet them. But what you want in a nurse is not a saint; it is a nurse. They aren't nurses, first and foremost and all the time. They're worried about this holiness of theirs. That's where they fall short. They fuss about with their souls, confessing and all that, taking themselves out and looking at themselves, and it distracts them. It takes them off their work. How can you think about what you are doing when all the time you are asking yourself, 'Am I behaving properly?' and keeping your mind off evil thoughts. Keeping their minds off evil thoughts indeed! Why! a real nurse like me just thinks of what she happens to be doing and lets her mind rip. The unholy things have come into my mind right under the nose of the doctor you'd hardly believe, Mrs. Rylands. And gone clean out of it again. Whereas one of them Roman Catholics would be all for laying hold of it and keeping it and carrying it off to tell her confessor afterwards like as if she'd laid an egg. And meanwhile with all that much of trouble in her, she'd be bound to do something wrong. Holy they certainly are I allow. But holiness is a full time job, Mrs. Rylands, and it only leaves enough over for nursing as will make a reasonably good amateur. And amateurs they are. So I keep to it I'm a Prodestant just to show I'm not that sort. Which is as much as to say if I don't nurse well I'm damned, and there's no excuses.

"And then all that purity of theirs. It takes a Prodestant to bathe every day," said Mrs. McManus. "These Catholics—they don't believe in it. There's nuns haven't bathed for years. And think all the better of themselves for it.

"And that's all about it," said Mrs. McManus, suddenly as if winding up her dissertation.

"There's your friend Miss Binny," she resumed. "A nicer lady I've never met. And she's just eaten up with this idea of being converted to Catholicism and all that. It's wonderful what she gives to it. They say she's visited nearly every image and picture there is in Italy where there's a Stella Maris, that being one of the Virgin-Marys they have. In a Rolls-Royce car. I've no doubt it comforted her greatly, if she happened to be wanting comfort, and

233

anyhow it was a grand occupation for her. Not having anything better to do. Catholic she is, like new paint. But would she have brought a Roman Catholic nurse along to you? She would not."

"That's very extraordinary," said Mrs. Rylands, considering it. "I never thought of that."

"Naturally," said Mrs. McManus. "It's only now that any occasion has arisen."

Her opinions upon the state of affairs in Italy were equally clear cut and novel to Mrs. Rylands. "These Fascists," she said, "are making a great to-do here—with their Mussolini and their black shirts and all that. Giving castor oil to respectable people and frightening them and beating them about and generally misbehaving themselves. They'll do a great mischief to Italy. They're just boys. There's not a Fascist in Italy would dare to stand up to a really formidable woman, who knew her own mind about them. There's suffragettes we had in London would tear them to bits. But they get taken seriously here, as if they were grown-up people. It's dreadful the precociousness of boys here. I could tell you things would astonish you. It's not having proper public schools makes these Fascists. We'll never get them in England, try though they may."

She reflected. "Those public schools of ours in England are by all accounts mere sinks of iniquity. If you believe the half you're told. And what better place could you send a growing boy to, seeing what divils boys are? And there they can work it off and get rid of it and take it out of each other. Whereas these young Fascists don't ever grow up to proper ideas even about cutting their hair."

"But don't they run the country?" asked Mrs.

Rylands. "Don't they at least keep the trains punctual?"

"The roads in Italy are a disgrace to civilisation," said Mrs. McManus. "I've had to bump my ladies over them. Let them mend their roads," and so swept Fascist efficiency away.

"All you hear of Italy is this Mr. Mussolini's propaganda," she expanded. "He's a great propaganding advertising sort of man. He's the voice of Italy and he's drowned all the other voices. Every one has been so shut up and so beaten and arrested and all that by these young divils that had a word to say against them, that now they don't even know the truth themselves. How can you possibly know anything about yourself if you won't hear a word about yourself unless it's praise? Well, that's where they are," said Mrs. McManus. "At bottom——" She sighed. "The trouble with a country like Italy is that there's no sensible women about to keep the young men in order. And speak plainly and simply to them about their goings on. They're just mere females and Catholics, these Italian women, and that's all there is to it.

"Would you believe it," said Mrs. McManus, "I was stopped by some of them young Fascists on the Pincio one day and told to go back from the walk I was taking. Up to some bedevilment they were. I wouldn't go back and I didn't go back. I just stood where I was and looked them in the eye and told them what I thought of them. Quietly. And what I'd like to do to them if I was their mothers. In English of course. After a bit they began to look sheepish and glance sideways at one another and shrug their shoulders and in the end they let me go my way. Of course I used English. It's always the best thing, especially with these foreigners here, to talk to them in English, if you happen to get into any sort of dispute with them. They're conceited people and they don't like to feel ignorant, and talking to them in English makes them feel ignorant. It puts them in the inferior position. If you talk to them in their own language you're apt to make mistakes and that sets them off despising you. Whereas if you talk in English they despise themselves and you get the upper hand of them. Exactly like talking quietly to dogs. Never lower yourself by talking to a foreigner in his own tongue. Never seem to try to understand him. Behave as though he ought to be ashamed not to understand every word you are saying to *him*. You have him at your mercy."

That too impressed Mrs. Rylands as a striking point of view. She made a note of it for future consideration.

Mrs. McManus professed an admiration for Casa Terragena and the gardens that was transparently a concession.

"They must have cost a terrible deal of money," she said, as if she wished that to be taken for praise. "Dragging these flowers from all the ends of the earth to make them grow here together! The industry of it! The ways of man! Hardly a thing on earth nowadays stays where God put it."

"If God did put it," said Mrs. Rylands.

"A manner of speaking," said Mrs. McManus. "There's that big lovely purple spike thing you say came from Australia. No, I'll not attempt to learn the name of it. Such things cumber the mind. It's standing up there like a regiment among the rocks with all its bells open, ranks and ranks of it—waiting for insects that are all round the world away. No one ever brought over the insects it was made for. You may say it is botany and science bringing it here, but I can't help feeling it's taking advantage of a flower that hadn't the power to help itself. It's making all the summer one long First of April for it bringing it here. Day after day, more of these bells. Open for nothing.

"It's like calling Caller Herrin' in the wilderness of the moon," said Mrs. McManus.

Mrs. Rylands saw her lovely garden from a new angle.

"Hundreds and hundreds of workmen it must have taken from first to last. I wonder what they thought they were doing when they made it. Anyhow—it's a very good place, what with the sea breezes, for you to be having your baby in."

Mrs. McManus went off at a tangent. "That butler of yours is a fine looking fellow and well set up. I doubt if Mr. Ramsay Macdonald has finer moustaches. It's a mercy he's so wrapped up in himself. He'd be a Holy Terror with the maids if he wasn't."

Perfectly true. But no one had ever remarked it before.

She regretted Philip wasn't available. "I'm no friend to separating husband and wife when there's a baby coming. Some people nowadays have a perfect fad for keeping them apart, just as though they were animals. But men are not animals in such respects and wives need to be comforted. Of course if he had to go back for the coal strike there's nothing more to be said. It's a pity."

She explained that she did not propose to walk about with her patient more than was necessary. "You've got your thoughts," she said, "and I have mine. I see you're carrying a little green book about to write in. I needn't chew the newspaper to make talk for you, thank goodness. The work I've had to do at times! But you don't want that. I'll hover. I'll just hover. You'll find I'll always be near and just out of sight—if ever you call. I've been trained to hover for years."

"You'll find it very quiet here," said Mrs. Rylands. "There's very little to do."

"I'll never want for something to do while there's a crossword puzzle to be found in the paper. Wonderful the uses men can find for things like words!"

"If you'd like to run in to Monte Carlo for an afternoon or so soon the car is quite at your service. There's really no need even to hover for a bit."

"Do you see me breaking the bank?" said Mrs. McManus.

"Shops."

"There again," said Mrs. McManus.

"There's English services in Mentone on Sunday. You must go for that."

"I will not," said Mrs. McManus.

"But as a Protestant—!"

"I'm no friend to extravagance in any shape or form. When I'm in England I go to the English church and when I'm in Scotland I'm whatever sort of Presbyterian is nearest, but going to English Church services in a country of this sort is like fox hunting in Piccadilly, I'd be ashamed to be seen going there, prayer-book and all."

An irrational impulse to make Mrs. McManus help with the little green book came to Mrs. Rylands. "But isn't God everywhere?" she asked.

"I was not speaking of God."

"But you are a Protestant."

"I am that."

"But Protestants believe in God."

"Protestants protest against Roman Catholics. And well they may."

"But you believe in God?"

"That is a matter, Mrs. Rylands, strictly between Himself and me."

§ 14

BUT the large clear *obiter dicta* of Mrs. Mc-Manus, those hard opaque ideas like great chunks of white quartz, were no more than an incidental entertainment for Mrs. Rylands. The main thread of her mental existence now was her discussion with her little green leather book, and with Philip, the discussion of her universe and what had to be done about it. For five days Philip sent nothing to her but three cards, not postcards but correspondence cards in envelopes from his clubs, saying he was "writing a screed" and adding endearments. Then in close succession came two bales of written matter, hard upon the sudden and quite surprising announcement in the French and English-Parisian papers that the general strike in England had collapsed.

These "screeds" were very much in the manner of his former communication. Some lavender-tinted sheets from Honeywood House testified to a night spent at his Aunt Rowena's at Barnes. But there were no more drawings; he was getting too deeply moved for that sort of relief. There was not the same streak of amused observation, and there was an accumulating gravity. He reasoned more. The opening portion was a storm of indignation against the *British Gazette,* the government control of broadcasting and the general suppression of opinion in the country. That was very much in his old line. He had taken the trouble to copy out a passage from the government proclamation of Friday and print and underline certain words. "*ALL RANKS* of the armed forces of the crown are notified that *ANY ACTION* they may find it necessary to take in an honest endeavour to aid the civil power will receive both now *AND AFTERWARDS* the full support of the Government." Something had happened, Mrs. Rylands noted! He had spelt "government" right! And an anticipatory glance over the pages in her hand showed that he was going on spelling it right. To these quoted words Philip had added in a handwriting that was distorted with rage, rather thicker and less distinct: "in other words, 'Shoot and club if you get half a chance and the Home Office is with you. You will be helped now and let off afterwards.' This is publicly asking for violence in the most peaceful social crisis the world has ever seen. I told you the government wanted to have a fight and this proves it. But this isn't the worst. . . ."

He went on to tell of how the Bishop of Oxford, the Masters of Baliol and University and a number of leading churchmen had called upon the government to reopen negotiations and how the Archbishop

of Canterbury had attempted in vain to get a movement afoot in the country to arrest the struggle and
revive negotiations. The Archbishop had preached
on this on Sunday and had tried to mobilise the pul-
pits throughout the country. He had found himself
treated as a rebel sympathiser and choked off. The
British Gazette had suppressed the report of this
church intervention and the government had prohib-
ited its publication by the British Broadcasting Company. "They *want* this fight. They *want* to get to
violence," wrote Philip, with his pen driving hard
into the paper, and proceeded to denounce "Winston's garbled reports of Parliament. Anything
against them is either put in a day late or left out
altogether. People like Oxford and Grey are cut
to rags. Cook said of the negotiations, days ago, 'It
is hopeless,' and the dirty rag quoted this as though
he said it of the strike. And we have a cant that
these Harrovians are real public school boys and
understand fair play!"

It was funny to find the faithful Etonian breaking
off in this way to gird at Harrow and make it responsible for the most unteachable of its sons.

It seemed Philip had been in the House of Commons on Friday and heard a discussion between Mr.
Baldwin and Mr. Thomas that more than confirmed
his suspicions that the petty *Daily Mail* strike and the
consequent break was a foreseen excuse, meanly and
eagerly snatched at by the government. Then came
a rumour, current at the time but with no founda-
tion in fact, that the King (or according to another
version the Prince of Wales) had wanted to say
something reconciling and had been advised against
such a step. "Jix as Mussolini," commented Philip,

quite convinced of the story. He stormed vividly but briefly at the broadcasting programmes and the talk in the clubs. Came a blank half-sheet, just like one of those silences in some great piece of music before the introduction of a new theme and then, on a new page and very distinctly: "I have had a damned row with Uncle Robert."

This was the motive of the next part of Philip's composition, written more evenly and more consecutively than anything he had done before, the *Largo* so to speak. He expanded and developed and varied his jangling sense of Uncle Robert, and gathered it altogether into a measured and sustained denunciation. He set out to convey with a quite unconscious vigour, his deep astonishment, his widening perplexity and his gathering resentment that anything of the nature of Lord Edensoke should exist in the world, let alone in such close and authoritative proximity to himself. At times his discourse might have borne the heading "The Young Man discusses the Older Sort of Human Male."

"He's damned," he repeated. "I never realised before that any one could go about this world without any stink or fuss, so completely and utterly dead and damned as he is." He jumped into capitals to say his worthy uncle was a "Bad Man, nerve and muscle, blood and bone." He declared that it was impossible to understand the general strike, the coal strike, the outlook in England, the outlook for all the world until Lord Edensoke had been anatomised and analysed. And forthwith he set about the business.

Philip made it quite clear that up to his early conversations with his uncle after his return to England, he had supposed Lord Edensoke to be animated by much the same motives as himself, namely by a strong if vague passion to see the world orderly and growing happier, by a real wish to have the Empire secure, beneficent and proud, by a desire to justify wealth by great services, and that he was prepared to give time and face losses that the course of human affairs should go according to his ideas of what was fine and right. These had always been Philip's own assumptions, albeit rather dormant ones. But—

"He doesn't care a rap for the Empire as an Empire," wrote the amazed nephew. "He sees it simply as a not too secure roof over a lot of the family investments." Lord Edensoke's sense of public duty did not exist. He despised his social class. His loyalty to the King amounted to a firm assurance that he diverted public attention from the real rulers of the country. People liked the monarchy; it saved public issues from the dangerous nakedness they had in America. "Otherwise if he thought there was a dividend to be got out of it, he would boil the king in oil." He didn't believe in social order, in any sort of responsibility that a policeman and a law court could not check. Frankly, in his heart, he saw himself to be a brigand, carrying an enviable load through a world wherein nothing better than brigandage was possible. Law was a convenient convention among the robbers and you respected it just so far as it would be discreditable or dangerous to break the rules.

Came an illuminating anecdote. At dinner Lord Edensoke had shown a certain weariness of Philip's political and social crudities. By way of getting to more interesting things he had opened a fresh topic with "By the bye, Philip, have you any loose balances about? I think I could make a good use of them."

He had proceeded to explain to Philip's incredulity that the general strike was bound to collapse as soon as the scared and incapable labour leaders saw an excuse for letting it down that would save their faces with their followers, and that then the miners would be left locked out exactly as if there had been no general strike—but with "diminished public support." "That fellow Cook" could be relied upon to keep them out and to irritate the public against them. His lordship did his best to disabuse Philip's mind of the idea that there would be any settlement for some time. "You mean *you* won't settle anyhow?" Philip had said. Lord Edensoke's reply had been a faint smile and a gesture of the hand. So, as Rylands and Cokeson would have thousands of trucks unemployed, and easily handed over to other uses, the thing to do was to buy foreign coal now, and release and distribute it later when the community at large came to realise all that Lord Edensoke knew. Coal would come back to fancy prices—higher than '21. "There's a speculative element, of course," he had said. "The miners *may* collapse," but as he saw it, there was, saving that possibility, anything from twenty-five to a hundred and fifty per cent. to be made in the course of the next few months upon anything Philip chose to bring in to this promising operation.

Philip ended his account of this conversation in wild indignation. "We are the coal-owners of Great Britain," he fumed, "and this is how we do our duty by the country that trusts us, honours us, makes peers of us! We starve the miner and strangle industry—and we make 'anything from twenty-five to a hundred and fifty per cent.' out of a deal in foreign coal. Naturally we do nothing to bring about a settlement. Naturally we are for the Constitution and all that, which lets us do such things." Philip's narrative wasn't very clear, but this was the point it would seem at which the "damned row with Uncle Robert" occurred.

Respect for the head of the family made its final protest and fled. It was Philip's last dinner with his senior partner. He seemed to have talked, according to his uncle's judgment, "sheer Bolshevism." It was doubtful if they got to their cigars. Philip returned to the Reform Club and spent the rest of a long evening consuming the Club notepaper at a furious pace.

Details of the final breach did not appear because Philip swept on to a close, unloving investigation of his uncle's soul.

"I seem to have been thinking of him most of the time since," he said.

What did Lord Edensoke think he was up to, Philip enquired. Clearly he did not suppose he was living for anything outside himself. He had no religion, no superstition even. He had a use for religion, but that was a different matter. For him religion was a formality that kept people in order. It was good that inferior and discontented people should be obliged to sacrifice to the God of Things as they Are. It set up a code of outer decency and determined a system of restraints. Nor had he any patriotism. The British Empire in his eyes was a fine machine for utilising the racial instincts of the serviceable British peoples for the enforcement of contracts and the protection of invested capital throughout the world. If they did not, as a general rule, get very much out of it in spite of their serviceableness that was their affair. They could congratulate themselves that their money was on a gold standard even if they had none, and they had the glory of ruling India if even they were never allowed to go there. He liked the English climate and avoided it during most of the winter. It was a good climate for work and Courtney Wishart in its great park just over the hills from Edensoke was a stately and enviable home, one of those estates that made England a land fit for heroes to die for. He had no passion for science. The spirit that devotes whole lives to the exquisite unravelling of reality was incomprehensible to him. He preferred his reality ravelled. It was better for business operations. He betrayed no passion for any sort of beautiful things. He would never collect pictures nor make a garden unless he wanted to beat some one else at it or sell it at a profit. He loved no one in the world—Philip would tell her a little later of his uncle's loves. In brief he lived simply for himself, for satisfactions directly related to himself as the centre of it all and for nothing else whatever.

One of his great satisfactions was winning a game. He was not, Philip thought, avaricious simply but he liked to get, because that was besting the other fellow. His business was his great game. He liked to feel his aptitude, his wariness, to foresee, and realise and let other people realise the shrewd precision of his anticipations. He played other games for recreation. He was reported to be a beastly bridge player, very good but spiteful and envious even of his part-

ner. He played in the afternoons at the Lessington
after lunch and Philip said rumour had it that
several other members of that great club would go
into hiding and get the club servants to report for
them, not venturing near the card-room, until Edensoke was seated at his game. He played golf bit-
terly well. Physically he was as good as Geoffrey,
the same sure eye and accurate movements. He
had been a memorable bat at cricket and still made a
devastating show at tennis. And he was a wonderful shot. Business kept him from much shooting,
but he loved a day now and then, when he could take
his place among the guns and kill and kill. He
would stand, with those thin lips of his pressed together, while the scared birds came rocketing over
him, wings whirring, hearts beating fast. He showed
them. But he had no blood lust. On the whole he
would rather play against a man than merely triumph
over birds and silly things that probably did not feel
humiliated even when they were shot. Besting people and feeling that the other fellow realises or will
presently find out that he has been bested was subtler
and far more gratifying. "You know that scanty
laugh of his," wrote Philip, "rather like a neigh.
The loser gets it." Just now he was besting the
miners. "The more he gets them down the better
he will be pleased." The profits were a secondary
consideration, important only like scoring above the
line.

He loved no one. "I don't think I have ever
talked to you about Aunt Sydney," said Philip, and
proceeded to explain the domestic infelicities of his
uncle. She had been a brilliant beautiful girl but
poor, one of the "needy Needhams." Uncle Robert

would never have married a rich and independent
wife because it would have been difficult to best her
and hard to try. He had kept Aunt Sydney down
for a time and she had been almost treacherously sub-
servient until she had got him well committed to
infidelity with a secretary, and had enticed him into
provable cruelty. She had been a patient Grisel who
had eavesdropped, stolen letters and bided her time.
A lover, well hidden, gave her sage counsel. Then
she had held her husband up with the threat of a
discreditable divorce. Uncle Robert had no stomach
for being "talked about all over London." It was
one of his essential satisfactions to be respected and
high and unapproachable, and he must have had
some bad hours over the affair. "We all rather like
Aunt Sydney on that account," wrote Philip.

She arranged a separation of mutual toleration and
wore her lover upon her sleeve in full view of her
baffled spouse. He became "Burdock, the chap Lady
Edensoke keeps," her watchful and not always comfortable shadow.

Lord Edensoke tried to make this seem to be his
own design and flaunted it with various conspicuous,
expensive and rather discordant ladies for some years
to show everybody just how things were. Then he
reverted to his more congenial pursuit of discovering,
seducing, exalting and throwing over, very young
and needy beauties from the middle classes. He
coveted them, bested them, got them, hated them
because so plainly he had bought them, and threw
them over with well established expensive habits and
a contemptible income. "He sets about it like a cat,"
wrote Philip. "I have seen him on the platform
at a Mansion House meeting, fixing some pretty girl

in the audience like an old cat spotting a nestling in a bush. He sets about it very quietly and cleverly. He has all sorts of secretarial jobs to offer, and I believe there is a friendly West End dressmaker. He can even seem to be influential round about one or two theatres if a girl has ambitions of that sort. He gets them and makes them submit to this and that, and they become afraid of him. They realise they are unsafe. He can turn them back to poverty and the streets, so easily. When he has got them thoroughly afraid of him, then I suppose he feels like God. In the end, it does not matter how they propitiate. Go they must. In his life, there must have been a score of these—*romances*."

Thus Philip, relentlessly. These were the interests and amusements of Lord Edensoke, the satisfactions that kept him alive and made the life he lived worth while, the besting of men, the abasement of women, the sense of conquest assured by the big balance, the big house, the many servants, the champagne you couldn't buy in the open market, the special cigars, the salutation of common men, the whispered "That's Edensoke," the rare visits to the House of Lords. What other reality was there? These were the things that kept the look of quiet self-approval on those thin lips and assured the great coal-owner that he had the better of the sentimentalists and weaklings about him, that he could rank himself above these other men who wasted their time upon ideas and causes, who kept faith beyond the letter of their bargains, and sacrificed and restrained themselves for their friends and their associates, their wives and their womankind. "My dear," wrote Philip, rising to the full gravity of his

Largo, "this is the analysis of Uncle Robert. These are his ends and all that he is! For the first time in my life I have looked at him squarely and this is what he is. And it is a hideous life. It is a hideous life and yet it comes so close to me that it is a life I too might drift into living.

"This is a common way of living among our kind of people now. Edensoke is no rare creature. There are more Edensokes than know they are [*sic*]. Edensokes with variations. There are hundreds of him now among the rich, and thousands and thousands as one goes down the scale to the merely prosperous. Some are a little different about their womenfolk and buy them dearer and make more of a show with them. Many are sillier—I admit he has a good brain. Lots are too cowardly for 'romances' and leave the women alone—but not so many as there used to be. Most have fads and hobbies that give them a little distinction, but all are equally damned. You and I could write down a score of names in five minutes. Not one that wouldn't rejoice to be in that deal over the foreign coal, if they knew of it and knew how to get into it. Not one, that wouldn't feel bested to hear of a coal miner with a decent bathroom, a Morris chair and a shelf of books. The government and the bunch behind the government, abounds in his quality. Soames Forsyte again!—how near old Galsworthy has come to him. The living damned.

"And in a world of men like this," Philip culminated, "we are waiting about for old Sempack's millennium to come of its own accord!"

Mrs. Rylands paused at the end of the sheet. The portrait of the contemporary successful man, for all the jerkiness of its strokes, struck her as devastatingly true. There was not a thing Philip was telling her about Lord Edensoke that seemed altogether new to her. Even the bilked mistresses she had known of, by intuition. And as certainly had she known, and yet never quite dared to know, that this was the quality of many men, of many powers, of much of the power in the world. The world into which she and Philip were now launching another human soul.

That too had to be reasoned out with the green leather book.

"What puts the sting into the problem of Uncle Robert," Philip continued, "is the fact that he is after all, blood of my blood and bone of my bone. When he isn't looking like an elderly shop-soiled version of Geoffrey coming home late, he is looking like me in thirty years time. The personal question for me is, whether he is the truth about me stripped of a lot of illusion and rainbow stuff and Wordsworthian 'clouds of glory' and such, or whether I am still in possession of something—I don't know— some sort of cleanness and decency, that he has lost. Which I need not lose. I'm all for alternative two, and if so, then the most important thing in the world for us is to know what has dried this up in Uncle Robert.

"I'm going to write something difficult, dear wife confessor. I can't help being clumsy here and it will sound priggish to the square of pi. But I see it like this. There is something in me that for want of a better word I might call religious. There is something else, unless it is the same thing, that holds me to you. Not just sex and your dearness, they hold me, but something else as well that makes me put not you, but something about you, over and before myself—before ourselves." (Marginal note: "I just can't get away from all these ambiguous somethings but I think you will see what I mean. When a man can manage his 'ones' and his 'somethings' and his other pronouns then I suppose he has really learnt to write.") This has to do with nobleness and good faith. This is in me but not so very strong, and I thank whatever powers there be that I met you. This wants help to keep alive, and you help it to keep alive, have helped and will help it tremendously. It may be illusion but that does not matter so long as it remains bright and alive. Lots of people keep it alive through religion, church I mean and all that, but nowadays that hasn't kept up, religion hasn't, and a lot of us can't make that use of it. Of any current sort of religion I mean. And it can go altogether. I have this in me, whatever it is, and so has Geoffrey and so perhaps had Uncle Robert. I am more like Geoffrey than you like to think and he is more like me. He didn't have my luck in getting you and having you thinking of fine things beside me, and before and always he has had the worse of that sort of luck and he is shyer than I am and more secretive. I've seen what I am talking about shrink in him, but I've watched it and it is there. I don't suppose there is any religion now strong enough to get him—or any sort of woman to pick him up. I don't know. Still something lingers. It makes him uncomfortable and he is disposed to hate it and try to sneer at it until it is dead altogether. And by the same reasoning Eden-

soke started like this. There was a time when he
thought of doing fine things and having something
in his life lovelier than scoring points in a game.
He had the illusion, or if you like, because practically it is the same, he had the sacred flame, whatever it is, flickering about in him. I expect Aunt
Sydney made a tough start for him. He hadn't my
luck. Suppose when they two were young he had
found out suddenly that she loved him—more even
than her pride. Suppose something had happened
like what happened to me. Infusion of blood saves
lives, but being loved like that is infusion of soul.
Shy men bury their hearts like that fellow in the
Testament who buried his talent. And when you dig
them up again, there's nothing. Hearts must have
air, have breathed upon them the breath of life. As
you did. The flame is hard to light again. Now
that there is no religion really, one is left to nothing
but love.

"I'm writing all this just anyhow and God knows
what you will make of this hotch-potch of ideas.
I've got to cut it short and finish.

"It is one o'clock, my dear, closing time for a
respectable club and I must turn out from here and
walk back to South Street to bed. Not a taxi to be
got."

This first letter had been sealed down after this
effort and then reopened to insert a sheet of South
Street notepaper and on this was scrawled: "I open
this letter again to tell you that Catherine Fossing-
dean has killed a man. I did not even know she was
in England. I thought she was still with you. But

she seems to have scuttled home directly the General Strike was begun. You know she is mixed up with the comic-opera fellow Fearon-Owen who stars it in the British Fascisti world. I can't imagine her taste for him. Looks to me like the sort of fellow one doesn't play cards with. Got his knighthood out of organising some exhibition. One of those splendid old English families that sold carpets in Constantinople three generations ago and was known as Feronian or some such name with a nose to it. Anyhow he's true-blue British now. Bull-dog-breed to the marrow. Union Jack all over him. And a terrific down on the lazy good-for-nothing British working man. Who really is British, blood and bone. In some irregular way this glory of our island race has got his fingers well into an emergency organisation of automobilists, for scattering Winston's *British Gazette* up and down the country, and suchlike public services. And he seems to have handed over a motor-car to Lady Catherine for moonlight rushes to the midlands.

"You know how she drives. Foot down and damn the man round the corner. Giving her a car to drive is almost as criminal as shooting blind down a crowded street. She got her man near Rugby. Two young fellows she got, but the other was only slightly injured. This one was killed dead. Tramping for a job, poor devil. *And she drove on!* She drove on, because she was a patriotic heroine battling against Bolshevism and all that, for God and King and Fearon-Owen and the *British Gazette*, particularly Fearon-Owen and the *British Gazette*. War is war. Nothing will be done to her. That's all. Philip."

§ 15

PHILIP'S other letter was much slenderer and had been posted only one day after its precursor. It opened with his amazed account of the collapse of the General Strike. "Everything has happened as Uncle Robert foretold, and so far I am proved a fool," it began.

He went on to express a quite extravagant contempt for the leaders of the Labour Party who had "neither the grit to prevent the General Strike nor the grit to keep on with it." It was clear that he had a little lost his equanimity over the struggle and that his criticisms of selfish toryism had tilted him heavily towards the side of the strikers in the struggle. And he was intensely annoyed to find his uncle's estimate of the situation so completely confirmed. The time had come to call out the second line, stop light and power and food distribution and bring matters to a crisis, and there was little reason to suppose that most of the men of the second line would not have stood by their unions.

But it would have meant the beginning of real violence and a grimmer phase of the struggle and the trade union leaders were tired, frightened and consciously second-rate men. They were far more terrified by the possibilities of victory than by the certainty of defeat. They had snatched at the opportunity offered by a new memorandum by "that Kosher Liberal, Herbert Samuel"—"Tut tut!" said Mrs. Rylands; "but this is real bad temper, Philip!" —which nobody had accepted or promised to stand by, and unconditionally, trusting the whole future of the men they stood for, to a government that

255

could publish the *British Gazette*, they had called the strike off. They had given in and repented like naughty children "and here we are—with men being victimised right and left and the miners in the cart! Nothing has been done, nothing has been settled. The railway workers are eating humble pie and the red ties of the Southern railway guards are to be replaced by blue ones. (Probably Jix thought of that.) The miners have already refused to accept Samuel's memorandum, and Uncle Robert's little deal is almost the only hopeful thing in the situation. He gets his laugh out of it sure enough."

Even the writing showed Philip in a phase of anti-climax. He was irritated, perplexed.

"Is all life a comedy of fools? Am I *taking myself too seriously* and all that? Here is a crisis in the history of one of the greatest, most intelligent, best educated countries in the world, and it is an imbecile crisis! It does nothing. It states nothing. It does not even clear up how things are. By great good luck it did not lead to bloodshed or bitterness—except among the miners. Who aren't supposed to count. And Catherine's kill of course. There was no plan in it and no idea to it. It was a little different in form and it altered the look of the streets; but otherwise it was just in the vein of affairs as they go on month by month and year by year, coming to no point, signifying nothing. Burbling along. Just, as you say old Sempack said, just Carnival. Where are we going?—all the hundreds of millions that we are on this earth? Is this all and has it always been such drifting as this? Are the shapes of history like the shapes of clouds, fancies of Polonius the historian? Now we expand and increase and now we falter and fail.

Boom years and dark ages until the stars grow tired of us and shy some half-brick of a planet out of space to end the whole silly business.

"I cannot believe that, and so I come back to old Sempack again with his story of all this world of ours being no more than the prelude to a real civilisation. Hitch your mind to that idea and you can make your life mean something. Or seem to mean something. There is no other way, now that the religions have left us, to make a life mean anything at all. But then, are we getting on with the prelude? How are we to get on with the prelude? How are we to get by Uncle Robert? How are we to get by Winston and Amery? How are we to get by all these posturing, vague-minded, labour politicians? My dear, I set out writing these letters to you to tell you how my mind was going on and what I was finding out to do. And in this letter anyhow I have to tell you that my mind isn't going on and that I am lost and don't know what to do. It is as if a squirrel in a rotating cage reported progress. I wish I had old Sempack here, just to put him through it. Is he anything more than a big bony grey squirrel spinning in a cage of his own? The great crisis came and the great crisis went, and it has left me like a jelly-fish stranded on a beach.

"The only people in all this tangle of affairs who seem to have any live faith in them and any real go are—don't be too startled—the Communist Party. I've had glimpses of one or two of them. And the stuff they teach and profess seems to me the most dead-alive collection of half-truths and false assumptions it is possible to imagine. For every one who isn't a Communist they have some stupid nickname or other, and their first most fundamental belief is that nobody who owns any property or directs any sort of business, can be other than deliberately wicked. Everything has to be sabotaged and then everything will come right. They don't work for one greatly organised world in the common interest, not for a moment. Their millennium is a featureless level of common people, and it is to be brought about by a paradox called the dictatorship of the proletariat. And yet they have an enthusiasm. They can work. They can take risks and sacrifice themselves—quite horrible risks they will face. While we—"

He had pulled up in mid sentence. The second fascicle began as abruptly as the first ended.

"I have just been to see Sempack at Charing Cross Hospital. I had no idea that he too had come back to England. I thought he was doing a walking tour in the Alpes Maritimes. But it seems that he was knocked down by a bus in the Strand this morning. They got through to me by telephone when he re-covered consciousness and I went to see him at once. There is some question whether the bus skidded, but none that the great man, with his nose in the air and his thoughts in the year 4000, overlooked it as he stepped off the kerb. He wasn't killed or smashed, thank goodness, but he had a shock and very bad contusions and a small bone broken in his fore-arm, and for two hours he seems to have been insensible. He was very glad to see me and talked very pleas-antly—of you and the garden among other things. Voice unabated. I could not have imagined they could have packed him into an ordinary hospital bed, but they had. There are no complications. He will be out of hospital to-morrow and I shall take him

to South Street and see that he is sent off properly
and in a fit condition to his own house near Swanage.
Perhaps I will take him down. I like him and it
might be good to talk things over with him. But
what can *he* be doing in London? He wasn't at all
clear about that. Has everybody come to London?
Shall I next have to bail you out at Bow Street or
identify the body of Bombaccio recovered from the
Thames?"

§ 16

IT was queer to turn one's mind back from the
social battles and eventfulness of distant England to life in the great garden. Here Mr.
Sempack was still a large figure of thought and Lady
Catherine simply lovely and florid and absurd. It
seemed as though it could be only little marionette
copies of them of which Philip told, Sempack ban-
daged in hospital and Lady Catherine become rather
horribly strident, with blood upon her mudguards.
She had killed a young man. She was such a fool
that she would not greatly care, any more than such
women cared for the killing of pheasants. That
young man would simply become part of the decora-
tion of her life like the dead and dying soldiers one
sees in the corners of heroic portraits of great conquerors. And Philip away there. But also he was a
voice here, his letters made him a voice very near to
his musing reader. In his letters there were also
little phrases, little reminders, that even an intimate
novel cannot quote. These touched and caressed her.
He seemed to be Philip close at hand telling of the
Philip who went about England in a state of peevish
indignation, accumulating rebellion against cold and

capable Uncle Robert and all that Uncle Robert stood for in life. And while the problems of this struggle in the homeland passed processionally before her mind, she had also in the foreground, great handsome chunks of the wisdom of Mrs. McManus and alternatively the religion of Stella Binny.

With Stella Binny Mrs. Rylands discussed theology. The green leather book had been planned on generous lines to open with metaphysical and religious ideas. Stella had just been received in the Catholic Church and had arrived in a phase of shy proselytism. So naturally both ladies converged on a common preoccupation.

But if they converged they never met. When at last Stella took her unremarkable departure for England and Mrs. Rylands could think over all that had passed between them as one whole, she was impressed by that failure to meet, more than by anything else in their arguments and comparisons. In some quite untraceable way the idea of God as of a great being comprehending the universe and pervading every fibre of her existence had crept into her mind during the past month or so. It was as if He had always been there in her mind and yet as if He was only now becoming near and perceptible. So long as she had been in her first phase of love for Philip she had hardly given this presence a thought; now in the new phase that was developing, the presence presided. It was something profoundly still, something absolutely permanent, which embraced all her life and Philip and everything in her consciousness out to the uttermost star. But when she set herself to compare this gathering apprehension of God with Stella's happy lucidities about her new faith, she found herself looking into a mental world that had not an idea nor a meaning in common with her own.

Indeed her impression was that Stella's religion, so far from being of the same nature as her own, was nothing more than a huge furniture store of screens, hangings, painted windows, curtains and walls, ornaments and bric-à-brac, to banish and hide this one thing that constituted her own whole faith. This cosmic certitude, this simplicity beneath diversity, this absolute reassurance amidst perplexity and confusion, this profound intimacy, had nothing in common with the docketed Incomprehensible of Stella's pious activities, who was locked away in some steel safe of dogmas, far away from the music and decorations. Stella became defensive and elusive directly Mrs. Rylands spoke of God. She gave her to understand that the Mysteries of the Being of God were unthinkable things, an affair for specialists, to be entrusted to specialists and left to specialists, like the mysteries discussed by Mr. Einstein. The good Roman Catholic hurried past them with a bowed head and averted eyes to deal with other things.

But Mrs. Rylands had not the slightest desire to deal with these other things. She found them not merely unattractive; she found them tiresome and even in some aspects repulsive. She had no taste for bric-à-brac in the soul. She wanted God herself. Belonging to a Church whose Holy Father conceivably stood in the presence of God, was no satisfaction to her. She herself wanted to stand in the presence of God. So far as Stella could be argued with upon this question, she argued with her about the Mass. "It brings one *near*. It is the ultimate nearness," said Stella, dropping her voice to a whisper. "It would take me a billion miles away," said Mrs. Rylands. She was naughty about the Mass and did her best to shock her friend. "I don't want to eat God," she blasphemed. "I want to know him." She said that invoking the spirit by colours and garments and music reminded her of the hiving of swarming bees. She objected scornfully to the necessary priest. "God is hard enough to realise," she said, "without the intervention of a shaven individual in petticoats—however symbolic his petticoats and his shaven face may be." She recalled some crumbs of erudition that had fallen from the table of the parental vicarage and cited parallelisms between the old Egyptian religions and religious procedure and the Catholic faith and practice. She hunted out controversial material from the *Encyclopædia Britannica*. And from more destructive sources.

The miscellaneous literary accumulations of Casa Terragena included several volumes about Catholic mysticism, and among others one or two books by Saint Teresa and the *Life and Revelations of Saint Gertrude* with many details of her extremely passionate worship of her "adorable lover." There was also Houtin's account of the marvellous experiences of the sainted Abbess of Solesmes, who died so recently as 1909. Mrs. Rylands had dipped in these strange records and now she returned to them for ammunition. She read the blushing Stella how every Christmas Eve the latter lady and her spiritual daughters nourished the infant Jesus, afterwards describing for the edification of the Abbey community "the chaste emotions of this virginal milking."

"Where, my dear," cried Cynthia, "is God, the Wonderful, the Everlasting, in ecstasies like that?"

Stella was ill instructed as yet in the new faith she had embraced. But she had learnt the lesson of confidence in the authorities into whose hands she had given herself. "All this can be explained. . . . It is a special side of the faith."

Mrs. Rylands propounding fresh perplexities had suddenly become aware that there was distress in her friend's voice, in her eyes, in her flushed face. Things had appeared in a changed light. Stella was large and very blonde, a creature so gentle that abruptly, as the tears showed in her eyes and the note of fear betrayed itself in her voice, her little hostess had seen herself like a fierce little rationalist ferret, tackling this white rabbit of faith. Surely she had not been discussing great religious ideas at all. How could one discuss such things with Stella? She had simply been spoiling a new toy that had been making her friend happy. "Oh, Stella dear! Forgive my troubling you with my elementary doubts," she had said. "I am very crude and ignorant. I know it, my dear. Of course there must be explanations."

Stella dissolved in gratitude.

"Of course there are explanations. If only you could talk to men like Cardinal Amontillado, you would realise how explicable all these things are. They make it so clear. But I'm not clever nor trained."

"I was just asking," Mrs. Rylands had apologised.

"Some things of course are simply given us to *try* our faith," Stella had said.

And Mrs. Rylands had changed the subject with the happy discovery of two pretty little birds flirting in a rose brake.

Now however that Stella had gone, Mrs. Rylands

could look back on all their disputations and utter her matured and final verdict upon the great system that had embraced and taken possession of her friend. And it has to be recorded that the matured and final verdict of Mrs. Rylands upon Roman Catholic Christianity, its orders and subjugations, its gifts and consolations, its saints and mysteries and marvels and the enduring miracle of its existence, was delivered in one single word: "Fiddlesticks," she said—aloud and distinctly as though she had hearers. She said it aloud as she walked in the darkness of her garden after dinner. As one might rehearse a one word part. Mrs. McManus no doubt was hovering, but she could hover so skilfully and tactfully that it seemed to Mrs. Rylands that she was entirely by herself.

With this word given out to the night Mrs. Rylands asserted her tested and inalterable Protestantism, her resolution to keep the idea of God clean from all traces of primordial rites, of sublimated sensuality and wrappings of complication, and her relations with God simple and direct. God might be invisible, indescribable, veiled so deep in mystery as to be altogether undiscoverable, but at any rate He should not be caricatured in mysticism, worshipped in effigy and made the mouthpiece of authority. Better the Atheist who says there is nothing than the Catholic who says there is such stuff as altars are made of.

And with that word of dismissal Mrs. Rylands ceased to think about Roman Catholicism and fell into a deep meditation upon the mystery and majesty of her God.

Her God, that Being was; the frame and substance

of her universe of which and by which all its things were made; the mighty essential reassurance of her particular mind. He was everywhere, but for her His seat was in her spirit and His centre was her heart. He had come as imperceptibly as a dawn and her life had ceased to be anæmic and dispersed and purposeless with His coming. Everything was suffused with tone and beauty because of Him. He had dawned upon her not as a dawn of light, for she knew no more than she had ever known, but as a dawn of courage. She perceived she could have as soon called him "Courage" as called him "God." The courage of the earth and skies. A courage mighty beyond thinking and yet friendly and near. No Name he had, nor need for a name; no prayers nor method of approach. His utmost worship was a wordless quiet. But in such stillness and black clearness as this night gave, under the laced loveliness of the star-entangling branches, he seemed to be very close indeed to her.

Dreaming, drenched in worship and the sense of communion, Mrs. Rylands walked in her garden. The familiar paths just intimated themselves in the obscurity sufficiently to guide her steps. One serene planet high in the blue heaven was the most definite thing in that world of shadows and obscurity.

The little white figure came to rest and stood quite motionless upon the bridge where Mr. Plantagenet-Buchan had discovered the flamboyant quality of the gorge, but to-night, now that the moon rose late, all that ascendant clamour of lines was veiled under one universal curtain of velvet shadow. Far, far above, minute cascades caught a faint glimmer from the depth of the sky, and plunged into an abyss of darkness.

For a long time she remained there and her soul knelt and was comforted.

At last she stirred and went slowly down a slanting path that led towards the Via Aurelia, a path that in its windings up and down and round about, gave little glimpses between the trees now of Ventimiglia and now of the stars.

§ 17

THE serenity of the night was broken.

Distant shouts ugly with anger and the crack of a pistol.

She stopped still and returned to the world of fact. The silence recovered, but now it was pervaded by uneasiness and clustering multiplying interrogations. What was it? The path she was on wound down among rocks and pines below the tennis court to where the work-sheds of the gardens showed dimly, near the old Roman road. The noise had come out of the blackness in which the road was hidden.

Suddenly again—voices!

And then little phantom beams of light, minute pale patches of illumination amidst the black trees. These flicked into existence and as immediately vanished again. There were people down there, a number of men with electric flash lamps, looking for something, pursuing something, calling to one another. As they moved nearer they passed out of sight below the black bulks of the garden houses, leaving nothing but faint intermittent exudations of light beyond the edges of the walls.

Then something appeared very much nearer, a crouching shape on the path below, moving, coming towards her, beast or man. A man with stumbling

266

steps, running. He was so near now that she heard his sobbing breathing, and he had not seen her! In another moment he had pulled up, face to face with her, a middle-sized, stoutish man who stopped short and swayed and staggered. He put up his hand to his forehead. Her appearance, blocking his path, seemed the culmination of dismay for him. "Santo Dio!" he choked with a gesture of despair.

"Coming!" came the voice of Mrs. McManus out of the air.

"What is it?" asked Mrs. Rylands, though already she knew she was in the presence of the Terror.

"I Fascisti m'inseguono! Non ne posso più. . . . Mi vogliono ammaazzare?" gasped the fugitive and tried to turn and point, and failed and stumbled and fell down before her on hands and knees. He coughed and retched. She thought he was going to be sick. He did not attempt to get up again.

"Coraggio!" said Mrs. Rylands, rallying her Italian, and took his shoulder and made an ineffective effort to raise him to his feet.

She thought very quickly. This man had to be saved. She was on his side. It did not matter who he was. She knew Fascismo. No man was to be chased and manhandled in the garden of Terragena. The pursuers were still beating about down in the black gully of the sunken road. They had not as yet discovered the little stone steps that came into the garden near the bridge, up which their victim must have stolen. He had got some moments' grace. But he was spent, spent and pitifully wheezing and weeping. He was sitting now on the path with one hand pressed to his labouring chest. He could make no use of his respite to get away.

He must hide. Could he be hidden? She surveyed the ground about her very swiftly. She remembered something that had happened just here, a caprice of her own. A little way back—

Mrs. McManus was beside her with her hand on her shoulder.

"Them Fascists," she remarked, with a complete grasp of the situation. "Is he badly hurt?"

"Help him up," whispered Mrs. Rylands. "Listen! Just a few yards back. Behind the seat. There is a hole between the rocks, where the romarin hangs down. One can be hidden there. I hid there once from Philip. Push him in. Oh! Oh! *What* is the Italian for *hide*? But he will know French. 'Faut cacher. Un trou. Tout preso!'"

"Inglese!" said the fugitive, helped to his feet and peering closely at their dim faces as he clung to the stalwart arm of Mrs. McManus. "Hide! Yes hide. Mes poumons."

"You help him there. I will delay them," said Mrs. Rylands, "if they come."

She showed the way to Mrs. McManus in eager whispers.

"Come," said Mrs. McManus.

The two dim figures, unsteady and undignified, retreated. The man seemed helplessly passive and obedient, and Mrs. McManus handled him with professional decision.

Mrs. Rylands turned her attention to the hunt again. It was still noisy down there in the trench of the road. It was just as well, for Mrs. McManus seeking the hiding-place and having to reassure her charge kept up a very audible monologue, and a considerable rustle of bushes and snapping of sticks were unavoidable. "But where the divil is it?" she asked.

The rustle and disturbance grew louder and ended in a crashing thud. "Ugh!" she cried very loudly and suddenly ceased to talk.

"Damn!" she said after a moment, spent apparently in effort. Mrs. Rylands saw only vaguely but it seemed that Mrs. McManus was bending down, busily occupied with something. What had happened? Had she found the proper hiding-place?

Mrs. Rylands abandoned her idea of standing sentinel and flitted up the path.

"He's fainted," said Mrs. McManus on her knees. "Or worse. We'll have to drag him in. Let me do it. Can you show me exactly where this hole of yours is? It's all so dark."

For a minute, a long minute, Mrs. Rylands could not find it. "Here!" she cried at last. "Here! To the right."

More crackling of branches. Loose stones rolled over and started off, as if to spread the alarm, down the slanting path. The two women spoke in whispers but the noises they made seemed to be terrific. It was wonderful that the Fascists had not discovered them minutes ago. How heavy a man can be!

A Fascist down below was yelping like a young dog. "Ecco! Ecco! E passato di qui!" He had discovered the steps.

"Come on with you!" said Mrs. McManus stumbling amidst the rocks and gave a conclusive tug.

"Pull that rosemary down on his boots," said Mrs. Rylands. "I can see the gleam of them from here."

When she looked down the path again, the noise-less beams of the flash lamps were scrutinising the white walls of the garden house. The Fascists, some or all of them, had come up into the garden. A group of four heads was defined for an instant against the pale illumination of the wall.

"We'd better go down towards them slowly," said Mrs. McManus. "And if you should happen to be feeling a little upset by all the hubbub they've made, well, don't conceal it."

"They've three paths to choose from at the corner of the sheds," said Mrs. Rylands. "The main one goes up to the house."

"So they'll send only a scout or so this way."

"But this way leads to the frontier."

Abruptly they were facing the scrutiny of the bright oval eye of a hand-lamp; its holder a shock-headed blackness. "Perche questa battaglia nello mio giardino?" said Mrs. Rylands in her best Italian, blinking and shrinking.

"Mi scusino, signore!" A boyish not unpleasant voice.

"Pardon me indeed," came the indignation of Mrs. McManus. "What are you after in this garden, troubling an invalid lady in the night and all?"

"Troppo di—what's light? it blinds me," Mrs. Rylands complained, and the white oval breach of the darkness vanished. "Che volete?"

The young man said something about the flight of a traitor.

"Don't bandy Italian with him," advised Mrs. McManus.

"You can speak French perhaps; Parlate Franchese?" said Mrs. Rylands and so got the conversation on a linguistic level.

The young man's French was adequate. That

traitor to Italy, Vinciguerra, she learnt, had been trying to escape out of his native country in order to
injure her abroad. He had been watched and nearly
caught in Ventimiglia two days ago, but he had got
away. Now he was making his dash for liberty.
He had fled through this garden. He had run
along the Via Aurelia and come up the steps by the
little bridge. The young man was desolated to in-
vade the lady's garden or cause her any inconvenience but the fault was with the traitor Vinciguerra.
Had she by any chance seen or heard a man passing
through her domain?

Mrs. Rylands found herself lying with the utmost
conviction. No one had passed this way. But she
had seen some one hurrying up the central path to
the house—perhaps five minutes ago.

"It would be about five minutes ago."

She had thought it was one of the gardeners, she
said. In the darkness the young man made an almost
invisible but evidently very profound bow. And
turned back to his friends. "I must sit down," said
Mrs. Rylands still in French and taking the arm of
Mrs. McManus, wheeled her round. "Sit on that
seat," she explained.

"Sit right on him," said Mrs. McManus. "Exactly."

At the same time the trees about them were suffused by an orange glow, that increased in a series
of gradations. The two women halted. Looking up
the hill they saw Casa Terragena, which had been
slumbering in the night, growing visible and vivid,
as Bombaccio and his minions put on the lights.
Evidently they had become aware of the uproar
and were illuminating the house preparatory to sally-

ing forth in search of their mistress. The framework and wire netting of the tennis enclosure became vividly black and clear against the clear brightness of the hall. A rapid consultation occurred at the garden sheds and then the whole body of Fascists went up towards the marble steps below the terrace. The voice of Bombaccio could be heard like the challenge of a sentinel, and replies, less distinct, in a number of voices.

"So it's Signor Vinciguerra we've got," said Mrs. Rylands, speaking very softly. "He used to be a minister."

"I'll go back to him. I wish I had some brandy for him."

"We'll go back together," said Mrs. Rylands. "If they make for the French frontier they may pass back along this path."

They returned to the hiding place. "Sit you down," said Mrs. McManus, and groped under the bushes towards the cleft in the rocks. She fumbled and produced a flash lamp of her own. Mrs. Rylands for the first time in her life saw the face of a horribly frightened man. He was crouched together in the hole with not a spark of fight left in him. His hand clutched his mouth.

"Sicuro," said Mrs. McManus with surprising linguistic ability. "Restate acqui."

"Put out that light," said the fugitive in English. "*Please* put out that light."

Darkness supervened with a click.

"Stay here until the way is clear," said Mrs. McManus.

"Sure," said Signor Vinciguerra.

"The garden is full of them," she said.

Inaudible reply.

She rearranged the trailing rosemary and returned cautiously to the bench. She sat down by her charge in silence.

"He must stay here until the way is clear," she said, and paused and added reflectively—"And then—?"

A silent mutual contemplation.

"What *are* we going to do with him?" said Mrs. Rylands in a low voice, glancing over her shoulder at the faint sound of a boot shifting its pose on the rock behind her.

Mrs. McManus also peered at their invisible protégé. "It's a very great responsibility to have thrust upon two peaceful women just as they are taking the air before bedtime. I hardly know what to advise. . . . We can't leave him there."

"We can't leave him there."

"He's done."

"He's done."

Mrs. Rylands contemplated the situation with immense gravity for some moments. Then she was seized with a violent and almost uncontrollable impulse to laugh at the amazing change of mood and tempo ten minutes could effect. But she felt that the fugitive would never understand if she gave way to it. Extreme seriousness returned to her.

§ 18

THE temperament and training alike of Mrs. Rylands disposed her to shirk this startling charge that fate had thrust upon her. Never in all her life before had she been in a position in which she could not turn to some one else to relieve her of danger or inconvenience. Her disposition now was to summon Bombaccio and the servants, tell them to order the Fascists out of the garden and take Signor Vinciguerra, give him refreshments, make him comfortable for the night and send him over the frontier in safety by the accepted route for fugitives, whatever that route happened to be, to-morrow. She realised the absurdity of this even as it came into her consciousness. She had no knowledge of Bombaccio's political views and still less of his susceptibility and the susceptibility of his minions to the Terror. This time she couldn't call upon Bombaccio. Even if he proved willing to help, it would not she perceived be fair to him to make him a party to the adventure. He and the rest of the Casa Terragena household were in Italy and had to go on living in Italy under a Fascist government. She was, the fact came up to her quite startlingly, doing something against the government under which she was living. For the first time in her life, the powers of social order and control would not be on her side.

The way of the lady, born safe and invincibly assured, would not do here. She who had always been quietly and surely respected and authoritative!

And if Casa Terragena was caught out at so directly an anti-Fascist exploit as this, what would be its worth to the Rylands family for the next few years?

Startling to think that the proper course before her, consistent with all the rest of her life, consistent with the lives of all the respectable people in the world, would be to go in and go to bed and just leave that frightened man in the hole to his fate, his probably highly disagreeable fate.

This thing was no mere adventure. It was a challenge, the supreme challenge of her life. She must risk herself, risk her home, risk failure and humiliating discovery. If she saved or did her utmost to save this man, she broke with limitations that had restricted and protected all her life thus far.

She clenched her hands together very tightly, for her fibre was nervous timid stuff. Then for an instant, one brief instant, her sense of her God who had been so near a quarter of an hour ago, returned to her. Wordlessly, in a breathing moment, she prayed. She stepped across the boundary and transcended State and government.

"We must save that man," she said.

No moral doubts about Mrs. McManus. "I'm thinking how. It's no light matter, M'am."

Mrs. Rylands stood up, with her heart beating fast and her head quite clear. She looked towards the house.

"I don't think they will come back by this path. They believed us that there is no one this way. They will take the way by the lily pond to the bridge across the gorge. They are sure to go west in order to block the escape to the French frontier. They will scatter up and down the rocks and spend the night there. I hope none of them catch cold. I think they have started already. I heard—something. Listen. Look up there; that's a flashlight. Along the path above us. Bombaccio is showing them—or one of the men. Very well. Now—"

She weighed her words. "There is only one place to put him where he will be safe from gardeners, servants, every one. Except perhaps Frant. . . . Mr. Philip's bedroom. Locked up—next to my little sitting-room. We can turn the key on the service stairs."

"We could do that."

"It is all we can do."

"But to get him there!"

"If he could walk in—in your hood and cloak. That cloak of yours with a hood. We can get the men out of the way. Listen. I am going to be very, very, very frightened. Hysterical. You are afraid for me. Very well, you go in and get Bombaccio to bring brandy *here*. *He'll* want brandy badly enough. Brandy and one glass; no tray. Take it off the tray and bring it yourself. And get your cloak and bring wraps for me. Oh!—and bring a pair of your shoes and stockings among the wraps. What? Yes—for him. I will be sitting here, terrified. 'Take those men away!' I shall repeat over and over. I shall be in terror at the idea of more people coming into the gardens from above. I shall be dreadfully shaken. You won't answer for the consequences if I see another strange man. . . . Will Bombaccio believe that?"

"Men will believe anything of that sort," said Mrs. McManus.

"Suppose he hangs about—sympathetically."

"No man ever yet hung about an ailing woman if he had any chance or excuse of getting away from her."

"Insist that he goes up to stop people at the gates and take the menservants with him. You cannot bear to think of his going alone and—unless I'm mistaken in him, *he* won't bear to think of his going alone."

"He shall take them."

"Have as many lights as possible put out. Say

they upset me. Tell the women not to be frightened on *any* account. Then they will be. It's just one *very*, very desperate man, tell them. Tell them to keep together and keep to their own quarters. Then when it's all clear he puts on your shoes and stockings and cloak and we just walk into the house and up to my room."

"If you'd been in the Civil War in Ireland, you couldn't have made a better plan," said Mrs. McManus.

"There's Frant? She'll be sitting up for me. She's the weak point."

"That maid of yours can hold her tongue," said Mrs. McManus. "I've got great confidence in her. I've heard Bombaccio trying to get things out of her. I'll just drop her a hint not to be surprised at anything she sees and keep mum. Maybe she'll have to be told about it. Later. But she's English and keeps herself to herself. You can risk Miss Frant."

"And Miss Fenimore?"

"She'll be in bed perhaps. Or maybe botanising." Mrs. McManus reflected. "We'll have to take the chances of that Miss Fenimore."

"The rest of it will work?"

"Please God."

The two women peered at each other in the darkness.

It was alarming, but exciting. They felt a great friendship for each other. "If you could look a bit dishevelled and sickish," said Mrs. McManus. "Instead of looking all braced up like a little fighting cock."

She reflected. "And when he's in that room—? But one thing at a time."

She departed towards the house almost jauntily. Mrs. Rylands, tingling not unpleasantly, returned to her seat. Seven years perhaps in a Fascist prison. But that would make a stir in England. The government of course was much too hand-in-glove with Mussolini to insist on her liberation. And yet Rylands stood for something in England. . . . Why think of such things?

There was a faint rustling and a painful grunting.

"Have they gone?" came a voice out of the blackness behind her.

She answered in a loud whisper: "Not yet. Have patience. We are going to hide you in the house."

Then she stood up and bent down towards the unseen refugee. "You prefer to speak English or French?" she asked and began to sketch out his part in her plan in French. But he insisted on English. "In America five years," he said. He asked various questions. "I shall sleep in a bed," he noted with marked satisfaction. "I have not slept in a bed for four nights. Possibly I may wash and shave? Yes?"

The plan worked. Presently came the brandy and Mrs. McManus. Much hurrying movement and quick whispers. He had to have his shoes and stockings put on him like a baby. But the brandy heartened him.

There were heart stopping moments. As Mrs. Rylands turned the corner of the landing with her cloaked and hooded refugee beside her and holding to her arm, Miss Fenimore came out of the little downstairs sitting-room with a book in her hand. "Going to bed?" said Miss Fenimore, yawning. "Good ni!"

"Good night, dear," said Mrs. Rylands and pushed her companion on.

"Good night, Mrs. McManus," cried Miss Fenimore.

"Put the sitting-room lights out, dear," said Mrs. Rylands instantly, with great presence of mind. And then as Signor Vinciguerra stumbled up the next flight of steps she whispered: "The door to the left and we are safe!"

Frant was in the ante-room immersed in a book and didn't even look up as they passed across it.

Mrs. McManus too had her disconcerting moment. Following discreetly, she discovered Miss Fenimore, just too late, in the sitting-room entrance. "I never did!" cried Miss Fenimore. "Why! I said good night to you on the staircase just a moment ago?"

"There's no harm in saying it again," said Mrs. McManus.

"But you went upstairs?"

"And came down again."

"It's not half a minute."

"I'm that quick," said Mrs. McManus, and left her still wondering.

"It's like second sight or having one of those doppel-gangers," said Miss Fenimore. "I just went into the sitting-room to switch off the light. I hardly did more than turn round. Hasn't there been some sort of trouble in the garden?"

"I heard a noise. Shouting and running it was," said Mrs. McManus. "We'll have to ask Bombaccio to-morrow. Good night to you," and she disappeared above the landing.

Alone with her God so to speak, Mrs. McManus

279

made a hideous grimace at the invisible Miss Fenimore.

She found Mrs. Rylands in her husband's room, having her hands kissed effusively by a weeping, dishevelled middle-aged man with a four days' beard. He had discarded the nurse's cloak and her much too tight shoes, but he still wore her stockings pulled over the ends of his trousers so that up to the waist he looked like a brigand and above that, a tramp. "Brave and kind," he sobbed over and over again. "I was at my ooltimate garsp." Mrs. McManus became aware that Frant had followed from the ante-room attracted by the rich sounds of the kissing and praise. "Miss Frant," said Mrs. McManus, closing the door on her, "we'll have to trouble you with a secret. Look at him there! A great political senator he was, and see what they have made of him! A friend of Mr. Rylands. He was being hunted to his death by them Black Shirts and we've got to hide him from them. None of the servants must know. They aren't safe not a single one of them. They may be Black Shirts themselves for all we know. We'll have to hide him and get him out of this country somehow or Murder it will be."

Frant's thin face expressed understanding and solicitude. She was a white-faced, whisp-haired woman with much potential excitement in her small bright blue eyes. "Have you locked the valet's door beyond the bath-room?" she asked, pallidly aglow. "I'll see nobody comes in from the passage."

One might have imagined that the rescue of fugitives was a part of her normal duties.

Mrs. McManus skilfully but tactfully disengaged

280

Mrs. Rylands' hands from the gratitude of Signor Vinciguerra. "The great thing here is Silence," she whispered, shaking him kindly but impressively. "There's Fascists maybe in the rooms above and Fascists maybe downstairs and they're almost certain to be listening outside the window. If you'll just sit down in that chair and collect yourself quietly I'll give you some biscuits and a trifle more brandy."

Signor Vinciguerra was wax in her hands.

Mrs. Rylands, disembarrassed, was free to make a general survey of the situation. She put two towels in the bath-room and found Philip's shaving things and a sponge. From the wardrobe she got a dressing gown and in the chest of drawers were pyjamas. The man seemed to be famished. Miss Frant could get some sandwiches without remark. Or Bovril. Bovril would be better. Unless Signor Vinciguerra made too much noise or talked too loudly in his sleep he could with reasonable luck be safe here for some days. Philip's room opened into the little sitting-room that gave on the balcony and into which her own bedroom opened on the other side. No one was likely to go into it. Signor Vinciguerra could lock himself in and answer only to an agreed-on tap. She could profess to be ill until definite action was called for and Miss Frant could make up a bed for Mrs. McManus on the couch in the ante-room, barring all intrusion of the maids. Food could be brought up; not much but sufficient to keep the good man going. And so having provided for the temporary security of Signor Vinciguerra the next problem was how to get rid of him.

He was left to his toilet in Philip's apartment.

Miss Frant, after a whispered consultation with Mrs. McManus in the ante-chamber, went downstairs to order and wait for a large cup of Bovril and toast and learn how things in general were going on. Mrs. Rylands drifted to the balcony and discovered the old moon creeping up the sky above the eastward promontory, picking out the palm fronds and patterning the darkness of the garden.

Extraordinary! It was long past her customary bedtime and everything was most improper for a woman in her condition, and yet instead of feeling distressed, fatigued and dismayed, she was elated. It was, to be frank with herself, a great lark. It would be something to tell Philip. It was still extremely dangerous and it might become at any time horrible and tragic, but it no longer appeared a monstrous and unnatural experience. She believed that on the whole she was likely to succeed in this adventure. Things so far had gone amazingly well. If one kept one's head they might still go well. The frontier was not half an hour's walk away. Being outside the law, fighting the established system of things, was after all nothing so very overwhelming.

Problem: to get him away.

That was going to be an anxious business.

There in sight were the lights of Mentone, France, freedom and security. The real Civilisation. And against that a dark headland, the edge of captive Italy. Where to-night the Fascists would be watching. Where always perhaps there were watchers, now that Italy was a prison.

Such a very middle-aged man he was!

In romances and plays a fugitive was at least able

282

to run. Most fugitives in fiction were high-grade
amateur runners. One thought of a young handsome
white face, with a streak of hair across it and perhaps blood, a white shirt torn open—a tenor part.
If only this were so now, one might give him a rest,
smuggle him down to the beach to-morrow night and
set him off to swim across that dark crescent of water,
to sanctuary. What could it be altogether? Four
miles? Five miles? Or put him in the bathing boat.
But that might be difficult. At times there were
search lights. Odd there were none just now! Perhaps that put swimming or a boat out of court even
for heroes. A really good swimmer might dive as
the lights swept by. Or one could have packed him
off up the gorge to clamber into the hills and escape
by precipitous leaping and climbing. But for that
a Douglas Fairbanks would be needed. Her mind
struggled against an overbearing gravitation towards
the prosaic conclusion, that the most suitable rôle for
Signor Vinciguerra would be that of a monthly
nurse, into which he had fallen already. In that
guise she could see herself taking him across the
frontier with the utmost ease in the well known and
trusted Terragena car, and she could imagine no
other way that was not preposterously impracticable.

§ 19

IT seemed incredibly late, later than any night had
ever been before; but Mrs. Rylands was in no
mood for sleep. She sat in her little sitting-
room, dimly lit by one shaded light, and listened to
the rambling astonishing talk of Signor Vinciguerra.
He had bathed himself and washed and shaved and

emerged to efface the first impression he had made of something worn out, physically over-fed and under-trained and mentally abased. In Philip's pyjamas, slippers and dressing-gown, he looked now a quite intelligent and credible Italian gentleman. He consumed his Bovril and toast with restrained eagerness. He talked English with a sort of fluent looseness and the only faults in his manners were a slight excess of politeness and an understandable jumpiness.

Mrs. McManus sat in a corner of the room, almost swallowed up in shadow, and she took only a small share in the conversation. At any time she might pounce and dismiss the talkers to their slumbers. Frant, after much useful reconnoitering, had gone to bed. Bombaccio and his minions had come back to the house, not too excessively excited, and gone to bed also, quite unsuspiciously. The Fascists it seemed had put a cordon round the garden and purposed to beat its thickets by daylight. Apparently they had an idea that in the morning Vinciguerra might either be caught exhausted or found dead within its walls. Mrs. Rylands determined to mobilise all her garden staff to make a fuss at the least signs of trampling or beating down her plants and flowers, while she herself telephoned complaints to the Ventimiglia police. It would look better to make a fuss than remain suspiciously meek under their invasion.

The respited quarry of the Fascists talked in weary undertones.

"To an Englishwoman it must be incredible. A man hunted like a beast! And for why? The simplest criticisms. Italy has embarked upon a course that can have only one end, National tragedy. Twice I have been beaten. Once in Rome in full daylight in the Piazza della Colonna. Once in the little town where formerly I was mayor. Left on the ground. I was carried home. Then my house watched by sentinels, day and night. Followed whenever I went abroad. It became intolerable. I could not breathe."

He shook his head. "I fled."

For some moments he stared in silence at his memories.

"Imagine! Your Bertrand Russell. Or your George Trevelyan, that fearless friend of Italy and Freedom. Men of that sort. Chased and beaten. Because they will not flatter. Because they will not bow down. To a charlatan!"

He said the last word in a whisper and glanced about him as he said it. He grimaced his loathing.

"We were in Civilisation. We were in a free country. And suddenly this night fell upon us. Truly—I learnt it in English at school—the price of freedom is eternal vigilance!

"This whole country is one great prison. A prison with punishments and tortures. For every one who thinks. For every one who speaks out. I made no plots. I went out of politics after the election of 1924. But I wrote and said Italy becomes over-populous. She must restrain her population or make war and war will be her destruction. I persisted that these facts should be kept before the Italian mind. . . . That was enough.

"Italy perhaps has never advanced since the Risorgimento. She seemed to do so after her unification, but possibly she did not. Only you Anglo-Saxons have won your way to real freedom, freedom of thought, freedom of speech and proposal. Slowly, by centuries, surely, you have won it. Perhaps the French too, Germany I doubt. You have your great public men, respected, influential, no matter the government. Your Shaw, your Gilbert Murray, your Sempack; Americans like Nicholas Murray Butler, Upton Sinclair, Arthur Brisbane. Free to speak plainly. Bold as lions. Free—above the State. But in Italy—that actor, that destroyer, that cannibal silences us all! Performs his follies. Puts us all to indignities and vile submissions. I can't tell you the half of things submitted. The shame of it! For Italy! The shame for every soul in Italy!

"I am a comfortable man. Not everything in my life has been well. I have been used to the life—eh, the life of a man of the world. Prosperity. Indulgence perhaps. But I had rather be this hunted thing I am than any man who keeps his peace with State and Vatican and lives now in Rome prospering. Yes—even here. In danger. Wounded and Dead perhaps, dear Madam, if it were not for you."

His voice died away.

"But is there no movement for freedom in Italy?" asked Mrs. Rylands.

"We took freedom for granted. We took progress and justice for granted. We did not organise for freedom and progress then, and now we cannot. No. All things in life, good things or bad things, rest on strength. Strength and opportunity. If you have things that you desire it is because you willed well enough to have it so. There was no liberal will in Italy but only scattered self-seeking men. Politicians were divided. Intellectual men, not very cordial, not banded together, not ready to die for freedom, one for all and all for one. Rather pleased to see a rival put down. No sense of a danger in

286

common. When I was young and read your Herbert Spencer and your liberal thinkers and writers I said the great time, the great civilisation, will come of itself. Nothing comes of itself except weeds and confusion. We did not reckon with the hatred of dull people for things that are great and fair. We did not realise the strength of stupidity to call a halt to every hope we held. We thought there were no powers of darkness left. And now— Now— . . . Progress has been taken unawares! Progress has been waylaid and murdered.

"But at least the freedom and progress of the English-speaking world is safe. Italy will not always be as she is now.

"Nothing is safe in life. Now I know. What has happened in Italy may happen all over the world. The malignant, the haters of new things and fine things, the morally limited, the violent and intense, the men who work the State against us, are everywhere. Why did we not see it? Man civilises slowly, slowly. Eternal vigilance is the price of civilisation."

"Yes," said Mrs. Rylands, "I begin to see—things I never suspected before, about me and supporting me. One may trust to servants and policemen—and custom. And live in a dream."

Signor Vinciguerra assented by a gesture.

Came a pause.

The little travelling clock upon the table pinged one single stroke and Mrs. McManus stirred. "One o'clock in the morning!" said Mrs. McManus, and rose masterfully. "You'll be wanting your rest, Signor Vinciguerra. There is much to be done yet before you are safe in France."

§ 20

WHEN at last Signor Vinciguerra was in France the whole thing seemed ridiculously easy. Mrs. Rylands was astonished to think the affair had ever seemed a challenge to her courage or a defiance of danger. For a day he lay hidden in Philip's room and no one, who was not in the secret, thought of going there. The next morning he walked out of Casa Terragena with Miss Frant, the maid, even as he had walked in, as a nurse. He was now carefully shaved, made up, dressed completely in garments hastily unpicked and resewn to fit him passably, and assisted by glasses. The men were already up the garden with the luggage, for Mrs. Rylands was going to visit her dear friends the Jex-Hiltons at Cannes for a couple of nights. Frant had let out to Bombaccio that her mistress had to see a great British specialist. Nothing to be really anxious about in Mrs. Rylands' condition but something not quite in order.

It was visitors' day for the gardens. If any one observed a nurse who was not Mrs. McManus, well, it was some other nurse. Or there are such things as consultations of nurses. Above waited Parsons the English chauffeur with the best car. Vinciguerra was left in a quiet corner and Frant went on to fuss about the luggage at the gates and send the man back for a thoughtfully forgotten umbrella and a book. Mrs. Rylands, assisted up the garden path by Mrs. McManus, was handed over to Vinciguerra at the trysting place. He produced an excellent falsetto and talked English as he helped his protectress into the car.

There was tension, certainly there was tension, as far as the Italian custom house at the roadside. But the douaniers gave but a glance and motioned the familiar car on with friendly gestures. A lurking Fascist young gentleman, just too late, thought the inspection perfunctory and was for supplementing it. He called out "Alo!" after the car. That was the greatest thrill. Parsons slewed his eye round for orders. He hated foreigners who said "Alo" to him. "Go on," said and signalled his mistress; "Go on!" said Frant, sitting beside him, and he put his foot down on the accelerator only too gladly.

She glanced back through the oval window at the back of the car. The young Italian gentleman was not pursuing. He had gone back to lecture the douaniers—on thoroughness no doubt.

The French douane was even less trouble. Bows and smiles. Mrs. Rylands, that charming neighbour, was welcome to France.

And this was all! They were purring smoothly along the eastern sea front of Modane. People promenading, people bathing. In bright sunshine, in a free world. It was all over. The danger, the stress.

"I have had to masquerade as a woman," said Signor Vinciguerra resentfully and took off the glasses which blurred the world for him. "But I am out of prison. I know I look ridiculous, I know— Dio mio!"

He sobbed. Tears filled his eyes.

"Il suo coraggio," he said, crushing her hand with both of his. "Non dimentichero mai quel ch' Ella ha fatto per me. Never. Never."

"In two hours or less we will be in Cannes," said

Mrs. Rylands, trying to save some of her hand. "Then you shall be a man again. . . . Don't! Don't!"

"I should have been beaten. I should have died like a dog."

He recovered abruptly. "This is absurd," he said. "Forgive me, dear Lady."

He was silent, but still intensely expressive.

"Don't you think this view of Cap Martin is perfectly lovely?" said Mrs. Rylands. . . .

Just at that very moment Mrs. McManus and Bombaccio confronted each other in the hall of Casa Terragena.

"But I thought you had gone with the Signora!" said Bombaccio.

"There's some telegrams in Ventimiglia. We thought of them at the last moment. I'll want the second car for that. Then I shall go on by train."

"*I* could have sent them on."

"What is that you've got in your hand there? a pair of shoes?"

"They were found in the garden," said Bombaccio. "They were found in a trampled place under a rock beneath the tennis court. And these—*affari*. Ecco!" Bombaccio held them out; the decorative socks of a man of the world but with a huge hole in one heel. "What can they be? And where are the feet they should have? Surely this is of the traddittore! Il Vinciguerra."

"Some of him," reflected Mrs. McManus. "Surely. His shoes and socks! Where did you say they found them?"

"Below the tennis court."

"Very likely if you look about you'll find some

more of him. He must have scattered to avoid them. Unless they found him and tore him to pieces—quietly. But then they'd be all bloody. Will you be ordering the car? For the eleven o'clock train."

Ahead of her the car with the fugitive ran swift and smooth through Monte Carlo, Beaulieu, Villefranche, Nice, Antibes. At Cannes Mary Jex-Hilton came running down the steps to receive her guest. "You felt dull, you darling, and you came over to us! The sweetest thing in the world to do! Trusting us."

"I'd a particular reason," said Mrs. Rylands, descending and embracing. She collected her wits. "Parsons, just help Frant with those bags into the house and upstairs."

Behind Parsons' back Frant turned round and grimaced strangely to assure her mistress that the chauffeur should be taken well out of the way.

"This nurse of mine, darling," said Mrs. Rylands, turning to the quasi-feminine figure that sat now in a distinctly heteroclitic attitude, bowing and smiling deprecatingly, "is Signor Vinciguerra, the great publicist. He has barely escaped with his life—from over there. I will tell you—how we found him, being hunted, in the garden."

"My dear! And you saved him?"

"Well, here he is!"

"You heroine! And it's Signor Vinciguerra!" Mrs. Jex-Hilton held out her hand. "We met in Milan. Two years ago! You don't remember, but *I* do. Won't you get out?"

Mrs. Rylands whispered. "He doesn't like walking about in these things. Naturally."

Mrs. Jex-Hilton thought rapidly.

"I'll get Ted's bathing-wrap. It's just inside the hall. It's more dignified. A toga."

It was true. The ambiguous nurse accepted the wrap, arranged a fold or so and became a Roman Senator, fit for the statuary. Except about the shoes and ankles. The round bare face assumed a serene and resolute civility. Signor Vinciguerra walked into the house, a statesman restored.

It was easier and easier.

When at last Mrs. Rylands sat down in the pretty white and green and chintz bedroom Mary had given her, to write to Philip and tell him all about it, the terror and stress of those dark moments in the garden were already impossible to recall. It was incredible that it should ever have seemed too mighty a task to help this fugitive. She was disposed to see the whole story now like some hilarious incident at a picnic. And for a time, all the great and subtle things she had thought about God and His infinite mightiness and nearness, had passed completely out of her mind. She knew she had much to write to Philip on that matter also, but now it was impossible. What did become clear presently was the grave import of the things Vinciguerra had said in her little sitting-room about the suppression of intellectual activity in Italy and the world. That stood out quite plainly still. She wrote of that.

Mrs. McManus arrived with the story of the shoes and socks in the afternoon. Later when she came against Parsons in the garden, he regarded her with perplexity.

"I say," he remarked. "Are you *another* nurse?"

"What nonsense! There's never another about me."

"But wasn't there another just now—with glasses?"

"Not it."

"I could have sworn. . . . Rummy! You look so changed."

"It's the air," said Mrs. McManus.

Little more was left to clean up of the Vinciguerra adventure. He was to lie *perdu* with the Jex-Hiltons for two or three days and then make his way to Geneva where he could appear in public and perhaps talk to an interviewer. It would be amusing to cast suspicion on Mont Blanc and suggest unsuspected passes in Savoy. It would help to divert any suspicion that might have fallen upon Casa Terragena. There still seemed some slight danger of leakage in the household, however. When presently Mrs. Rylands returned to her home, Frant found Bombaccio in a much too inquiring state of mind for comfort. It was almost as if some one had slept in a rug on the Signor's bed; and had any one tampered with his shaving things? Who had consumed the better part of half a litre of brandy? And made crumbs in the Signor's room? Then— He showed Frant the mysterious shoes and socks, and sent his eloquent eyebrows up and the corners of his still more eloquent mouth down. He explained them and thought Frant was densely stupid. "After that," said Bombaccio, "a man could not go far." He had shown them to no one else Frant elicited, but what ought he to do about them? He watched her closely as he spoke. He eyed her almost mesmerically. She did not watch him at all—she observed him with a wooden averted face. Then she reported adequately to her mistress. Mrs. Rylands decided to deal with Bombaccio herself.

She found him arranging the newspapers in the downstairs room. She went past him and out upon the blazing terrace and then called him to her.

"How beautiful the garden is this morning," she said.

Bombaccio was touched by this appeal for æsthetic sympathy and confirmed her impression richly and generously.

"Adam and Eve," she interrupted, "were put into a garden even more beautiful than this."

Bombaccio said that we were told so but that he found it difficult to believe.

"They were turned out," said Mrs. Rylands.

Bombaccio's gesture deplored the family fall.

"They were turned out, Bombaccio, for wanting to know too much."

Bombaccio started and regarded her as man to woman, through a moment of impressive silence. "There is nothing in the world the Signora might not trust to me," he said. "Have I ever been disloyal even in the smallest matter to the famiglia Rylands?"

"No," said Mrs. Rylands, and acted profound deliberation. She laid a consciously fragile hand on his arm.

"I will trust you to do the most difficult thing of all, Bombaccio. For man or woman. That is—not even to ask questions. As hard as that. For questions you understand are like microbes; they are little things, but if you scatter them about, they may cause great misfortunes."

She added, almost as if inadvertently: "Signor Rylands had reasons to be very grateful to Signor

Vinciguerra. It would have been sad if anything had happened in this garden to one to whom we are indebted."

Bombaccio's bow, finger upon his lips, put the last seal upon her security.

§ 21

MRS. RYLANDS had been back in Casa Terragena two days before the succession of little notes and cards from Philip was broken by a considerable letter again, this time a whale of letter, opening with a long account of the return of the prophet Sempack to his own home. This account seemed to have been written some days ago; the handwriting and paper were different from those of the latter sheets.

It presented that large untidy person in his own distinctive setting. Philip's curt, clumsy and occasionally incisive sentences, breaking now and then into a new-won fluency, portrayed Sempack like a big but prostrate note of interrogation, lying athwart the whole world. He had been rather more hurt it seemed than the doctors had at first supposed. There was a troublesome displacement of a wrist bone and there was something splintered at the end of a rib. Philip had had to wait longer than he had expected while X-ray examinations and a minor operation were carried out, and he had taken the great man down not in his own Talbot but in a special ambulance car to his home in Dorsetshire.

Philip was evidently surprised by Sempack's home. "I had expected something very ordinary, something like a small, square, serious house taken out of Clapham, with a rather disagreeable and unwilling house-keeper," he wrote, "but as a matter of fact he has done himself extremely well. In a compact but very pretty way." Apparently it was a house built specially for its occupant on the slopes and near the crest of the long hill that runs between Corfe and Studland; Brenscombe Hill said the notepaper. "There are no other houses about there, which is like him somehow, and also along the hogsback above him there are groups of tumuli, which is also in a way characteristic. He always straddles back to pre-history. If ever the man picked up a flint implement he would do so as if he had just dropped it."

The house was small but lined with books, it spread itself to the light, and the hill and a group of trees checked the burly assaults of the south-west wind. He worked before a big plate-glass window with a veranda outside, facing north of the sunrise. "It's got a tremendous view. Stretches of heath and then the tidal flats of Poole Harbour, blue razors of sea cutting their way through green weed-banks and grey mud-banks to Poole and Wareham and tumbled bits of New Forest to the north; with Bournemouth and its satellites low and flat across the waters, lighting up in the twilight. It is like old Sempack to have a window with a view that goes away into distance beyond distance for miles and miles and which has differences of climate, clouds or sluggish mists here and sunshine there. 'I can see thunderstorms gather and showers pass,' he told me, 'as if they were animals wandering across a field.'

"There's a Mrs. Siddon, a sort of housekeeper who can typewrite on occasion, a woman with an interesting face and a quiet way with her—over some-

thing that smoulders. Evidently she adores him.
She has the instincts of a good nurse. There is a
charming little girl of ten or twelve about the place,
with whom Sempack is on the best of terms, who
belongs to her. Sempack vouchsafed no explanations, but I have a sort of feeling that behind the
housekeeper is a story. Though he said nothing, she
dropped a phrase or so. It distressed and moved her,
more than it would move any one who was just a
common or garden paid servant, to get him back in
a broken condition. She liked me from the outset
because it was so plain I cared for him, and in the
emotion of the occasion her natural reserve gave way
a little. She has some tremendous cause for gratitude
to him. She was ripe for confidences, but I thought
it wasn't my business to provoke them. I guess and
infer that somewhen she had 'done something,' something pretty serious, I could imagine even a law
court and something penal—just a phrase or so
of hers for that—and he had fished her out of
the mess she was left in and treated her like any
other honourable individual. Put her on her feet
when she was down and said nothing much about
doing it. That may be all imagination on my part,
but anyhow our Sempack has a home, which I never
suspected; is extremely comfortable, which is still less
what I thought; is tenderly looked after and sits
among a loveliness, an English loveliness of rain and
green and grey and soft sunlight, which in its way is
almost as lovely as the glorious blaze, the stony
magnificence, the vigour and strength of colour of
dear old Terragena.

"I stayed three nights there and I may go down
there again if it can be squeezed in before I come back

to you. He can't write much. He's one-armed and one-handed for a time. He's rigged up on a comfortable couch before his big window and he lies watching the late English spring turn into the mild English summer. A pocket-handkerchief garden is foreground, and then comes all that space. This accident of his, the inaction that is necessary, and the other things that have happened to him recently and the way social and political things are going in the world seem all to have conspired to make him turn upon himself and his life and ask himself a lot of new questions. Like the questions we are all asking ourselves. He put it himself better than I can put it. He compared it to travellers going up into big mountains. For a long time you see the road far ahead, plain and sure. Then almost suddenly you realise that there is a deep valley, a gorge perhaps, you never expected. You come out upon it and you look down, and you lose heart."

Philip, his wife reflected, was learning to write and learning very rapidly. This would have been impossible a few weeks ago. Quick wits he had when he gave them a chance. He had evidently been reading widely and the uncertainty of his spelling was vanishing. All his latent memories of the look of words were reviving. There must be thousands of people, she reflected, who needed only sufficient stimulation to be released in this fashion from the sort of verbal anchylosis that had kept him inexpressive.

He went off into the question of Sempack's love affair with Lady Catherine. A note of wonder that anything so mature and ungainly could think of passionate love appeared in what he wrote. "We walk, my dear Cynna, in a world of marvels unsuspected.

talk, discuss, write, to hear criticisms, discuss, read in new directions and write again, has been after all just the easiest line of living for him. Catherine it seems had chanced to get her fingers through exactly that joint in his armour. She taunted him with it when he was already troubled by doubts. His present illness is quite as much his dismay at the prospect of having to change his loose studious way of life for some new kind of exertion, hurry, disputes, dangers, etc., as it is either broken rib or broken heart. His main trouble is getting acclimatised to a new point of view."

Philip and Sempack seemed to have talked for most of the time on that veranda that looked north of the sunrise. A phrase here and an illusion there conveyed the picture of Sempack sprawling ungainly, "like some Alpine relief map," beneath a brown camel's-hair rug upon his couch, talking still of that wonderful better time that was coming for an emancipated mankind, but talking also of the age of revolutionary conflict that was opening now and had to be lived through before ever the millennium could be won. The millennium was an old-fashioned theme, but the intervening age of battle and effort and the chances of defeat were new admissions. It was as if the facts wrung themselves out of him.

The talk must have rambled and Philip's memoranda rambled too. The writing varied. It was not clear whether he had written all this in Sempack's house or somewhere on his way to London. But the main conception that emerged was that the progress of liberal thought and of world development in accordance with liberal thought which had been practically free and unhampered for a century was now threatened with restriction and arrest, and had to be fought for and secured. Sempack spoke as one who belonged to the Nineteenth Century, and Philip added the note that "by his reckoning that means 1815 to 1914." Throughout this Nineteenth Century it seemed discussion had grown more free and bolder with every year. Towards the end one might propose, one might suggest almost anything. One might do so because throughout that age there had been no fundamental changes and people had come to believe there could be no fundamental changes. Liberal thought was free and respected because it appeared to be altogether futile. No one grudged the Great Thinker his harmless intellectual liberties. It was not until the second Russian revolution that this attitude came to an end. Then the ordinary prosperous man who had been disposed to tolerate every sort of idea and even to pat every sort of idea on the head as he chanced across it, discovered an idea that could turn and bite his hand. He discovered that projects for fundamental change might even produce fundamental changes.

Wilson also, Sempack thought, had frightened people with his League of Nations. There was hope and dismay everywhere in the world in 1919. People, great numbers of people, came to realise that what all these socialists and prophets of progress had been talking about might really begin to happen. There might actually be a world government which wouldn't so much "broaden out" from existing governments, as push them aside and eat them up. For a League of Nations was either a super-government or a sham. The British Empire and La France and Old Glory had in actual fact to go the way of the

Heptarchy, if this League fulfilled its promise. They had to be deprived of the sovereign right to war. And equally there might really be a new sort of economic life coming into existence. We might find ourselves positive, participating shareholders in a one world business, and all our individualism gone. Conduct was amenable to direction, with regard to health and work and all sorts of things, to an extent never suspected before the days of war propaganda and regimentation. Population might really be stanched and controlled. It was no dream. It was hard for most people to decide whether this was to be treated as a mighty dawn or the glare of the last conflagration.

And that he held was where we are still to-day. Still in doubt. The dreams of yesterday have become our urgent questions, our immediate possibilities. It stared every one in the face. Philip, either quoting or paraphrasing or extending Sempack, it was not clear which, went on to an amusing analysis of how the confrontation of a whole world with a common revolutionary possibility had reacted on different types of character. Some were for leaping headlong into the new phase, were prepared to discover it new-born and already perfect even in Moscow and Canton; many were terrified by the practical strangeness of it and bolted back to reaction. A lot did not want to be bothered. That was the common lot. They wanted to go on with their ordinary occupations like rabbits in a hutch eating lettuce when the stables they are in are on fire. Nobody saw yet what a gigantic, comprehensive, unhurrying, "non-returnable" thing world reconstruction must be; those who sought it saw that least of all. We were living in a period of panic and short views both ways. Fascism was panic, the present Tory government of Great Britain was panic, the people of Moscow were clinging, just as desperately as any westerns, to theories and formulæ they knew were insufficient, making Gods of Marx and Lenin and calling a halt to thought and criticism. The New Model of the Revolution, steadfast and sure of itself, always persisting and always learning, had still to appear. "'Clamour, conflict and muddle,'" quoted Philip, "'and so it must be until the great revolution has ceased to be a reverie, has passed through its birth storms and become the essential occupation, the guiding idea, the religion and purpose of lives like yours, lives like your wife's, all that is left of lives like mine and of a mighty host of lives. The socialist movements of the nineteenth century, the communist movement, are no more than crude misshapen, *small* anticipations of the great revolutionary movement to which all lives, all truly living human beings, must now be called. A new religion? It is that. To be preached to all the world.

"'Is this demand enormous and incredible?' he asked.

"'I said that to me it was enormous but not incredible.'

"'If it is incredible,' said he, 'there is nothing worth having before mankind.'"

From that point on Philip cited Sempack hardly at all and wrote, as it were, for himself. He had accepted and digested his Sempack and was even perhaps thinking ahead of him, crossing his *t*s for him and dotting his *i*s. He enlarged on this conception of revolution planned and wilful, as the coming form of mental existence. The scale of life was altering, and the new movement from the outset must needs be very great, greater than any other movement that has ever sought to change the general way of mankind. One thought of the outstanding teachers and founders of the past as mighty figures, but this movement must be far mightier in its ambition. The days when a single Buddha and a little group of disciples could start out to change the human soul, or a single Mohammed establish the rule of Allah on earth, or a single Aristotle set all science astir, had passed by. Countless men and women must serve—as men and women served science—and none be taken as a figurehead. This new world cult would have an infinitude of parts and aspects but it must never lose itself in its parts. It must be held together by a common confession and common repudiations. Its common basis must be firstly the history of all life as one being that grew in wisdom and power, and secondly the completest confidence in the possibility of the informed will to comprehend and control. Such ideas were spreading already like a ferment throughout the world.

It was just because this world religion, blind still and hardly more aware of itself than a newborn puppy, was nevertheless astir and crawling and feeling its way about, that reaction and suppression were everywhere becoming aggressive and violent. With the soundest instinct they were impelled to kill the new world—if it could be killed—before it accumulated the impetus that would abolish them. It is not only those who desire it who see the great order of the world at hand, but they also, those others who apprehend it as the shadow of a new state of affairs utterly unpropitious to and prohibitive of all their pride and advantages. They too believe it is possible and near. Violent reaction is the first cat's-paw to every revolutionary storm. And so for all further progress those who are progressives will have to fight, have to organise—for defence as well as aggression. It is a fight for the earth and the whole world of man. Who can live in peace, who can be let alone, in the midst of such a war? Who can be permitted the immunities of a friendly neutrality? The forces of reaction are not more powerful now but more manifest, more active and militant because only now do they begin to feel the strength and the full danger of the creative attack. To that effect Philip had written—though more discursively. He halted, he went back, he repeated himself several times; but she gathered his meaning together. It was Sempack written out again in the handwriting of a very young man—and touched with a nervous wilfulness that was all Philip's own.

There came a break in Philip's letter. When it resumed it was on the South Street notepaper. He was back in London. Sempack upon his couch at the window was no longer the presiding figure of the discourse. He was far away in Dorset, so far, so lost in perspective as presently to be invisible and disregarded. Philip had found his wife's letter about the Vinciguerra escapade waiting for him upon his desk.

"What a stir amidst the glories of Casa Terragena," he wrote, "and what a plucky front you seem to have shown! You write as if it was all a lark, but I think you must have been pretty plucky not to

scuttle indoors and have the shutters closed and the
bolts shot when the shooting and shouting began.
Reaction chasing Liberalism with intent to kill,
among the magnolias, under the palms, amidst moonlight and fireflies. This is theory coming home to
us with a vengeance. But there you are! The fighting is going on already, the old order takes the offensive—offensive defensive—and men are being
hunted and wounded and killed in the name of nations and tyrannies. Damn those fellows! If I had
been there that night there would have been some
shooting. I would have had them out of the gardens
faster than they came in—or there would have been
memorable events. I tingle at the thought,—the sort
of chaps we had to stiffen after Caporette! I don't
know whether it is liberalism or temper, but I'll
be drawn and quartered if I don't show all the fight
there is in me against these stupidities and violences
and oppressions on the part of the second rate, doing
their best to crush hope out of the world. Just as
it dawns.

"My dear, I'm for fighting. That little invasion
of our decent garden has stirred me like a trumpet.
And after poor old Vinciguerra of all people!"

"All the time that I have been away from you
I have been thinking over myself and over my world
and over our life as it spreads before us. I believe
that this project of a sort of continuing resolute push
towards one world system, is a feasible project and
the most sporting and invigorating invitation that
has ever been made to mankind. I want to go in
for it with everything I've got. I want to give myself to it for your sake and my sake and for every
reason in the world, and if I find little chaps in black

shirts or black coats or red coats starting in to stop me or my sort of people from going the way we mean to go, it's one of our lots will have to get right off the earth. What else is possible? How can we live in the same world with these castor-oil cads and their loaded canes? Still less with their cockney imitators! . . .

"This isn't mere wilfulness on my part. . . ."

The handwriting changed as if the letter had been left and resumed.

"There are damnable threads in me though they hide from you as wood-lice bolt from the sun. If I do not go this way then for all I can tell I may go the other way and end another Uncle Robert. And I dread coming to be like the Right Honourable Baron more than any Calvinist ever feared hell.

"But if we are to give ourselves to this Revolution of Sempack's, the great revolution of the whole world, as one religion, as one way of life, it means a new way of living for us both, dearest wife. For us and for that Dear Expectation of ours. I do not see us, serving the great order of the world from the drawing-room of Casa Terragena. I do not see our child or our children living aloof from this huge conflict in an enchanted garden. A Rylands. Neither from your side nor from mine is that sort of offspring possible. If we are going to realise the teaching of the prophet Sempack, there must be an end to Casa Terragena. We must give it over to the botanists if they will take it and send off Bombaccio to seek his fortunes in America.

The common English are our people and to England we must come; either to London because it is our natural centre or to Edensoke because it is our dominion. We must use our position in the Rylands properties to learn and experiment and find out if we can how to turn round the face of the whole system towards the new order. All our surplus wealth must go into the movement, and the spending of that we must study as closely as dear Uncle Edensoke studies his investment coups. No Rylands ever threw money away and I don't mean to begin. You don't see me pouring my little accumulations into the party funds of L. G. or Ramsay Mac. I shall probably begin by acquiring newspaper properties, and if I can make them do their duty by the movement and pay—so much the better. Then I shall have funds for the next thing. That will be organisation. I shall work like hell. That is the new, hard, serious, fighting, straining, interesting and satisfying life we have to face, my darling, and I am glad we have found it while we are still young. I no more doubt your courage to face it than I doubt that the sun can shine. We'll show all these infernal Tories, stick-in-the-mud liberals, labour louts and labour gentilities, loafers and reactionaries, what two bright young people can do in the way of shoving at the wheels of progress. We'll be such disciples of Sempack that we'll put his wind up. We'll start the move. We'll lug him out from his dreams into reality—blinking. . . . This house here in South Street, the agents say, will let quite easily."

The letter ended abruptly.

§ 22

FOR some days a great indolence had enveloped Mrs. Rylands, a lassitude of mind and body. She lay in bed now and thought over Philip's letter, so bold, tumultuous, and alive in this shadowed peace. The sheets lay on her counterpane and seemed to emit faint echoes of riot and battle. Quite certainly that night he would have gone out raging into the garden and fought. What else could he have done? He would have rescued Vinciguerra violently. Men might have been killed perhaps and everything would have been different. Well, she was glad that had not happened. But his letter was good, quite good, and he would keep his word, she felt, and play to win his games as old Edensoke won his games, but with great ends in view and his soul alive. It was good, but for all that just now that letter fatigued her and she made no attempt to read it over again once she was through with it. It was all right with Philip. For a time things must rest on that.

Life was a very pursuing thing. She recalled the figure of Sempack, so prone to fall into inactive poses, and how combative necessity, with a face singularly like Philip's, was forcing its way through his reluctant and comprehensive wisdom. She loved Philip, she had instigated Philip to give himself to these storming purposive activities, but just now also there was a shadowy resentment that he drove her along the path she herself had indicated. In her present mood Philip's energy blended in thought with the kicking, struggling energy within, behaving already like another Philip eager to get at issue with the world. She thought of her child still as It, and marvelled how little she had pictured its individuality or troubled about its outlook. She had questioned Mrs. McManus and learnt how widespread was this imaginative indifference of expectant mothers. She had had a few dreams of something

infantile and delightful flitting about the great garden, but they were always shadowy, and now it
seemed that It was not to spend its childhood in the
garden. Philip said they were to leave Casa Terragena. He, she and It. She did not want to leave
Casa Terragena. She did not want to leave this
room and this bed any more.

She knew this was a mood. She knew that when
the time came she would leave Casa Terragena with
a stout heart. Philip was her mate and captain and
leader and whither he led she would go. But this
afternoon she saw that without emotion, as an accepted fact of her circumstances and moral nature.
The garden had become very dear to her in these
last few weeks, very close and significant. Here it
was that she had first experienced that sense of God
at hand that comforted and sustained her now so
mightily. She would be loth to leave the place. But
God could be apprehended in many places. And she
would remember.

There was something here that her mind made
an effort to retain and examine. This apprehension
of God was a matter about which she had to write
to Philip. She had never told him about it. It was
very secret and difficult to tell. For some days she
had been brooding upon that. Yesterday and the
day before she had had a peculiar disposition to put
things tidy. She wanted everything in order, apple-
pie order. She had made Frant unpack her clothes
and linen from drawers and cupboards and helped
her to replace it with a meticulous precision. She had
put her writing desk in order and tapped her row
of little reference books into the exactest line. The
green leather book had been minutely corrected and

at last her mind had settled upon the one conclusive
act of tidying up that remained for her to do, to explain to Philip about her God. But she was as lazy
now as she was orderly. She had no sooner taken a
sheet of paper to write than she decided to lie down.
A queer disturbing sensation had come to her when
she had posed herself to write, a novel challenging
sensation. She would rest a little while and then she
would write.

It was very important that Philip should hear
from her about her God. It was the one thing
wanting, she found, in his latest letters. They
seemed so hard and contentious, quarrelsome was
the word, they were quarrelsome and aggressive, because they lacked any sense of this mighty serenity
that was behind and above and about all the details
and conflicts of life. Philip had discovered the imperative of right-living, but he had still to perceive
the Friend and Father who made all right things
right. "Friend and Father" one said, and "He," but
these were words as ineffectual as a child's clay
models of loveliness and life. One said "He" because there seems to be more will and purposiveness
in "He" than in She or It, but for all that it was a
misleading pronoun, cumbered with the suggestion
of a man. This that sustained the world for her,
was not a person, but infinitely more than a person.
As a person is more than a heap of stuff. And still
one had to say "He!"

Soon now and very near to her was the crisis of
maternity. She knew that to bear a child for the
first time is more dangerous than to follow the
most dangerous of trades. Irrational things may
happen. Yet she felt no dismay at this physical

storm that gathered for her. For some time now her mind had been tranquil as it had never been tranquil in her life before. It had been as though she drifted swiftly on a broad smooth stream that poured steadfastly towards a narrow gorge and inevitable rapids. Fearlessly she had swept forward through the days. On that unruffled surface everything was mirrored with the peculiar brightness and clarity of reflected things. Why was she not afraid?

Already there were eddies. The frail skiff of her being had turned about and rocked once and again. She could face it. She did not need Philip nor any comforting hand. Philip was all right and she loved him, but she did not mind in the least now that he was far away. She had her comfort and her courage, in herself and all about her. She whispered: "Though He slay me, yet will I trust in Him." She looked at the sheets of Philip's letter within reach of her fingers and withal it seemed ten thousand miles away. All that was in suspense now and remote and for a while quite unimportant; it could wait; for the present she was with God. So near, so palpably near was He to her that her whole being swam in His. He would be with her in the darkness; He would be with her amidst the strangeness and pain.

Something stirred within her and she put out her hand and took the little green leather book that lay on her bedside table. She had to tell all that to Philip. And it was so difficult to tell Philip. Now. Difficult to tell Philip at any time. She would set something of it down if she could in case— For some reason her hand was out of control but she contrived to scribble the words that sustained her: "Though He slay me, yet will I trust in Him."

There came a sudden pain, an unaccustomed urgent pain, that made her set aside her writing hurriedly and press the little bell-push that would summon Mrs. McManus to the fray. The green leather book fell on the floor, disregarded.

The rapids had begun.

§ 23

IN the evening when his account of Sempack at home was well on its way to his wife, Philip sat down and reflected upon what he had written to her. He tried to recall the exact wording of certain passages. He had written with a certain excitement and hurry. How would it affect her? He imagined her receiving it and reading it.

He pictured her as he had sometimes seen her reading books, very intent, turning the pages slowly, judging, pausing to think with a peculiar characteristic stillness. Her eyes would be hidden; you would just see the lashes on her cheek. So he remembered her reading in their garden. How clear and lucid was her mind, like a pool of crystalline water. He thought about the life he had led with her so far and the life they were going to lead together. He thought of the way in which all his interests and purposes had been turned about through her unpremeditated reaction upon his mind. He thought of the way in which fragility and courage interwove to make her at the same time delicate and powerful. So that for all that she was to him the frailest, most fastidious and inaggressive of women, she was plainly and surely his salvation. A wave of gratitude swept over his mind, gratitude for certain exquisite traits, for the marvellous softness of her hair, for her smile, for her fine hands and her characteristic movements, for moments of tenderness, for moments when he had seen her happy unawares and had rejoiced that she existed.

And as he thought of the steady, grave determination with which she must have set about this Vinciguerra business, of the touch of invincible humour that he knew must have mitigated her fear and steadied her mind, it was borne in upon him that never in their life, never for one moment, had he shown her the value he set upon her and given his love full expression. This letter he had so recently sent her was, he discovered abruptly, a shocking letter, altogether the wrong sort of letter to send at this time, full of *his* soul and *his* needs and his own egotistical purposes and taking no heed of how things might present themselves to her.

Was this the time to talk of leaving Casa Terragena and fighting all the powers of confusion in the world? Was this the time to foreshadow a harder life in England? To wave flags of revolution in her sickroom and blow bugle calls in her ear? She would be ailing, she would be a little faint and fearful, and she would be needing all her strength to face this initial tearing crisis of motherhood that was now so close upon her. And nothing from him but this clamour for support! She helped him; yes; and he took it as a matter of course. Now for the first time he perceived how little he had ever troubled to help her. That letter had gone, gone beyond recall, a day's start it would have and no telegram could correct a matter of tone and attitude, but he could at least send another after it to mitigate its hard preoccupation with the future, its hard disregard of any possible softening and fear in her. A love letter, it would have to be, a rich and tender love letter. Not mere "rubbidge" and caressing fun, but a frank and heartening confession of the divinity—for it was divinity—he found in her. Why do we lovers never tell these things? The real things? He began to search his mind for words and phrases to express his gathering emotion, but these words and phrases were difficult to find.

He sat down at his table and even as he pulled the writing paper towards him a telegram came, a telegram from Mrs. McManus.

A telegram so urgent it was, that he never wrote that letter. His intentions remained phantoms but half embodied in words which still flitted in his mind during most of his headlong journey to Italy. Latterly he had been finding far less difficulty in writing than at first; the necessity to affect whimsicality and defend his poor phrasing with funny sketches had disappeared, but now that it came to conveying the subtle and fluctuating motives of his heart, simply and sincerely, no words, no phrases contented him. Shadow and reflection and atmosphere, impossible to convey. Phrases that seemed at the first glance to say exactly what he needed became portentous, excessive, unreal, directly they were definitely written down. For this business, "rubbidge," the little language, peeping intimations and snatches of doggerel, seemed better adapted than the most earnestly chosen sentences. And still insufficient. He was pervaded by the idea that all his difference of spirit from the common Rylands strain was a gift from her. "Wife of my heart and Mother of my Soul" flitting into his thoughts like an inspiration, passed muster, and sat down and in two minutes had become preposterous. "You are my Salvation" became a monstrous egotism, when one thought of it as written on paper. But indeed she *was* his salvation, she *was* the light of his life, for him she was not only the dearest but the best of all things. Was he never to tell her these intense and primary facts?

"My life hangs on yours. My soul dies with yours. . . . We Rylands are things of metal and drive, unless a soul is given us. . . . With you I can be a living man. . . . It's Undine but the other way about. . . ."

It was profoundly true but it would read like rant.

"The world is a thing of cold fat, opaque and stupid, without your touch. You make it like a hand held up to a bright light; one sees it then as nerve and blood and life. . . ."

Would he never be able to tell her of such things as this? Never say more than "Cinna-kins" and "pet wife" to this firm and delicate spirit that could lead his by the hand? No better than dumb beasts we are, all of us who love, using just "dear" or "darling" as a dog must yap to express ten thousand different things! "The fireflies must be back at Terragena?" he wrote in this imagined letter, with an impotent poetic desire to liken her quick vivid thoughts, her swift deliberations, to those flashes in the darkness, in their brightness and their constant surprise. . . .

He was still thinking of that unwritten letter as he came through the little sitting-room of Casa Terragena to where she lay white and still, and looking now smaller than she had ever looked before. The weary little body curled up in that big bed reminded him grotesquely of a toy dog. A thing for infinite tenderness; "Wife, dear wife and mother of my Soul!" Why had he never told her that?

"I was just going to write to her," he whispered to Mrs. McManus. "I was just going to write to her. A real letter. I was sitting down to write. That last one—wasn't much good. And then your message came."

That last one was there on the toilet table. He saw it as he came in to her. That stupid heavy letter!

He threw himself down on his knees by the bed and very gently put his arm over that fragile body. "My darling!" he whispered. She had not seemed to know that he had come, but now very lazily one eye opened, searched its field of vision and regarded him with an inexpressive stare.

"Cinna dear! speak to me."

"Dju finka vim?" she murmured, dropping the aspirate from sheer inability to carry it. The eye closed again. Still so heavy with anæsthetics.

"That's all right," said Mrs. McManus with an experienced hand on the young master's shoulder. "Now let her have her sleep out and then ye can call her darling to your heart's content. Aren't you in the least bit curious to see what sort of first-born son she's given you? A fine fine boy it is and sparring at the world already with his little fists. *There!* D'you hear him?"

"And she is out of the least bit of danger?" he insisted, regardless of the Rylands' future.

"Just healthy fatigue. . . . After all, it's a thing a woman is made for."

THE END